A VALENTINE KISS

As soon as they stepped into the room, Antonio pulled Caroline into his arms and feasted on her sweet, red lips. Her fisted hand struck his shoulder, but he kept right on kissing her until she became pliant in his arms.

"You are a beast, Antonio," she said huskily when he stopped to draw breath. "You promised you would not do this."

"No, I did not," he said, breathing hard. "I promised I would let you go after a quarter of an hour. The thought of having you in my arms again is all that has sustained me in this wretched climate. This is the first time I have been warm since I left India."

He tipped her face up to his and stroked her cheek with his hand.

"I gather from the heat in your beautiful skin, *ma belle,* that I am not the only one. Does your English lord kiss you as I do?"

"That is none of your business," she said, pushing against him. "He is an honorable gentleman. He would never cast me off for another once he has married me."

"But will he love you as I do . . ."

—from *My Wicked Valentine,* by Kate Huntington

A VALENTINE WALTZ

Jo Ann Ferguson
Maria Greene
Kate Huntington

ZEBRA BOOKS
Kensington Publishing Corp.
http://www.kensingtonbooks.com

ZEBRA BOOKS are published by

Kensington Publishing Corp.
850 Third Avenue
New York, NY 10022

First Printing: January 2004
10 9 8 7 6 5 4 3 2

Printed in the United States of America

CONTENTS

MY DEAREST DAISY

Jo Ann Ferguson

Chapter One

Joshua Tremont was not quite certain why he was attending this gathering tonight. With Twelfth Night just past, the Season was still a few weeks in the future, but that had not prevented those already in Town from assembling to begin the rounds of parties and the cascade of gossip.

He could have been at his club with something marvelous to drink in one hand and a variety of cards in the other. He could have called on an old tie-mate and relived the excitement of an evening in the past. He could have spent time in the stables with his groom and his horse.

One thing he had most certainly not wanted to do was stay at the house near Grosvenor Square and listen to his mother remind him—as she had almost daily for the past year since his return from the Continent—that the announcement that she was adding "dowager" to her title was long overdue. Mother seemed unable to realize that he was well aware of the obligations he had to the family's title, which was almost as ancient as England itself. She believed she had found him the perfect woman to be his Lady Tremont, a young woman of excellent manners, agreeable visage, and a lineage as exemplary as his own. An introduction would be made when his mother returned from a call on a sick friend in the country.

None of that explained why he was *here*. Lady Higginson, the hostess, was a friend of long standing. She had been a young bride when he was a lad in the house next door. Eagerly he had taken tea with her, because he had believed her cook made the best pastries in London, and she had been amused by his interest in many topics she also found fascinating. She had been more like a beloved aunt than his own.

The other guests in the parlor were watching—transfixed, if he judged accurately—a woman standing at the front of the large room. She was dressed in a gown of a generation past and was performing a passage from Shakespeare. Lady Macbeth, he noted. Her voice flowed like beautiful music through the room, filling it from the marble floor to the ceiling decorated with nymphs in a bucolic setting.

Applause followed her bow toward the audience. Joshua took advantage of the break in the performance to slip along the back row of chairs to where Lady Higginson was seated. From here, she could keep an eye on her guests.

"Good evening," he said, as he put his hands on the back of her wooden chair.

Lady Higginson turned to smile. The streaks of silver in her black hair matched her gown. Few wrinkles, save for those from her many smiles, marred her face. "Joshua, I was wondering if you were coming this evening."

"Do you think I would miss one of your entertainments?"

She slapped him on the arm with her lacy fan. "Save your *bon mots* for others." She tapped the empty chair beside her. "Why don't you sit and tell me how your mother fares?"

Joshua sat beside her. "She fares very well."

"In her efforts to find you a bride?"

"Egad, I came here to avoid such talk."

Lady Higginson laughed. "You shall have to leave England to avoid it. The *ton* granted you time to recover from your sojourn in the military and to grieve for your late father. Now they will be unrelenting in their determination to see you in a state of wedded bliss."

"Wedded, at any rate." He smiled when Lady Higginson chuckled again.

Coming here was the prescription for his dismals. As he listened to two men perform a scene from some play he could not name, he glanced around the room. He recognized everyone in it. None of the young misses, who were about to be fired off, would be here tonight. They awaited their chance to make a grand entrance after the official beginning of the Season.

A flash of gold caught his eye, and he looked far to his left. In the front row, sitting with several empty chairs between her and the other guests, was a young woman he did not know. That was odd enough to draw his gaze back to her again and again as the quartet of actors—two men and two women—dramatized scenes both familiar and obscure.

His curiosity demanded satisfaction, so Joshua asked, "Who is that young woman sitting by herself in the front row?"

Lady Higginson raised her quizzing glass, peered through it, and then said, "Hmmm. I do not believe I have met her. She must be a friend of one of my guests, although it is strange that she is alone there." She aimed her quizzing glass back at him. "Why? Does she intrigue you, my boy?"

"She seems quite taken with the performances, especially those of Margaret Burroughs."

She laughed. "I should not be surprised that a young, virile man knows the name of the players who have come to perform for us tonight."

"No, you should not, as her name was announced before she read that poem shortly after I sat down with you."

"Oh, bother! I am beginning to see why your mother laments at you ever finding a wife. You are too practical and think only with your head."

"It *is* where one's thoughts begin." His gaze went again to the blonde. She possessed an ethereal beauty that suggested she might be a fairy called forth from a midsummer dream. Her gown was a creamy confection decorated with the same lace as on her fragile-appearing bonnet.

Joshua looked back at the actress, who was taking her bows to appreciative applause. When the guests stood and began chatting, he knew there would be an intermission while the performers prepared for the next scenes.

"Now you have your chance." Lady Higginson smiled.

"To find out her identity?"

"And whatever else you wish to find out."

He chuckled. "You are almost as persistent as Mother in this matchmaking."

"Nonsense. I am suggesting nothing more than a pleasant conversation. What you wish to suggest to the young woman is wholly up to you."

Joshua stood. "I do believe I would be wise to excuse myself before *this* conversation goes further."

"Very wise." She smiled. "Do share with me what you learn of her identity."

"And whatever else I wish to find out?"

"I leave that to your discretion."

Joshua bowed over her hand and edged along the row to the wall where he could walk, unimpeded, toward the front. The young woman was not rising to join the chatter. She sat with her hands folded on her lap, and, rather than looking at the guests, her gaze remained focused on where the scenes had been acted out.

"Good evening," he said, holding out his hand for hers. When she did not reply, he added, "I am Joshua Tremont."

Slowly her hand rose to settle on his. He bowed over it before releasing it.

"Good evening," she replied, her voice containing a lyrical warmth that brought to mind the actress who had read Lady Macbeth's soliloquy. "My name is Daisy Kendall."

"Miss Kendall, I trust you will forgive my intrusion into your solitude."

"Yes." There was some hesitation in her voice.

"May I?" He pointed to the empty seat beside her.

"Yes."

He did hope Miss Kendall would offer more to the conversation than these terse replies.

"Miss Kendall, is this your first visit to London?"

"No."

Another terse answer. Devil it! He must take care how he phrased his questions, so she could not reply so.

"I know I am being bold, Miss Kendall, but I cannot understand why we have not encountered each other before tonight. The Season may not yet be under way, but the Polite World is not large."

Waiting for her answer, Joshua was glad of the one asset every Tremont was born with. It was a gut-deep instinct of knowing when to push forward and when to give up. He had learned to trust those instincts, especially when they were this powerful. Now they told him that he would be a fool not to get to know this pretty blonde better. And few people had ever called Joshua Tremont a fool. At least, they had not addressed him so to his face. What was said outside his hearing had never concerned him.

"There are many paths in London," she said quietly. "Many of them never intersect."

He chuckled. "An astute observation."

Daisy Kendall smiled quickly. She could not guess why this man had singled her out for his attention. He was quite handsome, although his nose was a bit long and his jaw too square for Society's taste. His clothing, an elegant black coat and white waistcoat worn over dark breeches, announced his place in the Polite World. Most gentlemen in London would have only one reason to seek out a woman of her current station. She chided herself for the cold thought when he had done nothing more than try to begin a polite conversation.

"You are very kind," she said, "but I do not want to take you away from your friends."

He laughed again, a pleasing sound. "They have seen me so frequently over the years that we are eager for new faces. Will you grant me the boon of your company so I do not have to fall back on my own this evening?"

"You are very persuasive." Daisy watched Mr. Tremont. Or was it Lord Tremont? His clothing suggested the latter. She gauged his reaction to her forthright comment. She could be more brazen and speak the truth that she had not been unaware of how he had been watching her from where he sat beside Lady Higginson. That choice of seat told her that this gentleman was someone of importance, because she had seen how the countess's guests were arranged in a rigid hierarchy.

"So I have been told," he replied.

"Then I would be wise to accept the inevitable."

"I would prefer you did not make it sound like a terrible fate." A strand of his ebony hair twisted across his forehead that was as bronzed as the rest of his even features. This was a man who spent much time out-of-doors. A horseman, she guessed, for his hands were rough, and he had the strong shoulders of a man who had learned to control an unruly mount.

But she knew she should be careful in assuming too much from this short conversation. Appearances were not always all they claimed to be. She was an excellent example of that.

Daisy clenched her hands around her fan, which was leaning on her right knee. She drew it back before he might chance to see what she hoped her gown hid. She had sought this chair before most of Lady Higginson's guests arrived. That way, none of them could see how she limped when she walked to it. The plight that must have been an accident of her birth had brought pity to many eyes. She did not want to see the same in Joshua Tremont's brown ones.

"I am grateful for your company during the intermission," she said, then realized it was the truth. She had dreaded the idea of sitting here alone when she should be with her aunt, offering any help for the next scenes.

"Are you enjoying the performances?" he asked.

"Unquestionably." Honesty had a sweet taste. "I have always enjoyed my—Miss Burroughs's work." She held her breath. Had he heard her near slip of the tongue?

If anyone guessed she was not Lady Higginson's guest, but the niece of an actress here tonight, she would be escorted from the house posthaste. Speaking with Lord Tremont only increased the likelihood of her being discovered as a fraud. Yet, the chance to hear Aunt Margaret do a reading in this room with its splendid acoustics was something Daisy had not wanted to miss.

"She is exceptional," he replied.

Thank heavens! He had not heard her near mistake.

"Do you attend the theater often?" he continued.

"Yes." Again that was the truth. She frequently went to the theater to help her aunt with her performances. The hectic madness the audience never saw fascinated her. Everyone had to work together to make each show a success. She loved it, mayhap even more than Aunt Margaret did. She could let the stories on the stage carry her to a place where she no longer felt awkward and conspicuous. Although Aunt Margaret had told her, over and over, that her limp was barely noticeable, Daisy had seen the stares. "I always enjoy the chance to see new performers and new plays."

"Which theater do you prefer, Miss Kendall?"

"My family patronizes any one where Miss Burroughs plays. I have great admiration for her work." She struggled not to laugh at how she was twisting the truth and yet not telling lies.

He opened his mouth, but Daisy was saved from having to answer his next question when her aunt stepped into the center of the open floor serving as a stage. Aunt Margaret needed no jewels to enhance her simple gown, because she was, without question, the most beautiful woman Daisy had ever seen. Her hair was the shade of sunshine and her eyes jade green, unlike Daisy's gray ones. This gown was pale green with a high collar of lace beneath Aunt Margaret's chin. She always wore such collars, because of a tiny, rippled scar along the left side of her neck.

A frown marred her aunt's face for a moment, warning that Aunt Margaret was not happy to discover Lord Tremont by Daisy's side. Daisy knew there was a huge gulf between his world and hers. She knew the dangers when the two worlds intermingled. So many times, her aunt had warned of the very private entertainments the men of the *ton* sought at the theaters. Aunt Margaret was determined Daisy would not become some rich man's mistress before being passed to another. Daisy wondered why her aunt worried. No fancy lord would want a woman with a crooked leg.

As Aunt Margaret began to recite one of the French poems written by the popular poet Marquis de la Cour, Daisy knew she was beaming with pride. Her aunt's voice was as lovely as her appearance.

Her attention was brought back to her companion when he said, as applause marked the end of her aunt's recital, "Do not take my words the wrong way, Miss Kendall, but you seem to wish you were up there with Miss Burroughs."

"Me? Oh, no! I know my limitations, and I could never hold an audience enthralled as she does." She did not add that the stage was no place for a woman who hobbled.

She had little chance to think about that because Lord Tremont kept her busy answering questions between each performer's presentation. She wondered how he had learned to make another person feel as if their opinions were of the greatest interest to him. Mayhap she was too accustomed to theater people. Nothing mattered to them but the judgment of a theater owner or patron they were trying to impress.

When Lord Tremont stood as the actors were taking their bows, Daisy tried not to let her joy crash into despair that this magical interlude was coming to an end. He had been polite to keep her entertained with his questions, and she should be grateful for that.

"I have enjoyed our discussion," she said.

"As I have. I trust we may continue it while we dance later."

Glad her bonnet's brim would hide any hint of a blush, she answered, "I cannot."

"Are you betrothed or otherwise spoken for?" he asked, his smile wavering.

"No, but I cannot dance with you this evening. I am grateful for your invitation. However, I must decline it."

"I shall hope that you will change your mind."

Daisy did not want to tell him that she would be leaving with her aunt while Lady Higginson's guests had their late supper. She would be a fool to do so, for her charade would be ruined and Aunt Margaret and the others shamed.

"I cannot promise."

"Then promise we will continue this conversation soon."

"Let us see what the evening brings," she replied. There would be no *soon* for them.

"A splendid suggestion, Miss Kendall." He took her hand. When he raised it to his lips as he bowed over it, she drew in a quick breath. That soft sound brought a smile from him and a frown from her aunt, who was watching closely. "I look forward to continuing our *tête-à-tête* in whatever manner you deem appropriate."

Daisy tried to think of something to say, but no words formed as he released her hand and walked toward Lady Higginson, who was giving him an indulgent smile. Glancing up at her aunt, Daisy knew she should be relieved she had a reason to leave before the dancing began. She was not, for her mind refused to think of anything but how she might see Lord Tremont again and share a conversation and . . . she touched the hand he had kissed . . . a conversation and more.

Chapter Two

Climbing the narrow staircase in the house that smelled of too many meals in too much grease, Daisy listened to the familiar sound of Mrs. Bailey's children arguing on the first floor and her aunt doing voice exercises on the second. The bakery on the ground level was closed on Sundays, but tomorrow it would be busy.

She opened the door, and her aunt's voice became louder. Leaning her parasol against the door, she limped across the carpet that once might have been a variety of colors, but now was a sorry gray. She pushed aside the heavy drapes on the room's single window. Although the room was stuffy, she did not raise the window. Aunt Margaret did not like the whole street to "get a performance for free."

Aunt Margaret switched keys and began anew as Daisy sat on the bench by the window. The cushion was as worn and colorless as the rug. Gazing out the window, she did not see the street or the buildings. Thoughts of Lord Tremont filled her head. She was a widgeon.

"Home already?" asked Aunt Margaret as she came out of her bedroom. Her golden hair was piled casually on her head, and her cheeks were as pale as her white wrapper. Aunt Margaret was almost as proud of her perfect complexion as she was of her acting skills.

Daisy chuckled. "I am almost an hour late."

"Late?" Aunt Margaret's smile faded as she whirled to look at the clock on the mantel. It was finer than anything else in their rooms. On the right side, several pieces of the gilded decoration were missing. "Oh, dear! I had no idea so much time had passed. I need to leave for today's early rehearsal."

"An extra rehearsal?"

"For those who wish to have a chance at getting a lead role." She fluttered about like a flower caught in a wind. "Oh, dear! I had planned to get something for supper and—"

"I will make something for us." Daisy did not know when she had begun to protect her aunt from the realities of their tight finances. Mayhap it had been from the moment Daisy had been trustworthy enough to buy their food, when she was no more than five or six years old.

Aunt Margaret loosened her hair. Shaking her head, she frowned. Immediately, her lips turned upward. She would not chance any lines that would mar her appearance. In the past few years, she had stopped introducing Daisy as her niece.

"Remain here and allow no one in while I am at the theater," Aunt Margaret said. "I do not want that man you spoke with last night calling here."

"How could he call here? He has no idea where we live." She smiled. "His name is Joshua Tremont. He was charming, nothing else."

"Daisy, you know I have warned you about charming men." This time, her frown did not ease. "You are too trusting."

Daisy sagged against the bench as her aunt went into her room. Aunt Margaret knew about men who tried to beguile their way into a woman's life, for she had been dealing with them since she first walked the boards.

But Aunt Margaret was wrong about Daisy being too trusting. She could not even trust her own heart. She had learned that after having a *tendre* for a handsome young actor who had plied her with attention until he discovered she could not help him advance himself within the company. That lesson had taught her to be leery of men.

"But Lord Tremont wants only to talk to me," she whispered sadly. Even that, she knew was now impossible.

"Who is he?"

Daisy put the sleeve she was embroidering for Aunt Margaret's costume on the bench. On the room's only chair, Georgette Noone was sewing another costume. Georgette was an aspiring actress. Her red hair and bright blue eyes revealed her enthusiasm about everything around her. Although she had done no more than serve as an assistant for several renowned actors, she dreamed of applause and admirers waiting for her after each performance.

"Who is who?" asked Daisy.

"Whoever is making your face glow like a sunny day."

"I don't know what you are talking about."

Georgette wagged a finger at her. "Don't try to trip me the double. I have known you since we were children. I have seen that expression on your face only once before." Her nose wrinkled. "I never understood what you saw in that man."

"Neither do I. Now."

"So who is this new man who has caught your fancy?"

Daisy knew demurring would be a waste of time. Georgette would keep asking until Daisy owned to the truth. "Someone I met at Aunt Margaret's last performance."

"At Lady Higginson's house?"

"Yes."

"Did you attract the attention of the butler, Daisy? Do tell me you have not let a mere footman intrigue you."

"I have not been intrigued by a footman, nor did I get even a passing glance from the butler, who was old enough to be my grandfather. I met a gentleman."

Georgette grinned. "A gentleman, you say. Does this gentleman have a name?"

"Joshua Tremont."

"Lord Tremont?" Georgette's eyes widened.

"Have you heard of him?" She wanted her friend to say no, that Lord Tremont was not one of the rakes who loitered near the theater in hopes of a liaison with an actress.

"Yes."

"Oh."

Georgette laughed, the sound like a cheerful fountain. "Don't look down-pinned. It is not as you think. I have heard of him because members of his family have been generous patrons at several theaters in recent years. His father was fond of classical plays while his mother seems to prefer farces."

"Then she would enjoy this conversation."

"Especially the part where you act as if you don't care if you see Lord Tremont again."

"I never said that. I—"

A knock came at the door. Daisy's heart leaped with excitement before she silenced it with a reminder that Lord Tremont could not be calling.

When she opened the door, she saw a boy waiting on the landing. "Yes?"

"Miss Carver asked me t'bring this t'ye, miss."

Adelia Carver was Aunt Margaret's dear friend who had helped her in the theater. Miss Carver had had a rich protector for almost a decade, and she lived in a lovely home.

"Thank you," Daisy said, holding out her hand for the folded page he was drawing from beneath his tattered but clean coat. "I will see my aunt gets it."

"Not fer yer aunt, miss. 'Tis fer ye."

"For me?" She had never received a letter, although Aunt Margaret received requests for performances. None of them came to this address. Daisy was not quite sure why Aunt Margaret used her friend's address.

The boy nodded.

Daisy took the page. "Wait here." She went to where she kept her bag. Fishing in it, she found a penny and gave it to the boy.

He tipped his cap, grinned, and ran down the stairs.

"I do hope," Daisy said as she closed the door, "he will not lose that penny in some game of chance."

"More likely some tavernkeeper will have it in his pocket soon." Georgette motioned for Daisy to sit. "Who has written to you?"

"I have no idea."

"Then open it and find out. If it is bad news, it will not get better by waiting. If it is good news, why would you want to delay?"

Daisy looked down at the page that was sealed with green wax. She started to peer at the symbol pressed into the wax, but Georgette urged her again to open the letter. She slipped a finger between the edges and broke the seal, the pieces of wax sprinkling on her lap. Unfolding the single sheet, she read:

My dear Miss Kendall,

Forgive my impertinence in writing you. I am sorry our conversation at Lady Higginson's soirée was cut short. On the morrow, I shall be enjoying fresh air in Hyde Park. If the weather permits you to consider an outing, we may have the opportunity to continue that conversation.

I am,

Your humble servant,
Joshua Tremont

"What does he have to say?" asked Georgette.

"He?" Daisy wondered if her friend had suddenly mastered the skill of reading her mind.

"It is that glow. It is back!"

Daisy folded the page and put it into her sewing basket. "Don't be want-witted."

"*I* am not." Georgette leaned toward her. "What *rendezvous* has he suggested?"

"Did you read through the page?"

"No, because you did not hold it up to the light." She giggled. "Daisy, the only reason a gentleman would write to you or me is to suggest a *rendez-vous.*"

"You need not make it sound tawdry."

"Tawdry? I was thinking of the excitement."

"Think as much as you wish." Daisy reached for her aunt's costume. There was still the other sleeve to complete.

"Your aunt will be pleased that he has contacted you."

"You are mistaken. Aunt Margaret would be greatly displeased to learn of this. You must not say anything to her."

Georgette regarded her with bafflement. "Does she have higher aspirations for you? An earl, mayhap? After all, she has insisted that you learn all a woman must know to be a part of the *ton.*"

"I shall never be a part of that world."

"Even a lord's mistress may come into contact with the Polite World."

"This conversation is silly. I have no interest in becoming Lord Tremont's mistress." A quiver raced through Daisy as she thought of his powerful gaze and his gentle touch.

"Oh, Daisy," Georgette moaned. "If you will not consider going to meet Lord Tremont for yourself, go for me."

"For you?"

"I shall fade away from curiosity about what Lord Tremont is like."

"You are being absurd."

Georgette held up the costume she had been working on. "If I wear this, he will assume I am your maid. Then I can see him, and, more importantly, he can see you."

"You are wasting your time playing matchmaker. He is of the Polite World, and I am not."

"To own the truth, I am wasting more time on my curiosity. A chance meeting with a handsome viscount, Daisy, and your life has been changed. I want to discover why."

"You have been too long in the theater. You believe in the fairy tales on stage."

"Why not? Don't you?"

"I used to," Daisy whispered.

"Then why not see if you can again? We can borrow a carriage from my friend and meet Lord Tremont in Hyde Park as he requests." Georgette smiled, and Daisy knew she was still having an *affaire* with the second son of a baronet. "Don't say no, Daisy."

Picking up the letter, she read it again. She would not say no, for while she might hide the truth from her friend, she could not hide from it herself. She wanted to see Lord Tremont again. After all, what could come of it but a pleasant memory?

Chapter Three

Hyde Park was quiet as snow drifted through the air. The day was chill, but not unbearable.

Joshua walked his horse slowly along a path. Would Miss Kendall accept his invitation? He would have preferred to ask her to call at his house, for January was not the time to meet out-of-doors. Such a suggestion would have scandalized the young lady, and he suspected she would have refused, telling him not to bother her again.

But was Daisy Kendall a lady or an imposter? She had the polished manners of a young miss, but nobody at Lady Higginson's house had ever met her. That was a puzzle, and he liked solutions for puzzles.

In the three days since Lady Higginson's gathering, he had sought to find that answer. He had been pleased when he learned that Lord Hird's convenient had worked in several productions with Miss Burroughs. A request through Hird to Miss Carver for directions to Miss Kendall's house had been denied, but she had assured him that his message would be delivered to Miss Kendall. Although Joshua was baffled why Miss Carver refused to tell him where Miss Kendall lived, Lord Hird had mentioned that those in the theater had many peculiar superstitions. Mayhap one was not revealing the residence of one's patrons. Joshua found that difficult to believe, for the theaters where his family served as patrons knew quite well how to find them to ask for more money. He had not wanted to get into a brangle, so was grateful for the promise that the letter would be taken to Miss Kendall.

Like Cinderella, the pretty blonde had appeared and vanished without a clue to her identity. Not even a slipper remained behind. Was she a shy lady or a woman with aspirations far above her station? If she came to the park, he might discover the truth to the mystery surrounding her.

As he turned his horse toward the path leading down toward the Serpentine, Joshua heard a grumble behind him. He smiled at his companion, who had made no secret that he thought this outing had already gone on too long.

Nate Mithen, the son of a successful industrialist, had everything, save a title, to make him welcome in the Polite World. His pockets were plummy, as evidenced by high-stakes wagers at the gaming table; he frequented the best tailors and was the envy of the dandy-set; he provided a well-stocked cellar; and he had a honed wit that got him into trouble and back out with alacrity.

"How long must we ride in circles?" Mithen muttered, drawing his gray horse even with Joshua's chestnut mount. His round face lengthened almost to match his horse's as he shivered. "It is dashed cold."

"If you wish to return to your house," Joshua said, scanning the shore where the Serpentine broadened, "do not let me keep you here."

"She is not here."

"Yet."

"It is not like you to chase after a woman who turned you down when you asked her to stand up with you."

He smiled. "You are right. It is not at all like me."

Mithen scratched his brown hair and settled his tall beaver back on his head. He slowed his horse, but called, "You usually are the most sensible of us."

"True, but a man can get bored with being sensible."

"*That* most definitely does not sound like you."

Joshua chuckled, but wondered how his friend could not understand that a man should not always do just as it was anticipated he would. Mithen was outrageous, but on occasion, he could be almost philosophical, revealing a most unexpected aspect of himself.

His laugh faded when he espied the golden fire that had caught his eyes at Lady Higginson's house. A simple open carriage was driving toward them from Oxford Street. That must be Miss Kendall, for he had never seen another with hair that color. Resisting the temptation to ride neck-or-nothing toward her, so he might get some answers to his questions, he chose a pace more appropriate for the park.

Miss Kendall wore a dark green bonnet and spencer. A heavy blanket covered her lap. Beside her sat an attractive redhead huddled beneath another blanket, only her hands emerging to grip the reins. Her clothing identified her as an upper servant. Everything appeared to be exactly as it should for a lady enjoying an outing. Yet . . . no one knew her.

Joshua tipped his hat toward the carriage. "Good afternoon, Miss Kendall."

"Good afternoon, my lord." She put her hand on the one he held out as he had on their first meeting. She must have seen him glance at her companion because she added, "Georgette, please bring the carriage to the side of the path." Looking back at him, she smiled. "I wondered if you would be foolish enough to ride on this brisk day." Color flashed up her already burnished cheeks. "I did not mean to suggest—"

"You are right. I was foolish to suggest meeting here on a wintry afternoon. However, we are well met."

She laughed. "That sounds like one of the lines spoken during the Shakespearean scenes at Lady Higginson's recital."

"I appreciate you coming out in the cold."

"Fresh air does one good." She glanced at where he still held her hand.

He did not let her draw her fingers out of his. He had not guessed her slender fingers were so strong and so delicate at the same time. "Shall we walk along the Serpentine?"

"I am sorry. No."

He frowned as he looked at his friend flirting with her maid. The redhead was responding with an inviting smile. "Miss Kendall, now it is my turn to apologize if my words gave you the wrong impression. I did not mean to suggest anything untoward."

"I did not mean to suggest you did."

"Then will you walk with me so we may speak more comfortably?" He chuckled. "I was quite spoiled by our first conversation. Sitting side by side in a parlor allows for easier discourse than this."

Daisy smiled even as she wished she had not let Georgette persuade her to come to the park. She could not fault her friend because the chance to speak with Lord Tremont again had been so tempting. But she must be wiser in the future. Not only did each encounter increase the chance that he would discover she was not of the *ton*, but devising excuses not to walk in his company would become ever more difficult.

"It is very cold," Daisy said. "I fear I am not dressed for a promenade."

He swung off his horse. Holding the reins, he rested the elbow of his dark blue coat on her carriage. "Now you will not have to strain your neck to look up at me."

"You are kind, but won't you take a chill standing here?"

"Not if you entertain me with your wit."

She laughed. She could not halt herself, for his entreating expression appeared so heartfelt. "I am unsure how entertaining I shall be, my lord."

"Why not tell me how you happened to be at Lady Higginson's soirée? You are quite the lady of mystery."

"I was there with my aunt. Her last name is not the same as mine, so that may be why nobody realized."

"So no mystery?"

"Not really. Are you disappointed?"

Lord Tremont chuckled, but she noted how his eyes remained narrowed as if still trying to figure out her secrets. Oh, what a simpleton she had been to come here!

"Quite to the contrary," he said. "I am glad to have that question out of the way, so I might ask you another."

"And what is that?"

"Would you allow me to call so we might talk under warmer circumstances?"

"That would not be wise." She reached for the reins.

"No?"

"No."

"Why not?" he asked.

Daisy had no quick answer to give him. "Forgive me, my lord, but I must be returning home. I came here only to let you know that I received your kind note. If I am tardy, my aunt will be concerned for me."

"Your aunt? You live with your aunt?"

She smiled. This was a safe topic to bring this to an end. "I live with Aunt Margaret. She has had the responsibility of me since I was a very young child."

"When your parents died?"

"Yes."

"A straightforward answer."

"I would like to have known my parents, my lord, but Aunt Margaret tells me stories of them. She is a skilled storyteller, and through her, I have come to know them."

He folded both arms on the side of the carriage. "I guess it is not possible to mourn for someone you never knew."

"Yes, it is impossible to mourn their deaths, because I have never known them other than as characters in one of Aunt Margaret's stories. However, I do long for the chance to know them better."

"I can understand that." Without a pause, he asked, "Miss Kendall, when can I see you again?"

"Again?" She shook her head. "I am not sure that is possible."

"But why? Haven't you enjoyed our conversations, both today and before?"

"Yes, very much."

"Then do say you shall agree to have me call."

"No!"

Lord Tremont drew back at her vehemence. "If I have done or said anything to distress you, Miss Kendall, please accept my deep apologies. Such words were unintentional."

"You have done nothing." She slapped the reins on the back of the horse.

Both Lord Tremont and his friend jumped away as the carriage rolled out into the middle of the path. Beside her, Georgette gasped in shock.

"Slow down!" Georgette cried, holding onto the side of the carriage. "You shall run someone over."

Daisy drew back on the reins.

Her friend pouted. "I was having a lovely conversation with Mr. Mithen. Why did you take off with no warning?"

"Lord Tremont was insistent about calling on me."

"That is good."

Daisy scowled at her friend, then looked forward again as she drove the carriage into the traffic on Oxford Street. "Are you out of your mind? I cannot have him calling on me. If he saw where I lived, he would . . ."

"He would know you had lied to him."

"I have made a jumble of this. What shall I do now?"

Georgette turned on the seat and sighed. "You do not need to fret. We are not being followed. I doubt you need to do anything. Lord Tremont clearly saw your actions as a request not to call."

"I hope so."

"Do you?"

Daisy almost said, "No." She stayed silent. She could not be silly, because she knew all the reasons why his call was impossible. Yet she did not want to lie to her friend, so she decided not answering would be the wisest thing she had done today.

Chapter Four

"Let's go in here." Georgette pointed to Mr. Dedham's china shop near St. James's Square.

Daisy laughed. "An excellent idea. We might find just what we are looking for."

"I did not mean to buy anything. I simply wish to look at his wares."

"We shall look, and mayhap we can find what we need."

"Are you certain the director would want us to shop here?" asked Georgette as she walked with Daisy into the shop.

Daisy smiled. "Why not? The scene is set in a fine house. When my aunt throws plates to shatter against the set's wall, they should look like ones used in a fine house."

"These will be more than we can afford."

"Let's hope not. We found nothing suitable at Mr. Blyde's shop in Golden Square. Just musty old bottles and dishes that did not look elegant enough. Mayhap there is something here we might afford."

"I doubt it." Georgette went to a table where bowls and teapots appeared as if they would topple to the floor if one was moved. "Although there may be some chipped pieces they would have to throw away otherwise."

"They may be willing to give us a discount."

Georgette grimaced. "You are always an optimist, aren't you?"

"Yes." She looked at ewers with animals painted on them.

Lifting one, she examined it closer. Aunt Margaret would prefer something a little more feminine.

"Is that why you had that expectant look on your face when you opened the door to me? Were you hoping to see another letter from Lord Tremont?"

Daisy put the ewer back on the table. "You are silly."

"You are, too, Daisy, if you keep thinking about him. Your parting last time made your intentions quite clear. I am sure he has turned *his* intentions elsewhere."

"I would rather not speak of this." Daisy took care that her uneven steps did not brush her against one of the tables or shelves. Sending the merchandise crashing to the floor would incur a debt greater than the production could afford. She admired the delicately decorated pieces. "This might do." She picked up a plate decorated with Chinese figures. "The blue is bright, and it would look fancy to the audience."

"How many do you think we should get?" Georgette asked. Her sigh signaled she had reluctantly given up discussing Lord Tremont.

Daisy wished it was as easy to get him out of her thoughts. He had lingered the past few days, refusing to be budged. Forcing herself to concentrate on what Georgette was saying, she replied, "A score should be enough for the scheduled performances." She counted out the plates, setting them on a wide windowsill. "Will you find a clerk to help arrange for these to be delivered to the theater?"

As Georgette went along the narrow aisle between the tables and the wall, Daisy reached for more plates. She froze when she heard the voice that had sifted into her dreams. Lord Tremont! What was he doing here? She started to turn to see if her ears had deceived her, then looked down at her weak leg. She sat on the bench by the window and rearranged her cloak to hide her right leg.

Would Lord Tremont even notice her pretending to examine the plates on the windowsill? She was unsure if she hoped he would or would not. No, she was not unsure. She wanted both.

Georgette rushed to her and said in a taut whisper, "Daisy! *He* is here!"

"I know."

"What are you going to do?"

"I must be honest with him. This charade has continued too long."

"No! You must not." Georgette's eyes were wide. "If the truth angers him, he could withdraw his family's patronage from the theaters. That would be disastrous for your aunt."

Daisy gulped. She had never considered how yearning to see Lord Tremont might affect her aunt's career. She would do nothing to risk Aunt Margaret.

"Miss Kendall?" asked a deeper voice.

She looked up to see Lord Tremont standing in front of her. He was elegantly dressed as always, and his boots shone with his valet's attention.

"Good afternoon." She glanced at Georgette, hoping her friend had some suggestion.

Georgette sat beside her on the bench.

"We are again well met," Lord Tremont said.

She smiled when he did. She must give no sign of the true directions of her thoughts. "In far more clement conditions, my lord."

"Joshua, if you would."

"Really?" Daisy stared in astonishment. When Georgette jabbed her with a hidden elbow, Daisy hurried to say, "That is very kind of you, and my name is Daisy."

"I know." He picked up a dish decorated with white and yellow flowers. "Just like on this design. Do you like it?"

"No." She laughed, amazed that she could. Then she realized, no matter what the circumstances, she enjoyed talking with him. As they must not meet again, she would savor every word. "I have to own to disliking the flower I was named for. It is a silly blossom covered with insects."

"Do you prefer roses?" He put down the dish and offered his arm. "Shall we see what we may find of that sort here?"

"If you would forgive me, I must say no. I am waiting for my order to be completed."

Georgette said quietly, "I shall go and see what is keeping him, Miss Kendall."

Daisy hoped Joshua—how delightful it was to think of him that way, for it suggested no chasm existed between them—did not see Georgette's mischievous grin.

"May I?" Joshua asked, motioning toward the bench.

"Of course."

"Are these what you are buying?" He sat and lifted a plate from the stack on the windowsill.

"These are for my aunt."

"Ah, your mysterious aunt whose name is not the same as yours. Do you gain pleasure from being cryptic?"

She met his eyes evenly, wishing she had her aunt's skills as an actress. Mayhap some of the hours of practicing scenes with Aunt Margaret would help her now. "I thought I was answering your questions."

"Answering, yes. Fully, no."

"I am sorry if you find my answers inadequate." She gave him a smile to ease the sharpness of her answer. "Mayhap, if I were to ask *you* a question or two, I might be shown what responses you expect."

"What sort of questions?"

"I thought it was my turn to ask questions."

He chuckled. "You are quite right. Ask what you will, Daisy."

Words threatened to disappear from her mind, banished by the warm sound of her name in his voice. She must take care, or her delight would betray her into revealing too much.

"What brings you into this store today?" she asked.

"You."

"Me?"

He smiled. "I was passing by on my way to meet friends, and I saw you through the window."

"That is an amazing coincidence."

"You sound dubious."

Daisy shook her head. "Not in the least. Only in stories are coincidences forbidden. I find, in real life, they happen all too often. I seldom come here. If Georgette had not insisted—"

"You are kind to heed the desires of your maid."

"Georgette has been a part of my life for as long as either of us can remember," she said, glad to be back on the solid ground of the truth. "I have to own I would prefer to shop at a bookshop than here."

"I suspected you might have something of a bluestocking about you."

She laughed. "That is very insightful of you, for I enjoy poetry as well as prose."

"And plays, I surmise."

"Yes."

"If you will forgive another question, allow me to ask what your favorite bookstore is."

"Mr. Homsby's bookshop on Old Bond Street. It is a bit dusty, but I find his selection of books unmatched in London." She was talking too much. She would be wise to bring an end to this conversation before he discovered what she was hiding. "I fear I am keeping you from your friends, my—" She corrected herself when he gave her a feigned frown. "I am keeping you from your friends, Joshua."

"You always seem anxious to see me on my way. Do you find my company bothersome?"

"Another question?"

"I am afraid so. You are a puzzle, Daisy. Will you answer that one question?"

"Gladly. I don't find your company bothersome. I do have another query of my own."

"What is that?" He laughed. "Forgive me for yet another question."

"Are you always so persistent with women?"

His eyes slitted as they had by the carriage, and she wondered if she might be seeing the real man behind the jovial rogue. There was an intensity that fascinated her, giving her the same feeling she got on an opening night when everything could go wrong or be gloriously splendid.

"That is quite the question," he replied.

"Yes, it is, but I daresay it is a fair one."

"It is a fair question, unquestionably."

"If you would prefer not to answer it, you need not." She scanned the shop. "I wonder where Georgette has taken herself off to."

"No."

Daisy looked back at him, astonished at his peculiar response to her comment. "No?"

"No, I am not usually this persistent with women."

"Oh." She had no idea what else to say.

When Georgette walked toward them, a clerk following with a wooden box to hold the plates, Daisy almost jumped to her feet to rush to her friend. She halted that impulse as Joshua stood and stepped to one side so the clerk could gather up the plates on the windowsill.

"I shall leave you to your business," Joshua said as he took her hand. "Thank you for yet another most unusual conversation. I trust I shall see you again."

"That is possible."

"Possible?" He laughed, but again that forceful gleam brightened his dark eyes. "I would say it is quite likely. A man who owns that he is persistent should not disprove his words with the very next breath."

"I did not think you would."

"How well you have come to understand me when I have figured out so little about you."

She saw the clerk was done putting the dishes into the case. In moments, he would be asking for payment, and she did not want Joshua here when she stood and hobbled after the clerk to the counter.

"Good afternoon, Joshua."

"Good afternoon, Daisy. Until next time we meet . . ." He brushed her hand with a swift kiss that sent fire through her.

Daisy watched as he walked to the door. When it closed behind him, she twisted on the bench to see him through the window. His easy, confident stride announced he was a man who knew what he wanted and intended to get it. In only a few steps, he had vanished along the street.

Her hand was squeezed, and she looked at her friend. Georgette was grinning as broadly as Aunt Margaret did after receiving a part she had hoped for.

"Until the next time you meet?" gushed Georgette. "I believe that viscount is much taken with you, Daisy, and you are much taken with him."

"Yes." Not owning to the truth would be ridiculous when her friend saw it quite clearly.

"So what shall you do now?"

"Do?"

"He is going to seek you out again."

Daisy shook her head. "You know he must not be allowed to find me. Aunt Margaret will be aghast that I have had these conversations with him." It was easy to forget that when she was laughing with Joshua. His attentions made her feel beautiful and perfect in every way.

"He is going to seek you out again," Georgette repeated, her smile fading. "You must decide what you shall do."

"I know that I must." As she rose so she could pay the clerk for the dishes that by the end of a fortnight would be nothing but shards, she wished she had some idea what she should do next time she encountered Joshua Tremont. She knew what she wished to do, but letting him kiss more than her hand was an invitation to further complications. If she were honest with him . . .

Her heart denounced the very thought. It was, she realized with a pulse of dismay, already too late to halt further complications.

Chapter Five

My Dearest Daisy,

I trust you will forgive my presumption in addressing you so. You have been much in my mind in recent days.

"Egad," groaned Nate Mithen from over Joshua's shoulder. "Why not beg her to see you again and have it over with?"

Joshua pushed back his chair from the writing table, forcing his friend to step aside. "When did you get into the habit of reading one's private correspondence while it is being written?"

"Shortly after you started writing these ardent letters to Miss Kendall." He frowned as he dropped onto a chair, stretching his legs across the dark rug. "I have to say something I never thought I would say to you."

"What is that?"

"You are pathetic!"

"I would rather you spare yourself from saying that again." He rested one elbow on the writing desk.

"I gladly would if you would spare me from having to watch you chasing after this young miss's skirt. It is absurd. You don't know anything about her. She is leading you on a merry chase, knowing quite well that her mysterious aura intrigues you."

"I am interested in discovering the truth."

"Just what she thinks as well." Mithen's mouth twisted as he ground out, "She is playing you for a fool, my friend."

"You are mistaken."

"Then she is married."

"Married?" he asked, astonished.

Mithen laughed as he propped his foot on his knee. Flicking mud from his boots onto the patterned carpet, he said, "She has no interest in you calling. In fact, she gets agitated at the very idea of you giving her a look-in. That suggests she has a husband or mayhap a jealous lover she is anxious to keep you from discovering."

"Now you are the one being absurd."

"Then what is your explanation?"

"I have none."

His friend exploded up from the chair. "This is not like you, Tremont."

"On that, I agree." He watched as Mithen stormed about the room like a cat on the prowl for a hapless mouse and finding no prey. "And I like that this is nothing like how I would customarily act."

"Aha!"

Joshua sighed as his friend faced him. "Do excuse me from watching such theatrics."

"I see what you are up to. You are meeting her to spite your mother's plans to have you in the Parson's Mousetrap before the upcoming Season reaches its end."

"An excellent theory, save that my mother has not yet returned to London. She should be arriving within the next few days."

"Then why are you continuing this chase?"

Coming to his feet, Joshua went to a table where wine and glasses awaited. He poured two glasses and held one out to his friend. As Mithen gulped it down, Joshua walked to the window that offered a view of the street.

Why *was* he continuing this chase? He had given that question no thought because he had simply been enjoying the encounters with Daisy. She was unlike any other woman he had met. She was straightforward on most subjects, except her family.

No one he knew within the *ton* recalled seeing her before the evening at Lady Higginson's house. Even though her polished manner suggested she belonged in the Polite World, she showed a commonsensical approach he had not encountered in a young miss before. Was he fascinated with her solely because, as his friend suggested, she was an enigma? Those secrets were part of his preoccupation with her. He was fascinated, as well, with her kindness to her maid, her quick mind, and her charming countenance.

"No answer?" asked Mithen, bringing the bottle of wine to refill Joshua's glass. "This is a very sad sign."

"Sad?"

"Or featherbrained, which may be closer to the truth. Only a fool would fail to see that this young woman is luring you into a snare." His friend sighed. "A most permanent snare that even your mother's machinations have failed to get you to spring."

"You have it backwards."

"How so?"

Joshua took a sip of the wine, then smiled. "Here is a woman who may or may not be a part of the *ton*. She has not made any demands upon me to escort her to any gathering. She seems interested only in conversation and friendship."

Mithen shook his head with a wry smile. "Don't you know that it often begins that way? First she beguiles you, then she draws you into that trap in front of the parson."

"Daisy is not like that."

"Are you sure?"

"As sure as any one person can be about any other person." He almost laughed, but the situation was not amusing. It had been almost a week since he had chanced to see Daisy at the china shop. Yet his curiosity refused to be quiescent. "I suspect on our next meeting I shall learn what I need to get answers to my questions."

Mithen rolled his eyes and sat heavily. Putting the back of his hand to his forehead in a melodramatic pose, he intoned, "My friend, you are showing all the classic symptoms."

"Of?"

"Falling in love." He groaned. "I fear you are doomed."

Was she being followed?

Daisy looked over her shoulder at the carriage rolling slowly down the street. The carriage's black sides glistened with care, and its green wheels were bright in the harsh winter sunshine. The coachee steered the horse around trash, keeping it out of the gutters.

It was a gentleman's carriage, sleek and yet able to travel long distances on rough roads with speed. She saw other residents of the street turning to stare. Rarely did such a grand conveyance come here, and each time it meant one of the actresses living in the mazes of cramped rooms had found a protector who offered her a more elegant dwelling. When an actress returned here, she usually came in a simple cart along with whatever possessions her lover allowed her to take. There was a constant cycle of women leaving in hope and returning, dejected but determined to obtain another paramour.

Daisy had seen many such carriages, but today the sight made her uneasy. What if Joshua happened to pass by and spotted her on the walkway? Her stomach twisted at the thought of him making arrangements for an actress to become his mistress.

His smile thrilled her. Could he look at her like that and still be seeking a convenient? She knew so little about men, other than the actors at the theaters where her aunt played. They treated her like a little sister and saved their flirtations for rich matrons and dowagers. Aunt Margaret's only lessons on this topic had been that a young woman could easily make a wrong decision. If a man looked more than once in Daisy's direction, her aunt made sure that he had no chance to talk to her.

The carriage kept pace with Daisy. She walked as quickly

as she could without calling undue attention to herself. The carriage drove faster. When she reached the steps to her door, she climbed them, holding her cloak close.

"You are panicking over nothing," she said to herself.

She knew she should not look, but she could not resist as she opened the door. She peered around it as the carriage drove past. The man inside was not Joshua, for he was a generation older and had white hair. The carriage stopped in front of a house farther along the street.

Daisy breathed a sigh of relief, then chided herself as she climbed to the uppermost apartment. Why had she thought Joshua would send his coachman to find her? He had no idea where she lived, because she had been careful to offer him no clue.

Yet a part of her had hoped it *was* Joshua in the carriage. In the days since she spoke with him at the shop, she had thought of little other than him. She enjoyed recalling the sound of his voice, the sparkle of his smile, how his eyes narrowed and twinkled when he laughed. It was not enough. She wanted to see him again. Not just for a brief flirtation while she guarded every word she spoke, but long enough so she could learn more about the man who beguiled her heart.

She was being silly. Joshua had offered her kindness, nothing more. She halted on an upper landing. That was not true. He had offered her that dizzying kiss on her hand, and she had seen the barely banked flames in his eyes. He was a man of strong emotions, which he was restraining in her company. Did he, as she did, wish for more than such a chaste salute?

She climbed the topmost staircase. Such thoughts would obtain her nothing but misery. Seeing Joshua again would be addlepated. Even Georgette could comprehend that now. What had begun as a game had become an invitation to disaster. She needed to forget about Joshua.

That thought brought tears to her eyes, but she dashed them away as she opened the door. She was glad she did when she saw her aunt standing in the middle of the main room, a grim expression on her face.

Daisy closed the door behind her. Her aunt should be at the theater now, having one final rehearsal for the play opening tomorrow evening. Had there been a change in plans?

She must choose her words with care. To ask if the play or her aunt had some difficulty could cause more distress. She forced a smile as she slipped off her cloak and hung it by the door. "Aunt Margaret! What a surprise! I did not think you would be home so early."

"Obviously." Her aunt stormed toward her, holding out a slip of paper. "I found this slid under our door."

"This?"

"A letter to you that begins 'My Dearest Daisy.' Who is Joshua Tremont?"

Daisy did not consider, even for a moment, lying to her aunt. Aunt Margaret had always been honest with her.

Taking off her bonnet, she hung it next to her cloak. "Don't you remember? Joshua Tremont is Lord Tremont. I met him the evening you performed at Lady Higginson's house."

"That handsome man I saw sitting with you?"

"Yes."

Aunt Margaret tossed the page onto the table. "You told me that you did not know him."

"I did not . . . then."

Her aunt stared at her for a long moment, then sank into the chair beside the table. Her voice sounded strangled as she asked, "And since then?"

Daisy knelt beside her aunt's chair. "I have seen him twice, each time well-chaperoned, I assure you."

"Well-chaperoned?" Aunt Margaret laughed sadly. "If all young women were as sensible as you . . ." She frowned. "Whether you had a watchdog or not is not the issue. The issue is that you have met Lord Tremont without seeking my permission."

"I knew you would not allow it."

"So you went behind my back?"

"Yes."

Aunt Margaret raised a brow. "Honest as always, aren't you, Daisy? However, that virtue does not excuse your behavior. How many times have I told you what a peer wishes of us?"

"Many times, but Joshua—"

"You address him so?"

"He asked me to, and I saw no reason not to comply." She put her hand on her aunt's arm. "Aunt Margaret, he has been a gentleman with me."

"They start that way, then they offer an arrangement which is much to their benefit. It might appear to be to your benefit, but when they tire of you, you find yourself tossed from that comfort. I have taken care not to compromise myself in hopes of protecting you."

"And you have protected me, Aunt Margaret. I have heeded your words, and I know the peril awaiting an unwary woman in the theater."

"In spite of that, you let the first lord you meet sweep you off your feet."

Daisy flinched and looked down.

Aunt Margaret asked in amazement, "He doesn't know about your weak leg?"

"No."

Aunt Margaret brushed Daisy's hair back gently. "You must bring this to an end. You may believe he is a good man, but he has been interested only in using you."

Daisy closed her eyes. Her aunt said *has been interested*. Aunt Margaret believed Joshua would want nothing more to do with her if he discovered how she hobbled. Tears bubbled into her eyes, and Daisy knew she believed that, too. Otherwise, she would not have gone to such extraordinary lengths to prevent him from seeing her walk.

"Those men," Aunt Margaret continued, "are accustomed to having every whim catered to, and they believe any woman connected to the theater offers an air of danger which appeals greatly to them. Those two things in combination have created many broken hearts. Dear child, do you think Lord Tremont's family will accept him offering his attentions to the niece of an actress? Not even a renowned actress, who could have found welcome within the Polite World." Her eyes glittered with tears. "I once believed I would have that opportunity."

"And then you had the responsibility for me." Daisy smiled sadly. "I am grateful, dear aunt. You have sacrificed so much for me. If you had not had to consider me when deciding which parts to take, you would be renowned from one end of England to the other."

"Your faith in me is amazing." Cupping Daisy's cheek, she said, "So believe me now when I tell you that Lord Tremont's family, upon discovering the truth, will insist he rid himself of you posthaste. Even if he has a true *tendre* for you, he could offer you a life only as his mistress. I suspect, in spite of how you have defended him, that is his intention."

"But Joshua has no idea I am connected with the theater."

Aunt Margaret stared at her, speechless.

"I have not lied to him," Daisy went on before her courage failed her. She wanted Aunt Margaret to admire Joshua as she did. "He assumed I was one of Lady Higginson's guests. He has asked to call, but I have found kind ways of saying no. All he knows of me is that I live with my aunt."

"Did you tell him my name?" Her aunt grasped Daisy by the shoulders.

Shocked by her aunt's abrupt fervor, Daisy whispered, "I told him I live with my aunt whose name is Margaret."

"Oh, my!" Aunt Margaret surged to her feet. "You didn't, did you? Not really."

"I did. I didn't think there was a reason not to. What is wrong, Aunt Margaret?"

"Oh, my!" Wringing her hands, she went into her bedroom and slammed the door behind her.

Daisy stared after her aunt. Of all she had said, mentioning that she had told Joshua the name of her aunt had distressed Aunt Margaret the most.

Why?

Chapter Six

Daisy watched the walkway. Last night's rain had turned into sleet near dawn. Although it was vanishing with the day's sun, ice remained in shadowed spots. She used her folded parasol to test the walkway in front of her because slipping in public would be humiliating.

There were not many shoppers, other than she and Georgette, abroad on Old Bond Street this early in the day, which was why she preferred to be doing her errands now. She would not come here in the afternoon when the Bond Street Loungers, dandies with not a single rational thought among the lot of them, bothered anyone who did not meet their sartorial standards.

Even at this hour, Mr. Homsby's bookshop might be busy. It was rumored the Marquis de la Cour's newest book of poetry was available. Aunt Margaret hoped to use selections from the Frenchman's latest collection of love poems for a reading this evening at a duke's house. So many in the Polite World adored his poems, and an inspired reading would be a way for her aunt to obtain the applause she craved.

"Is your aunt done with flying up to the boughs?" asked Georgette who flashed a smile at a young man walking in the other direction.

"She is, once she found out that I had torn up the letter from Joshua."

"You tore it up?" Georgette gasped. "Without reading it?"

"I read it first." Daisy could not imagine shredding the

page without reading what had begun with, "My Dearest Daisy." She had read the rest quickly so her heart did not have time to plead with her to join Joshua at an assembly the following evening as he requested.

"Did he ask you to meet him again?"

"Yes."

"And will you?"

"I cannot. Aunt Margaret is adamant about that."

Georgette edged around a patch of ice. "Mayhap she knows something about the viscount that you do not."

"I asked her that, and she denied it." Daisy did not add that, for the first time, she doubted her aunt's honesty.

"Excuse me, miss," came a voice from behind them.

Georgette moved to the inner part of the walkway, and Daisy stepped toward the curb. She was accustomed to letting those in a greater hurry squeeze past her.

"Excuse me, miss."

At the impatience in the man's voice, she wondered how much smaller he expected her to make herself against the edge of the street. If she moved any farther from the middle of the walkway, she would be stepping in front of a carriage.

"Excuse me, miss."

Daisy turned, tightening her hold on her parasol so she did not do something absurd like falling on her face. Her sharp retort went unspoken as she stared at Joshua. Even as joy swirled through her at the sight, she realized, in dismay, that he must have seen her uneven steps. All her efforts to keep her impairment hidden had been for naught.

She glanced at Georgette, who was staring, wide-eyed and wide-mouthed, at Joshua. How long had he been walking behind them? Had he heard the course of their conversation?

"Good morning," he said with a tip of his hat. As always, his clothes were stylish and his boots shone like the patches of ice.

"Good morning." Daisy kept her hands folded on the handle of her parasol, waiting for the questions that always came when someone saw her walk. *What is wrong with your leg? How did it happen?* Those were always followed by looks of pity. She did not want to see that pity in Joshua's eyes.

"We are again well met." He smiled.

Daisy blinked, astonished that he had not pelted her with those hated questions. "Y-y-yes." Was it possible he had failed to notice her lopsided gait? No, that was impossible. He had been walking behind her long enough to ask her to excuse him three times.

Joshua motioned along the street. "May I walk with you to the bookstore, Daisy?"

"How did you know we were bound for the bookstore?"

"Aren't you?"

"Yes, but how did you know?"

"You spoke of how you enjoyed shopping at Mr. Homsby's bookshop, so I decided to take the chance you might be going there." He chuckled. "To own the truth, I have taken that chance each day for the past four days."

"What? You have been lurking here solely in hopes of encountering me?"

His smile twinkled in his eyes. "Not solely, for I have had business here. I simply chose to do that business along Old Bond Street when it was possible you might be doing yours as well."

Heat scored Daisy's cheeks when she saw Georgette hiding her smile. "I should not have suggested otherwise."

"Why not? I have been curious why I received nothing, not even a dismissal, from you in response to my latest letter." He held out his arm. "Shall we continue to the bookshop?"

He did not say anything when Daisy hesitated before putting her fingers on his arm. She was glad he kept his pace slow. Her weak leg supported her as long as she did not do something careless. Something else careless, for she should have guessed he would be curious why she had not written back. She kept waiting for him to ask the questions she had considered inevitable. Instead he talked about the wares displayed in the shops they passed.

She paused at the curb. Keeping her gaze on the street, she edged down with care. She did not want to topple on her face.

He waited patiently, then matched her steps across the street. He put his hand over hers on his arm when they reached the curb. Although she wanted to tell him that going down a curb was much more unsettling than going up, she let him assist her. She lifted her hand away and thanked him as Georgette joined them. Her friend would not want to miss a word.

"You are welcome." His smile remained warm, and she did not see pity in his eyes.

Joshua offered his arm again to Daisy. He was not surprised when she hesitated as she had before they crossed the street. He wanted to assure her that, as a gentleman, he would have offered his arm then and now no matter what. He had been shocked by the sight of her unsteady steps, but he admired how she used her parasol as a cane. She was a woman who let nothing stand in her way, not even her own malady.

Questions about why she walked as she did pounded through his head, but he would not embarrass her by asking them here. Some of the mystery about her had been solved, because he understood why she had declined to dance at Lady Higginson's and not walk along the Serpentine. The injury must not be recent, because she handled herself with the ease of having done so all her life. Was *this* what kept her from taking a greater part in the Season?

At first, when he received no answer to his letter, he had been vexed. Why would she react with such warmth to his touch, proper though it had been, and then disappear? He had been enjoying the flirtations, and his curiosity about what she refused to discuss remained unsatisfied.

As a few days passed, he had realized his reaction was not just irritation. He missed her teasing and kindness and her unique insights that were such a change from the young misses who seemed to think only of marriage.

Then more time went by, and he began to fear that she could not meet him because something appalling had happened. What if she were ill? He considered finding out where she lived, but the idea of showing up at her door and being asked to leave because she would not receive him was bothersome. So he decided to watch for her on Old Bond Street. Now this plan had reached fruition, and all he had were more questions.

The bookshop's two windows were filled with books that had recently been published. There was a large stack of bright blue books with gold leaf pressed into the leather to form the book's title. He recognized it as the latest book by the French poet. He grimaced. Each time Marquis de la Cour had another book published, nobody seemed able to speak of anything but the poetry.

As Joshua opened the door to the sound of a tin bell, the hush from the bookshop reached out to invite them in. Daisy stepped past him, and he was treated to a flowery fragrance that seemed perfect for her. Light and ethereal and impossible to capture. She looked especially lovely with the sunlight upon her creamy cheeks. Her dark green cloak and straw bonnet were ones he had seen her wear before, and they suited her far better than the cumbersome parasol with its wide border of lace.

Her sweet scent was overwhelmed by the musty odor within as he followed her maid into the bookshop. If Mr. Homsby ever cleaned his murky shop, there was little sign of it. A fine layer of dust clung to every surface. The bookshelves were close together, every shelf overflowing with books. The table in the center of the shop had books piled high on it. Even a sneeze threatened to send everything crashing down.

Daisy went to the counter at the rear of the shop, her maid following closely. Mr. Homsby stood in front of a crimson curtain that separated the shop from whatever he kept behind it. The stout man had a bushy mustache the same gray as his hair. He reminded Joshua of a well-fed curate.

Mr. Homsby's eyes were wide, and Joshua guessed the quarto had not expected to see Daisy with him. Joshua wondered what Mr. Homsby might know about the secrets Daisy hid. Asking was something a gentleman could not do, even though the thought was tempting.

"Good morning. Do you have the book I have been waiting for?" Daisy asked.

"One moment, Miss Kendall." The bookseller reached under the counter.

She accepted a package wrapped in brown paper and paid him. "Thank you, Mr. Homsby."

"You were wise to order the book early. In spite of what you see in the window, most of the copies of the marquis's book have already sold." He grinned, and Joshua guessed that a good share of the profits was going into Mr. Homsby's purse.

Daisy turned, and he saw her uncertainty when she discovered he still stood by the door. He did not move. There were answers he wished to obtain, and he would not allow her to slip away again before he got them.

The door bumped into him, and Joshua stepped aside, opening the door wider for a pair of elderly ladies. He closed it and blocked Daisy's exit again. She frowned at him, but he remained where he was.

"Where are you bound next?" he asked, keeping his tone conversational.

"Home."

"I would be glad to give you a ride in my carriage."

"No. No, thank you. That is not necessary, and you have your business concerns to attend to."

"My foremost concern now is to find out why you did not answer my most recent letter."

She took a step forward and reached out her hand. Did she

think he would move aside if she confronted him boldly? She was right, he had to own, and he cursed the manners so well drilled into him.

As she opened the door and went past him, he caught her arm. She looked at him, shocked, but he would not let her astonishment halt him again. Drawing her hand within his arm, he took a pair of steps. He thought, for a moment, that she would be stubborn and remain where she was. Then she acquiesced and walked beside him.

"So you enjoy the marquis's poetry," he said in the same casual voice.

"It is a gift for my aunt." Dismay rippled across her face, and he wondered what part of the innocuous answer had upset her.

"When shall I have the honor of meeting your aunt?"

She stopped and lifted her hand off his arm. "I must ask you to excuse me, Joshua. I fear I forgot other matters I need to attend to this morning."

He put his hand on her sleeve again. "Daisy, I deserve the courtesy of an answer to such a simple question."

"This is not the place for a discussion."

"We can sit in my carriage." He motioned toward a vehicle, and it rolled along the street toward them.

"You cannot think I would sit with you in your carriage without a chaperon."

"We have a chaperon. Your maid is here."

Daisy looked again at her friend. Georgette grinned, and Daisy knew Georgette was relishing every moment of the debacle. Would she have let Georgette talk her into the meeting with Joshua at Hyde Park if she had guessed the situation would become such a bumblebath? There was no need to wonder. *She,* not Georgette, had been the one to decide to go.

"You should have brought a footman with you," Joshua continued. "If the Bond Street Loungers decided to go abroad earlier in the day, you could find your situation troublesome."

"My eagerness to obtain this book led me to make a poor decision." She shifted, hoping he would release her arm.

He did not, as the carriage slowed next to them. He opened the door and motioned to Georgette to climb in. When Georgette was seated facing backwards, Daisy handed her the wrapped book. She let Joshua hand her in, glad that he made sure she was steady on her feet. He shouted to his coachee before entering the carriage. He drew her down to sit next to him on the other seat as he closed the door.

The carriage bounced into motion. Georgette giggled as she ran her fingers along the fine black velvet on the seats.

"Where are we going?" Daisy asked, unable to share her friend's excitement. This was a catastrophe of the first order.

"Green Park." Half-turning on the seat, Joshua asked, "Daisy, why won't you be honest about why you did not respond to my letter?"

"I should—"

"I would like an explanation, an honest explanation."

She stared at his taut face. He had every right to be angry at her bizarre behavior. And he *was* right. She did owe him an explanation. She considered spinning him a tale worthy of one of Aunt Margaret's scenes, but he had asked for honesty. She should give him that, no matter how difficult it was for her to say and for him to hear.

"My aunt does not wish me to see you again," she said quietly. She ignored Georgette's sharp breath.

"Is that so?" His mouth tightened, and she realized he believed her aunt thought him an unsuitable companion for her niece.

She wanted to laugh and tell him how mistaken he was, but she feared he would find the truth even less amusing. Instead she said, "My aunt is the only family I have remaining. I trust her to know what is best for me."

"So you share her opinion?"

"No . . . I mean, yes . . . I mean . . ." She paused to halt her babbling. "Joshua, you are assuming things that are not so."

"I am assuming your aunt believes I will cause damage to you in some way. Is that wrong?"

"No." She put her hand on his sleeve. "But I have assured her that was not so."

"Then you assured her wrongly."

"What?"

He clasped her shoulders and drew her closer. His gaze captured hers, refusing to relinquish it, as his voice dropped to a husky whisper. "Daisy, she is not wrong. When I see you and hear your bright laughter, the thoughts in my head would be very damaging to you if I acted upon them."

"You should not speak so."

"It bothers you to hear the truth?"

"In this case, yes." She drew out of his grip and edged away, even as she wanted to move closer and urge him to do as he imagined. "Joshua, it would be prudent for us to bid each other *adieu* now and leave with our fond memories."

He cupped her chin in his broad hand. "Fond memories may be enough for you, but I find that those memories haunt me when I am not with you. Are memories truly enough for you?"

"No," she whispered.

"Then—"

"Do not say something you will regret, Joshua."

"You are right. I should not *say* something I shall regret when I could *do* something I know I shall *not* regret."

Daisy gasped when he tilted her face up and brushed his lips across hers, so quickly that she had no time to react. No, that was not true. Liquid fire flowed through her, teasing her to melt against him.

His thumbs brushed her cheeks as he said, "I was wrong."

"You regret that you . . ." She could not say the words that blemished the delight of this kiss.

"I regret that I did not kiss you like this."

When his arms swept around her, bringing her up against his hard chest, his mouth found hers. This kiss was not a mere grazing across her lips. This kiss was searing as his lips urged hers to return it. Her fingers curved up around his shoulders, tentative, then more certain as she stroked his nape. The very touch of his skin thrilled her.

He lifted his mouth and murmured a question. She understood only her name as he sprinkled kisses across her face. She whispered a yes, because she could not imagine telling him no when he held her close.

When he had the carriage stop near Buckingham House, so that she and Georgette might alight as she requested, he held her hand, reluctant to let it go. She stared after the carriage while it continued toward James Street.

"Are you out of your mind?" cried Georgette as the carriage vanished into the traffic along the busy street.

Daisy looked at her friend. "I must be." She sighed as she touched her weak leg. She could never marry, for she chanced having her children born with this wretched leg as she had been. Knowing that made the stolen kisses even more precious.

Georgette grasped her shoulders. "Daisy, how are you going to explain to your aunt?"

"I was not going to tell her I kissed Joshua. If you say nothing—"

"Not about kissing Lord Tremont, but about agreeing to meet him at the Olympic Theater tomorrow night."

"The Olympic Theater? What are you talking about?"

Her friend screwed up her face as she shook Daisy gently. "You air-dreamer! Lord Tremont asked you to attend with him, and you told him yes."

"Oh, my!" She had been so lost in the pleasure of his kisses she had been oblivious to what he was saying.

"What will you do?"

"I don't know."

"If you don't go, he will come looking for you again."

Daisy felt color drain from her face. "That must not happen."

"What will you do?"

"I will have to meet him and put an end to this." Her voice

broke on the last words. Her heart did, too. She had been a fool to let this continue, and now grief was the price she must pay. "Will you help me, Georgette?"

"If your aunt finds out I have been helping you, she may have me banished from the theater."

"The only way to keep her from discovering the truth is to help me bring this to an . . . to an end." She bit her lip to silence her sob.

"All right," Georgette said with a sigh. "Why couldn't you have developed a *tendre* for another man?"

"If I could answer that question, I would be a genius." A drop of rain struck her bonnet. "We need to hurry. It is going to storm." Daisy started along the street. When she noticed Georgette was not with her, she looked back to see her friend wearing a very chagrined expression. She asked, "What is wrong?" A silly question. Everything was wrong.

She was even more sure of that when Georgette hurried to where she stood and said, "I left your aunt's book in Lord Tremont's carriage. What if he tries to find you to return it?"

Daisy just stared at her friend. She had no answer.

Chapter Seven

Daisy arrived early at the Olympic Theater in Wych Street near Drury Lane, which was not far from where she lived. The half-dozen narrow columns out front offered nowhere to hide. She must not be seen by someone who had worked with her aunt. That would destroy her charade. She had put on her best dress, which had been remade from one of her aunt's costumes. It was a delicate cream satin with netting of the same color. She had persuaded Georgette to borrow a gauze turban from the theater. Its trio of feathers touched the curls across her forehead. She had taken the elbow-high gloves and a dark blue cloak from her aunt's cupboard, and the fan was the simple one she had carried to Lady Higginson's soirée.

Although Georgette had pleaded with her not to come to the theater tonight, Daisy knew not meeting Joshua was a guarantee that he would come looking for her. If Joshua discovered what she really was, he might denounce her as a liar. She had not lied, but she had not been honest, either.

Good sense told her to remain at home. Her heart led her here.

Daisy breathed a sigh of relief when Joshua arrived in his fine carriage. His black coat and white breeches were the perfect complement to her elegant ensemble. When he took her hand and bowed over it, for a moment she could believe she was a part of the *ton*.

"Good evening," he said with a smile that sent happiness careening through her.

"Good evening." She laughed. "Aren't you going to say we are well met?"

His laugh resonated off the roof. When people milling around the columns glanced in their direction, she hoped no one would recognize her.

"I am glad you agreed to join me here tonight," he said. "After the performances, I will give you the book you left in my carriage."

"You are kind to return it."

"It will cost you, my dear."

She could not keep from smiling, for joy burst within her heart at the endearment. "Really? What?"

"That we can discuss inside." He gestured toward the theater's open door.

Putting her hand on his arm, Daisy went with him. She bit her lower lip when she saw a familiar face just inside the theater. Dorian had been selling drinks in theaters for as long as she could remember. She had not realized he had left Drury Lane to work here.

Before Dorian could see her, she raised her fan quickly and bent toward Joshua as if whispering a secret. She was glad when Dorian was called away to the other door.

"Are you all right?" Joshua asked. He was looking at her as if he feared she had lost every bit of her mind.

Mayhap she had, but not now. She had lost it when she agreed to join him here.

"Just excited," she replied quietly. "I have not been to this theater before."

"Its renovations were completed not very long ago, so this is my first time here as well." He led her toward the stairs. "Our box is this way."

Daisy smiled as she walked with him past a plush curtain on the upper level. Entering the box, she gasped. "This is remarkable."

"We have no poles to block our view of the stage."

"Amazing," she said, not wanting him to guess she had been talking about the box itself.

It was as grand as the stage. She let him take her cloak and seat her on a plush chair. Although she had spent her life in and out of theaters, she never had viewed a performance from a luxurious box. So many times, she had hidden in the wings and watched the glittering ladies and their escorts arrive for the evening's entertainment. Glances out during the entr'acte showed her that the entertainment was not limited to what happened on the stage.

She looked down at her gloved hands. She was here without a chaperon. What must Joshua think of her?

The curtain at the back of the box was pushed aside again, and she saw the man who had been with Joshua when he met her in Hyde Park. The pretty miss with him was introduced to her as Miss Katherine Stubbs. Her clothing was of the latest style, and she wore enough jewelry to buy the building where Daisy lived several times over. The man was Mr. Mithen, but she did not hear his first name because Miss Stubbs began to prattle about how exciting this evening was and weren't they thrilled to be here and had they heard the latest *on dits* and she was just speechless with anticipation of the performances to come.

Joshua folded his arms over his chest and tried to stop listening to the chatterbox. He shot a scowl at Mithen, but his friend seemed enraptured with Miss Stubbs. His frown became a smile as he recalled how Mithen had agreed to escort this young woman as a favor to his grandmother. Mrs. Mithen was as anxious to see him married as Joshua's mother was to see *him* leg-shackled. How ironic if Mithen was caught in the very snare he had lambasted Joshua for tempting.

Tempting . . . that was the very word for Daisy tonight. Although those silly feathers had bounced several times up into his face, threatening to make him sneeze, as they came into the theater and to this box, she looked even more lovely than usual tonight.

He put his elbow on the edge of the box and said beneath Miss Stubbs's patter, "I hope you will enjoy this evening."

"I already am."

"About the fee you owe me for returning your book . . ."

Her eyes twinkled as brilliantly as the jewels around Miss Stubbs's neck. "Yes, you said you would tell me my debt to you when we were inside."

"It is quite simple. I want—" He was halted by Mithen calling his name. Devil it! "What is it, Mithen?"

His friend hooked a thumb toward a lad who was carrying a tray. The box attendant, Joshua realized, coming with tea they could enjoy before the performance started.

"Would you like a cup?" he asked, looking back at Daisy.

He was astonished to see her fan open and against her face again. "No, thank you," she said, her voice low and rushed.

"Are you certain? The air is dry tonight, and—"

"No tea!"

The box attendant backed out as Joshua motioned him away. As Miss Stubbs began chattering again, Joshua put his hand on Daisy's arm. He lowered her hand away from her face and asked what was wrong.

"How can anything be wrong tonight?" she asked with a lightness he knew was false. She had never been coy with him before, and he found it unsettling. "Joshua, I am happy to be here with you."

That he believed, for there was a sincerity in those words that had been missing in her question. As the play began, barely slowing Miss Stubbs's prattle, he found himself watching Daisy's face more than the stage. She laughed along with the jokes, and tears filled her eyes when the heroine's plight became desperate. He had never seen a more expressive, open face, and he smiled when she did and slipped his arm around her waist when those tears almost overflowed. She looked up at him, setting his heart to beating so fiercely he wondered how anyone could hear the lines from the stage.

Then, more quickly than he guessed, it was time for an intermission. As Miss Stubbs talked about the performance as if none of them had seen it, he saw the curtain at the back of the box shift again.

Joshua came to his feet as his mother stepped into the box. He nudged Mithen, who was clearly blinded with his admiration for Miss Stubbs, to stand, too, then bent to give his mother a kiss on the cheek.

"Will you join us, Mother?" he asked.

His mother, who had not been taller than he since shortly after he left for his first school, wore jewels twisted through her hair. Her gown, a sedate dark purple, was edged with wide lace at the bottom. She had been thrilled when the war with the French was over so she could once again buy lace that had not been smuggled into England.

"I am sitting with my friends," his mother replied, "but I thought I would see how your evening is passing. Very well, it appears." She looked directly at Daisy. "Joshua, I do believe there is hope for you yet." She smiled. "I am Louisa Tremont, Joshua's mother. I do not believe we have met."

"No, my lady." Daisy returned his mother's smile, and he could see she was relieved. Why? Who had she expected to appear through the curtain? "My name is Daisy Kendall."

"We met at Lady Higginson's house a few weeks ago," Joshua said before his mother could put Daisy to an interrogation. As he had guessed, his friend's name brought a wider smile to his mother, who had been trying to enlist Lady Higginson in her matchmaking schemes.

"You must call on me tomorrow, Miss Kendall," his mother said.

It was not a request, but a command. Daisy realized that, too—he could tell by how she swallowed roughly.

"I would like that very much, my lady," Daisy said, "but I

have other plans for tomorrow that I cannot change. My aunt would be heartbroken if I did. Mayhap another day?"

"Of course." His mother was taking her refusal far better than he had expected. "I am always at home on Thursday, so do call Thursday next."

Daisy nodded, knowing she could do nothing else. When Joshua's mother turned to speak to Miss Stubbs, greeting her warmly, Daisy let her breath sift out. Lying to his mother was horrible, but what else could she have said? She was grateful when Miss Stubbs nattered on and on, because that kept Daisy from having to say anything else. Even when Joshua's mother bid them good evening and the curtain on stage rose again, Miss Stubbs did not slow.

When Joshua escorted Daisy from the theater at the evening's end, he asked, "How long do you think our ears will ring with her prattle?"

"Your friend seems quite taken with her."

"Quite the surprise, although he may be more interested in the fact her father is a baron with no sons than he is in her chatter."

"What an awful thing to say!"

He regarded her with astonishment as they stepped out onto the columned portico, which was teeming with other theater-goers. "Awful? Mithen would not be the first man to marry to get a title for his son."

"But he should have some affection for her. She—"

Joshua pushed her aside roughly. Before she could do more than gasp, she saw him seize a lad's wrist. A knife clattered to the ground. Joshua kicked it into the shadows and gave the boy a shove in the other direction. The boy turned and started to snarl a curse, then stared at Daisy.

She recognized him as one of the boys who did errands for the actors at her aunt's theater. Before he could say anything to betray her, she slipped her hand into Joshua's arm and stepped out into the falling snow with him.

"He would not have hurt you," Joshua said, misinterpreting her silence. "He wanted your bag."

"I know that." She glanced back to make sure the boy was not following them. The wrong word now could be disastrous. She knew what she had to do. She had to tell Joshua good-bye.

"An interesting end to an interesting evening," he said.

" 'Interesting' is one way of describing it."

"I am sorry if Miss Stubbs distracted you from the performance."

"You have no need to apologize." She rubbed her hands together as snowflakes drifted down around them. "I was not myself tonight."

"On that matter, I concur completely. I should have considered the effects my invitation to the theater would have on you."

"Really?" She must take care not to speak out of hand. But had he discovered the truth?

"And on me. You owe me an apology."

"I do?"

He smiled. "Miss Stubbs may have distracted you, but you distracted me. I could not tell you a single word that was said on that stage tonight." He drew her closer as they walked along the street.

Daisy stepped away. "Joshua, I should have told you before we went into the theater, but . . ."

"You cannot see me again."

"Yes."

"You know I will not accept that edict from your aunt without trying to persuade her to be sensible."

"She will not change her mind."

"If I speak with her, she might."

"No!"

He frowned. "Is that no to changing her mind or to speaking with her?"

"Both."

"Daisy, you are making no sense. What is wrong with me that your aunt will not receive me?"

Tears flooded her eyes. "There is nothing wrong with you."

"Are you suggesting that something is wrong with you?"

Before she could answer, a slight form pushed between her and Joshua. Lady Tremont, she realized, when she heard, "Have you lost your mind, Joshua?" Fury bristled from the viscountess like an explosion of fireworks. "How could you escort a woman like *her*?" She pointed at Daisy.

"Mother," he said in the coldest tone she had ever heard him use, "I would ask you to lower your voice and not to belittle Daisy."

"I am not belittling anyone." She glanced at Daisy and away, obviously dismissing her. "I am thinking of this family and your obligations to it. I will not have you paying court on a woman who is not . . ." She faltered.

Daisy tightened her hold on her cloak. Lady Tremont believed Joshua should not pay court on a woman unable to walk without lurching like a cart with a broken wheel.

Joshua's voice grew cold. "Mother, you owe Daisy an apology."

"It is not by my doing that she is as she is." Lady Tremont's anger dimmed for a moment. " 'Tis a shame, for she is a lovely young woman, but your son cannot be crippled."

Joshua asked again for his mother to apologize, but she continued to argue.

Daisy slipped into the shadows. The fairy tale was over. Cinderella had to leave with the chiming of the clock, and she must be careful to leave no clue, not even a slipper, to allow her beloved to find her. Blinking back tears, she knew she should have heeded her aunt. There was no place for her in Joshua's life, and letting him into her heart had been foolish.

As she went along the walkway, clinging to the darkest spots where he could not see her, she heard him call her name. She fought her yearning to run back into his arms, but that would only hurt him more. His mother was right. A viscount must have healthy sons.

The sound of his voice, filled with pain and despair, remained in her head as she hurried to her street only a few blocks away. As she climbed the stairs, the memory of his distraught voice trailed her, still urging her to turn around and go back to him. With her hand on the banister, she thought of how his arm had felt as unyielding beneath her fingers. She would never feel it again. This was the best thing for both of them, she knew, but had never guessed how hard it would be to do what was right when her heart ached to be his.

Chapter Eight

"I have the grandest news," Aunt Margaret said as she came out of her bedroom two days after Daisy's disastrous visit to the theater. She was smiling, and her steps were lighter than usual.

Daisy looked up from her mending and hoped her eyes were no longer ringed with red from tears. She did not want her aunt to learn of her humiliating evening. Forcing a smile, she asked, "What is it?"

"I have been offered the lead female role in a production of *As You Like It.*"

"How wonderful!" She stood, embracing her aunt.

Aunt Margaret could not stand still. She bounced about the room like a child. "It *is* wonderful, Daisy. I have longed for this part for many years."

"And now you have the chance to play it. Which theater will it be at?"

"It is not at one of the London theaters. It is with a traveling company. We shall be giving productions throughout the south of England, culminating with one at Stratford-upon-Avon, the great bard's birthplace. Isn't that wonderful?"

"A traveling company?" She could not imagine her life without her aunt. These cramped rooms would seem so empty when Daisy was alone.

Aunt Margaret sat, facing her. "I grew up in daisyville, as you know. I miss the fresh air one cannot enjoy in London."

"I know you do, for you speak of it often."

"We shall be gone for almost a year. Imagine, Daisy, getting to see so much of England while I have a chance to be the lead in such a delightful play!"

"It is wonderful. When do you leave?"

"Me? You are coming, too. I would not think of leaving you here alone."

"I should have realized that." She put her hand on the chair, gripping it, as she tried to control her heart that begged her to tell her aunt it was impossible to go to the country as long as Joshua was in Town. "When do we leave?"

"It will be a fortnight before we can go. Our first performance is scheduled in Dover for the evening of Valentine's Day."

"That is not much time." Did her voice sound as strangled to her aunt as it did in her own ears?

Her aunt's smile faltered. "You are unhappy about leaving London."

"I have never lived anywhere else."

"Not since you were a baby."

"I thought I was born in London."

Aunt Margaret stood. "There is so much to do to prepare for our time away. Daisy, will you go to Mme. Bellepont's millinery shop and bring back the hat I ordered? I must look my best now that I am going to be the female lead."

"Of course." Why had her aunt never revealed that Daisy was not born in London? And to leave now . . .

"Daisy, I would not have accepted this role if I didn't think it was for the best for you, too." Her aunt stroked Daisy's cheek.

"I know." Mayhap it was for the best to put as many miles as possible between her silly heart and Joshua. "Is it true that time heals a broken heart?"

Her aunt lowered her eyes and turned away. "I don't know."

"You have never had a broken heart?"

"Why don't you go to Mme. Bellepont's now? That way you will be back before it gets dark."

Daisy nodded. Her aunt had refused to answer so many other questions over the years by pretending she had not heard them, but never as many as today. Was this frustration welling up inside her, choking her, the same as Joshua felt when she evaded his questions? If so, she owed him a heartfelt apology. It was too bad she never would be able to give it to him.

Daisy dragged her dreary spirits behind her as she went along the street toward the milliner's shop. Every time she tried to persuade herself it was for the best that she not see Joshua again, she knew her heart would not let her lie. The time with him had been enchanted, for he did not seem to care who she was or that she limped on every step.

Lights were already lit in the shops, for the clouds were as low as her mood. She did not pause to look at the wares in each window. She must hurry if she was to get home before icy rain fell.

In front of Mme. Bellepont's shop was a wooden sign shaped like a bonnet topped with large flowers. This was one extravagance Aunt Margaret never denied herself, for she believed—rightly so, it appeared—that one must look the part of a great actress if one wished to be offered leading roles.

Daisy reached for the shop's door, then stepped back as she saw an unmistakable figure inside. Joshua! He was in the shop. What was he doing in a milliner's shop? She edged into the shadows and peeked in.

Joshua was standing with his hands clasped behind him as he watched Mme. Bellepont place an elegant bonnet on a young woman's black hair. The miss gazed up at him in expectation. Although Daisy could not hear her words, the pose spoke loudly. The young woman wanted Joshua's opinion of the bonnet. When she put her fingers on his arm with a suggestion of intimacy, Daisy backed farther away.

Her throat was tight with tears. This should be what she

wished for Joshua. He should have the company of a young woman who would be an appropriate Lady Tremont.

But how could he turn to someone else so quickly? Her heart refused to surrender its yearning. He remained in too many of her thoughts, and, during the past two days, she often wished she could share some tidbit of her day with him.

He had found another woman.

Mayhap Aunt Margaret was right. Mayhap leaving was for the best. Daisy wished she could believe that.

Joshua stepped from his carriage. How long would this chase go on? He had come here as soon as he escorted Miss Lofting home from Mme. Bellepont's shop. The idea of him going with the young woman to the shop had been a mistaken thing from the very beginning, something both of them discovered quickly. She had seen that his heart longed to be with another woman and that he was with her only as a favor to her brother, who had turned matchmaking eyes on the two of them. Miss Lofting could not hide her expectation of an offer from a man she had loved since she was little more than a girl, and Joshua offered his best wishes on her upcoming betrothal before hurrying back to the milliner's shop.

He had seen Daisy through the window, her stricken face as she discovered him there with Miss Lofting sending a blade of pain deep into him. Although Miss Lofting had urged him to go after her, by the time he reached the street, Daisy had vanished.

As he climbed the steps to the elegant town house not far from Soho Square, Joshua tried to get his jumbled thoughts in order. It was impossible.

The door opened as he reached it. A tall man in flawless black livery greeted him.

"Please express to Miss Carver," Joshua said, "that Lord Tremont wishes the indulgence of a few moments of her time."

The footman nodded and opened the door farther to allow Joshua to enter. The entry hall was decorated with the latest styles and colors, and he wondered how long Miss Carver had been living here. She was testing the limits of her lover's generosity.

Joshua followed the footman to a sitting room as exquisitely decorated as the foyer. Miss Carver, a lovely brunette, was sitting on a white satin settee. She looked up as her footman announced him. She blanched to the color of the satin. With a scowl at her footman, she stood.

"I am sorry, Lord Tremont," she said, "but you should have been informed I am not at home today."

He nodded. "Forgive me for intruding, Miss Carver. I shall take my leave as soon as you tell me why my letters to Miss Kendall have come to your house."

"Lord Tremont, you are asking for answers I cannot give."

"Cannot?"

"Will not." She picked at the buttons on her blue-sprigged wrapper.

"It would be most ungentlemanly of me to interrogate you further," he said, swallowing his frustration. "However, as you do know how to arrange for a message to reach Miss Kendall, I beg a boon."

"Do not ask for me to arrange for another message to be delivered to her from you, my lord. That is impossible."

"Will you let her know I called?" He clasped his fists behind him to hide his exasperation.

"If she asks, yes." Miss Carver hesitated, then said, "Lord Tremont, she plans to leave London within the fortnight, so it is unlikely I will be able to pass along your message."

Joshua bid her a good day. He tried to gather his thoughts together as he left the house and walked toward his carriage. How in all of London—in all of England or mayhap even the world, for Miss Carver had not said where Daisy was bound—could he hope to find Daisy now?

As if in answer to the question he had not spoken, he heard, "Lord Tremont, I may be able to help you."

He turned and stared. "You are Georgette, Daisy's maid."

"No, I am her friend. Do not be angry at her for the deception. It was my suggestion when I saw how much she longed to meet you in Hyde Park. She wanted to tell you the truth, but I warned her what she risked if she did."

"Risk? What do you mean?"

She glanced in both directions along the street. "Before I say anything else, my lord, I must know why you came here looking for Daisy."

It was, he owned, a reasonable request from someone who was most clearly, like Daisy, not what she claimed to be. "I wish to know where she is."

"If you are seeking her out solely to satisfy your curiosity about her, then I must bid you farewell. I will not have her hurt by you again."

"It was never my intention to hurt her at any time."

Georgette smiled. "I had hoped you would say that, which is why, when I saw your carriage, I waited here for you."

"You are a good friend to Daisy."

"I hope so, because I have never told anyone what I am about to tell you, my lord." She lowered her voice. "I think it would be better if we did not discuss this in the street."

Joshua opened the door to his carriage and handed her in. After he ordered his coachman to drive toward Grosvenor Square, he said, "All right, Georgette. Tell me what you can."

As he listened, more questions filled his head. He needed to get answers, and he had less than a fortnight to find them.

Chapter Nine

Daisy folded the nightgowns and placed them in the bottom of the box. Surrounded by everything she and her aunt owned, she was trying to get it into this one trunk that was all her aunt was allowed to bring when they left at dawn.

When someone knocked on the door, she said, "I will answer it, Aunt Margaret." She hoped it was Georgette, for she had not seen her friend in days. She did not want to leave London without saying good-bye . . . as she must with Joshua.

"Have you seen my green hair ribbons?" her aunt called from the bedroom.

"I believe they are on your bed," Daisy shouted back as she went to the door. Opening it, she gasped, "Joshua!"

"As you recognize me," he said, "I assume you will allow me to enter."

"What are you doing here?"

"Giving you a long overdue look-in." His voice remained icy.

As his mouth grew taut, she followed his gaze around the room. She wanted to explain away what he was seeing, but he was, at last, seeing the truth.

"May I come in?" he asked.

"I don't think that would be wise, Josh—my lord." Her heart shattered anew, but what he had discovered took away the privilege he had given her to address him by his given name.

"Wise?" He pushed past her. As she faced him, he said,

"Forgive me for doubting your ability to see what is wise when you plan to leave Town without telling me the truth."

"I should have been honest right from the beginning."

"You should have."

Daisy had never imagined his eyes drilling into her so coldly. Ignoring her heart imploring her to remain silent, she said, "I wanted to, but I feared that, once you learned how I had deluded you, you would withdraw your family's patronage from the theaters where my aunt works."

"You believed I would do such a thing?" Shock replaced the fury in his eyes, and she knew her words had wounded him.

"I did not want to believe you would, but you have every right to be furious with me, my lord. The deception was all mine. My aunt asked me to stop seeing you."

"So that much was true? You live with your aunt."

"Yes."

"And what else?"

My kisses, my love for you. She would be foolish to say that.

She was still trying to devise an answer when she heard, "Who was at the . . ." Aunt Margaret frowned. "Who are you?"

"Aunt Margaret," Daisy said, barely above a whisper, "this is Joshua Tremont."

"Lord Tremont?" Aunt Margaret folded her arms in front of her. "I had been led to believe, Daisy, that you had given Lord Tremont his congé."

"She did," Joshua replied. "I assume you are Margaret Burlingame, or do you prefer to continue the role of Margaret Burroughs within these walls?"

"Role?" asked Daisy.

Aunt Margaret's voice was tight. "You should leave now, Lord Tremont."

"I shall take my leave if Daisy honestly tells me why she has no interest in learning the truth about her weak leg."

"My leg?" Daisy asked, startled. She clutched the door as she looked from Joshua to Aunt Margaret and back. Both of these beloved faces wore a stubborn expression. Neither was ready to relent. This was not how she had imagined her aunt and Joshua's first meeting; it was how she had feared it would be.

Joshua went to her and folded her hands between his. "Daisy, do you wish to know the truth?"

She wanted to shout, *Yes!* but how could she betray her aunt? Aunt Margaret had raised her, and Daisy knew her aunt loved her. *And I love Joshua.* That unbidden thought refused to be silenced.

"You cannot know the truth!" Aunt Margaret cried. "The truth is dead and buried long ago."

Joshua smiled coolly. "Truth has a way of not staying dead and buried. You have to tell Daisy what happened to you and to her."

Aunt Margaret seemed to fold into herself. Sinking to the chair, she said, "Daisy, I have tried to protect you from the truth."

"About what?"

"About my greatest crime."

"Crime? You?" Daisy shook her head. "That is impossible."

"No, it is true," Aunt Margaret said. "Your leg's weakness has nothing to do with your birth. You were born perfect." Tears burst from Aunt Margaret's eyes and down her cheeks. "You were a beautiful baby, and when I saw you, all I could think of was how I wanted one just like you."

"If I was not born with this weak leg . . ." She glanced at Joshua and quickly away, a teasing warmth swirling through her. Aunt Margaret's words banished her fear that Daisy could pass on the frailty to her children.

"It was an accident," her aunt whispered. "I should have listened to Papa. He told me not to meet Louis again, but I could not bear never to see him again." She looked up at Daisy. "I did not want you to make the same mistakes I made. The same horrible mistakes." She hid her face in her hands. "I don't want to think of it. Lord Tremont, don't force me to think of it."

"Daisy deserves to know the truth."

Before Aunt Margaret could answer, Daisy said, "The truth is not worth making my aunt cry."

He took her hand, drawing her to him. "This is not the time to think with your tender heart. You need to know the truth, Daisy."

"And you know it?"

"Yes. With the help of Bow Street and others, I know it."

Daisy sat on the battered bench and brought him down beside her. Folding her hands in her lap, she said, "Then tell me. Do not force Aunt Margaret to say what brings her so much sorrow."

Joshua looked at her aunt for a long minute, and Daisy thought he would insist Aunt Margaret reveal what had been unspoken for so many years. Then, softly, he said, "There was a fire. Your aunt saved your life by tossing you out a window. It was snowing that night, and she must have hoped the snow would cushion your fall. It did, but something happened to your leg."

"She saved my life. That is nothing to be sad about."

"That is not all that happened that night." He took her hands again as he said, "Your parents died in that fire." He cleared his throat. "As did Louis Gatewell, your aunt's paramour."

"And Papa," choked Aunt Margaret. Once started, the words burst from her in a deluge. "I was upset when Papa discovered my tryst with Louis. I fled the room while they argued. I remember bumping a table and knocking a lamp to the floor, but kept going. Suddenly I smelled smoke and then I saw fire coming along the hall. I tried to put it out, but I could not. By then, it was too late to alert everyone." She whispered, "Daisy, I knew you would be in a room close to where my sister and her husband—your parents—slept. I was able to get to you, but they never got out. I don't know if they were in their room or where they were. I panicked. I could not face what I had done, and, if it had not been for you, I fear I would have killed myself. But I had to take care of you. I came to London in hopes of becoming a great actress, because on the stage, I could be someone else, someone who had not, through disobeying her father, killed her family." She hid her face in her hands. "That is why there is no one else, Daisy. You and I are the only ones to survive the fire."

"No, someone else did." Joshua went to the door and opened it wider. "Please come in."

An elderly man entered the room. He was as straight as a soldier, and his face looked familiar. Not because Daisy had seen his features before, but . . . She put her hands up to her own face. She had seen his features when she looked into a mirror.

Aunt Margaret leaped to her feet and flung her arms around the old man's neck. "Papa! Papa!"

Daisy stared in disbelief as her aunt hugged the old man, and they both wept. Slowly she stood.

When Joshua came back to stand beside her, he said, "Daisy, this is your grandfather, Sir Leander Burlingame."

The old man released Aunt Margaret and stared at Daisy. Tears washed down his face, and more welled up in his eyes. "You are the image of your mother."

"My mother?"

"My daughter, Lady Henry Sherson, but I see much of your grandmother, for whom you are named."

"Lady?" Daisy whispered.

"Your father was a baron," Joshua said almost as softly. "Your cousin now holds the title."

Her grandfather hugged her. "I feared I would never find you and Margaret after I recovered from the fire. You had disappeared."

"Papa," began Aunt Margaret.

"I heard everything from the other side of the door." Sir Leander looked around the room. "I believe you have punished yourself long enough for what was an accident. It is time for you and Daisy to come home."

Aunt Margaret tried to speak.

Daisy blinked back tears. For her, Sir Leander Burlingame

was a stranger, but her aunt's joy at this reunion would, she hoped, presage the happiness Daisy would have in knowing her grandfather.

"You don't need to ask," she said, "for I forgive you, Aunt Margaret. How could you believe otherwise?"

"I took you from the home and the life that could have been yours because I could not face my shame."

Daisy kissed her aunt's cheek. "You took me into your home and into your heart when you must have been sad and afraid. You have given me love and happiness." She smiled. "And a chance to meet your eccentric friends in the theater."

"But your parents . . ."

"You are the only mother I have ever known, Aunt Margaret. Your love has been everything to me." She looked at Joshua. "Thank you."

He cupped her chin. "When I realized after you fled from the theater that this was more than a flirtation, I wanted to find you. I saw your dismayed face during our joint trip to the milliner's, and I discovered there was no need for anyone to play matchmaker because I love you. Since then, I have been trying to find you and the truth, so I might tell you that. Will you marry me, my dearest Daisy?" He smiled. "With your grandfather and your aunt's permission, of course."

"Of course."

"Is that a yes to my offer?" He chuckled. "Or are you creating another puzzle for me to solve?"

"Which do you think?" Her laugh vanished when he captured her lips with the love she wanted for the rest of her days and every night in his arms.

Epilogue

Valentine's Day dawned with a hint of the spring to come. Daisy knew it was just a tease, but she could not help wondering if the weather was extraordinary because the day was special.

Today she would exchange vows with Joshua while her aunt and grandfather watched proudly. Even his mother had acquiesced to obtaining a special license for this wedding once she had a chance to meet Daisy's grandfather. The granddaughter of a baronet was an acceptable match for her son.

The door to the luxurious bedchamber in her grandfather's Bedford Square house opened, and Aunt Margaret came in with a smile. "This was just delivered for you."

Daisy broke the familiar seal and opened the page. Why was Joshua sending her a note when she would be seeing him at the altar within an hour?

My Dearest Daisy,

I wanted the chance to write you one final time a note that begins with "My Dearest Daisy," so excuse this silly missive. From this very special Valentine's Day through the rest of our lives, any letter I write to you will begin with "My beloved wife."

It was signed, *Your adoring husband, Joshua.*

CUPID'S CHALLENGE

Maria Greene

Chapter One

"By Jupiter, I'm bored beyond redemption," Vincent, Lord Ecton, said and drained his claret glass and put it down on the table. "Why are we closeted here at Watier's when there are any number of nubile females in London who are waiting for our ministrations?"

"We could at least have brought some Opera dancers around to entertain us," Eddy Miles said, and passed around another bottle of claret. "I'm getting foxed and in the mood for some dalliance."

Vincent put the empty bottle in the center of the green baize-covered table with the fifteen others. He was a four-bottle man himself, with one more to go before he would fall under the table.

"There's a new one, a plump blonde that I have my eye on," Freddy Longman said, and brushed back a floppy blond curl from his forehead. "She smiled at me the other night in the green room, and pouted at me. By Gad, I wanted to kiss her red mouth silly right then and there—and more."

Lucien Montclair sighed. He was growing more tired by the minute listening to these old arguments. Was there nothing else to talk about? Opera dancers were all the same; they claimed respectability, which they sorely lacked. Some had great wit and charm, yet underneath it all lay the desire for funds—*his* funds, which in the end didn't make them any different from prostitutes. He longed for someone, that elusive woman who was a lady, yet had some dash. She seemed to grow more intangible with every Season he spent in London. Perhaps such a female didn't exist; he certainly hadn't met anyone.

The brandy haze in his mind rejected any thought of entertaining Opera dancers tonight. He still enjoyed the odd evening of drinking and gambling with his cronies, but why bring in females? They brought nothing but complications.

"What about you, Montclair?" Freddy asked.

"I'm staying out of your plans, Freddy. Opera dancers don't carry an allure tonight."

"'Pon rep, what's wrong with you?" Monty Blaine asked, his red-rimmed eyes round with surprise. "You've never complained before."

"I'm tired, I'm jaded, I've had enough of Opera dancers," Lucien said with a shrug. *For a lifetime,* he wanted to add.

Monty snorted. "You sound *old,* my friend. Don't tell me you've tired of the creamy soft skin, luscious ankles, and heaving bosoms that they offer?"

"I have," Lucien declared. "If that's all they're offering. I like a quick mind, something more."

"They haven't tired of you, you handsome devil," Freddy said. "They fall all over you—literally fight to get your attention."

"I ought to be envious," Monty said, "but I can see why the attention could get tedious."

Montclair continued, "I've paid handsomely for their services in the past, and I resent that they are never content. No matter how well you treat them, they are never content. I'm swearing off women."

The men fell about laughing. "That's a dashed maggot-witted statement if I ever heard one," Eddy Miles said, and pushed a hand through his limp brown hair. His high shirt points had started to wilt and his face glowed red. "You can no more live without women than you can breathe, Lucien."

"Devil take it, Eddy, you make me sound dependent on the creatures, which I am not." Lucien knew it to be the truth at this point in his life, and it made him very world-weary—blue-deviled, in fact.

"Truthfully, aren't we all dependent on their attention if we admit it?"

"If you let them lead you by the nose, you surely are, Eddy," Lucien said. "In the end, empty attention leaves you with a hollow feeling inside."

An uneasy silence fell for a moment, and the men replenished their glasses.

"Well, they are better than the society females," Monty said. "At least you get something back from the dancers. The so-called society ladies are seeking to ruin us, and most of them don't even have anything to recommend themselves, except possibly lineage and land. They faint at the merest mention of male needs. They faint at everything. I can't abide them, and more often than not, they are horse-faced, vapid, humorless, and too high in the instep. Or they are poor and beautiful. They snare you with flashing smiles and seductive glances, and when you succumb, all that charm is turned off, and their greedy hands are held out for wads of blunt, and you end up supporting their entire family. No thank you."

"Listen to the cynicism," Freddy said, and flicked some ash off his black evening coat. "I don't agree with you on that score. I daresay some of us will make advantageous matches in due time. I, for one, plan to set up my nursery."

"Ha! You with your snout, Freddy?" Monty said good-humoredly. "All you'll be able to attract is someone from the hinterlands of Cumbria."

Freddy looked offended, his long nose quivering, and Lucien held up his hand. "Gentlemen, we're here to support each other, not to insult each other. Freddy can't help that his mother was a sow."

Everyone except Freddy laughed until tears streamed down their faces. "Devil take it, I resent your comments," Freddy said. "I want to suggest a wager."

Monty stopped laughing, his massive body growing still. "Wager? What kind of a wager?"

"Since all of you are so blasé, I suggest we make a wager on women."

"That's ludicrous, Freddy," Lucien said. "I won't be part of any blasted wager involving women. It would be insulting to them, and to us."

"Whyever not a wager?" Monty asked. "You're just as involved in this issue as we are, Montclair. You have to do your part."

"I have no interest."

"Then you ought to change that—this will give you a new spark in your eyes."

Lucien laughed. "Hardly. Perhaps I'll enter a monastery—"

"That's ludicrous. You're too young to swear off females. Twenty-eight is no age to turn celibate," Monty replied. "I know you won't be able to stay celibate for very long."

"You're in your cups, Monty, old fellow. Tomorrow you won't remember a word of this."

"Blast it all. Let me finish," Freddy said, his face covered with perspiration. "I suggest we collect the names of the least attractive ladies of the *ton* and then set out to court them. The first to win the lady's heart in question gains a thousand pounds."

"Of all the harebrained notions," Eddy said. "I can't picture myself at the feet of some flat-chested bluestocking when I can have a ripe peach in my hand any time I desire."

Freddy waved away his objection. "Let's bring in some paper and a quill." He ordered the footman at the door to fetch the desired writing implements, and within minutes, he was throwing out names. Another claret bottle emptied and joined the others in the middle of the table, and the footman uncorked one more.

"Agatha Ponsonby," Freddy cried with sudden excitement. He quickly wrote down the name.

"She's been on the shelf uncountable years." Monty said. "She's her stern father's handmaiden."

"Perfect," Freddy said, and rubbed his hands in glee.

"Letitia Wells," Monty said, and Freddy wrote, the quill rasping unsteadily against the paper.

Monty continued, "She's in love with bonbons and nothing else. She had an admirer once upon a time and when he turned to someone else, Letty went into a decline."

"Lucy Mottingrow. She loves nothing but horses, and she doesn't have a feather to fly with," Eddy said.

"Angela Valentine," Freddy said. "Sharp-tongued, and known to have a mind of her own. Dark as a gypsy, which ain't fashionable, but I don't mind the coloring myself. The family is poor but of good lineage."

"I would be sharp-tongued as well if I'd been on the shelf for three years," Lucien said. "Didn't some scandal involve her name?"

"Yes . . . I believe she was about to be married once, and the groom left her at the altar and fled to the Continent so that he didn't have to face the consequences of a breach of contract," Monty said, and wiped his forehead with a folded napkin.

The smoke in the room grew so heavy they could barely see each other. Lucien's eyes ached.

"Rosamunde Knoll," Vincent said uneasily. "She squints but is said to have a sweet disposition. I don't know."

"I suggest we put these names in a hat and each of us draw one. The first to bring one of these ladies to declare her love, wins the thousand pounds." Freddy wrote quickly and started to fold the billets.

"Now wait here, Freddy," Eddy said. "There's no challenge in this, and we're setting ourselves up for future difficulties. The women will fall over themselves to marry us. We are from old families and we're reasonably plump in the pocket. None of these women has any dowry and nothing else to recommend herself to us. The only one with any kind of lineage is Miss Valentine, but I believe her grandfather gambled away the family fortune, so it has fallen upon her shoulders to make an advantageous marriage to save the family."

"Freddy, you're a coxcomb if you think I'm willing to court one of these charmers," Lucien said. "I would *never* consider marrying one of them, and when it comes to ladies, you have to be careful so as not to be trapped. Their mothers will have you sign some kind of nuptial agreement before you've smiled twice at one of their daughters."

"I'd say you're wrong," Monty said. "We can behave as foolishly as we want so that they ultimately jilt us, but they have to succumb to our charms. The first one who can get the words 'I love you' out of the lady whose name he draws wins the money."

"That's outright cruel," Lucien said, and drank some more wine. "I won't be involved in breaking someone's heart. It's indecent, that's all. I don't want to cause some innocent lady any pain. Just think of it—if one of them was your sister, you would be livid. I wouldn't want to be the cause of someone's tears."

"As if your path weren't strewn with tears already," Monty said with a snort. "Don't turn sanctimonious."

"You're wrong, Monty. I've never deliberately gone out with the purpose of crushing someone's tender feelings. I don't care how undesirable these women are, they still have hearts."

The other men looked at each other.

"Shall we take a vote?" Freddy asked, his nose quivering.

The men—all except Lucien—gave shouts of encouragement.

He was immediately outvoted, and he wondered if this silly bet wouldn't be the downfall of some of them.

"Montclair, when did you ever care about the feelings of others?" Eddy asked, his lips pinching into a thin line.

"You might not know all of my good sides, Eddy, only my indifferent ones."

"Good sides?"

They all had a good laugh at that, and Lucien contemplated how empty the night that stretched ahead of him seemed, despite his rambunctious company. Claret was not the voucher to happiness, nor were Opera dancers, and it pained him to see how shallow his friendships had become.

To be truthful, he didn't know where to find happiness, and he dreaded the thought of living another forty years like this. To drown that disturbing thought, he drank some more claret, but at that moment he felt trapped, and he couldn't drown the truth with wine.

"We're going to draw names now," Freddy said loudly, and put the folded pieces of paper into a beaver hat. "You shall have to go into this venture wholeheartedly or face our ridicule for the rest of your days."

"Halt right there," Lucien said. "We can't be careful enough. After all, you don't want to be trapped into matrimony, do you?"

They all shook their head and waved unsteady hands. "No! We're too needle-witted to get leg-shackled to any of these maidens," Monty said.

"The thought of Parson's Mousetrap gives me hives," Eddy said, squirming. He undid his tight neck cloth and patted his brow with a handkerchief as if to cool the bright red color of his face.

"We draw the line at one dance at Mrs. Barton's ball," Montclair said.

"The St. Valentine's ball at Mrs. Barton's estate in Greenwich? Hmm," Freddy said, rubbing his chin. "It's the only ball between the Seasons. All the sticklers are *expected* to attend or forever be outcasts. As you well know, we're not welcome due to our reputations, and if we do attend, no chaperone will allow her charge to dance with us. We shall be asked to leave if we show ourselves there."

"Exactly," Lucien said. "It'll take some ingenuity on your part. Besides, we can't bring any witness along to hear declarations of love."

They all agreed, with cheers. A whole claret bottle turned over as Monty flailed his arms, and the wine soaked into the green baize. The footmen looked askance and set to clearing the table.

"The ball on Valentine's Day. That gives us some weeks to get closer to our goal, not counting the Christmas season. Our targets should still be in London."

"The little season is almost over," Monty said. "They'll be leaving for the country shortly."

"Then we have to busy ourselves with this mission," Freddy said, and started passing around the hat.

The men groaned in pain as they pulled the name. "I got . . . Letty Wells. She sh-swells like a sh-ship on a . . . sh-stormy sea." Monty looked bleary-eyed, and it wouldn't be long before his face fell forward into the wine stain on the baize cloth.

"I have no idea what you're talking about, Monty," Lucien said, looking heavenward.

"The Ponsonby female falls to me," Freddy said with a shrug of his padded shoulders. "If I don't look too closely, I'll be fine . . ."

"You're rather critical, aren't you, Freddy?" Lucien said, and put aside his wine. The metallic taste in his mouth made him long for something salty.

"What?" Freddy stared at him, his gaze unfocussed. "Who did you get?"

Lucien dipped into the hat and unfolded the paper. "Angela Valentine."

"Ugh," Eddy said. "She's a challenge. If you're not careful, she'll rake you over the coals."

"Nonsense." Lucien pushed his chair away from the table. "Good evening, gentlemen. Consider yourself losers of this bet. By Valentine's Day I will have her exactly where I want her."

The others laughed drunkenly. Lucien pushed the door open and left. As he went out into the damp, foggy evening, he pulled a deep sigh of relief. He could breathe again, and he swore he would stay away from smoky clubs for a while.

* * *

In a stately mansion in Mayfair that had seen better days lived the impoverished Countess of Figdon, Angela Valentine's aunt. The Oriental rugs and the faded draperies could no longer be called elegant, and the walls desperately needed painting. The furniture, or what was left of it, had held up the best under the onslaught of time. Lighter squares on the wall showed where pictures had been taken down and sold. The rooms held a damp cold that no fire could quell.

Angela finished a minuet on the pianoforte, and placed her cold hands on her lap. She tried unsuccessfully to pull the long sleeves down over them. Her aunt sighed and patted her eyes with a handkerchief. She wore an expression full of pity. "Angela, my dear, you have a heavenly gift—I always said so—but it won't put food on your table. You really have to focus on what is important."

"I know, Aunt Elvie." Angela had heard this litany so many times she could mouth the words by heart, but if her aunt saw such frivolous behavior, she would make her displeasure known with a fit of the vapors.

"I'm distraught to remind you that you've now been on the shelf for years, Angela. This cannot continue."

Angela followed the words silently as her aunt spoke them. Her aunt's recriminations had hurt her in the past, but now she felt only a slight exasperation. She couldn't help that she was uncommonly tall, and that her complexion did not have the rose-and-gold tints similar to those of the current favorites of the *ton*.

Au contraire, her skin was rather sallow, and her hair was as dark as a raven's wing, with more curl than she liked. Someone had once said she had wild, uninhibited curls, but her life was far from wild and uninhibited; sometimes she wished she had been born a gentleman so she could travel or go about town without restrictions.

She chafed under the constant supervision of her aunt. She loved Aunt Elvie, but the woman was unpredictable at best. When Angela wanted her aunt to protect her against unwanted attention from some gentleman, the old lady would only encourage the man. *I am trapped and I abhor it,* Angela thought.

"This is your last chance, Angela. The Season is nearly over, and we're not going to return next spring."

Angela mouthed the words, and this time the statement made her immensely weary. It had fallen on her to secure some kind of income for her almost destitute uncle, Henry Valentine, Lord Figdon of Figdon, in Yorkshire, her longtime guardian, and Aunt Elvie, who had lived in this mansion for most of her life. "Yes, Auntie. I shall do my best." But she knew she had no desire to attract some gentleman's attentions. She would never marry. She was tired of all the tedious men who turned as slippery as eels when she had the instruction to charm them at the social gatherings. She hated the game with a passion. The eels never pursued her, and it went against her grain to pursue anyone.

Marriage wasn't going to happen, but how could she find a way to support her family? It should've been her brother's worry, but he'd gone off to the Colonies on adventure, and it was unlikely he would ever return to this mausoleum of a house. Angela didn't judge him one bit. Had she been a man, she would've traveled to the ends of the earth as well to search for new opportunities. She saw no way out of her predicament.

Chapter Two

Lucien stood with Monty Blaine outside one of the modiste shops in Bond Street and pretended to be deeply involved in a discussion. Wearing their finest coats and neck cloths, they had followed Miss Angela Valentine and her chaperone to Bond Street in the hope of attracting the young woman's attention. Lucien was of two minds about the challenge, as he really didn't want to make Miss Valentine's acquaintance, or take part in his cronies' wild schemes, but he'd allowed himself to be pulled in.

He looked down the street. The fog had barely dispersed; it still hung in dirty tatters over the rooftops, and the mud in the street splattered his boots and clothes with every step.

Christmas was coming, and he knew his dragon of a mother would demand his presence at Montclair during the holidays. He didn't mind, but his parent was a severe hypochondriac and he did not cherish listening to her complaints, which were always new and highly obscure. For all he knew, she could have contracted malaria this Christmas, and he didn't want any part of nursing her imagined ills.

"This is deuced folly," he said to Monty and straightened the sleeves of his drab overcoat.

"Miss Valentine towers over her chaperone, but I'd say she has an elegant neck, and she moves with grace and pride. She's rather striking," Monty said.

"I believe there's Italian blood in that family, if I remember correctly," Lucien said.

Monty pressed his hand against his forehead. "My poor head is pounding from that brandy I drank last night."

"Moderation, old fellow. I, for one, am tired of headaches and other miseries attached to drinking too much. I must be getting old."

"Sanctimonious fellow." Monty groaned, his eyes bloodshot and bleary. "I don't know why I accompanied you here."

"Because I went with you to spy on Miss Wells."

"I didn't like the way she was smiling at me when I picked up her dropped handkerchief," Monty said. "I'd liken it to the smile of a shark—avid and hungry. And deadly."

Lucien laughed. "You're exaggerating, surely. Miss Wells's smile was amicable." He stole a furtive glance toward the modiste shop, but there was no sign of Miss Valentine as yet. "Perhaps we should go inside. She might've slunk out the back door."

"I can't picture her slinking anywhere, Lucien."

"You're probably right."

"We won't miss her on the way out."

"I don't want to stand here like a nincompoop."

Lucien moved with purpose toward the door, and Monty followed, emitting hissed protests. He looked miserable, but Lucien felt no pity for his friend's self-inflicted suffering. Mayhap Monty would drink less next time.

Going inside, he looked around the room. Bolts of fabric covered every table; fans and reticules lay spread across a counter. Miss Valentine was holding a painted chicken-skin fan and scrutinizing the design.

Her chaperone was arguing about some pale yellow fabric with one of the seamstresses at the other end of the shop. One of the shop attendants gave him an apprehensive glance and stepped forward to ask if she could help. Rarely did a gentleman venture into this wholly female establishment, unless he was collecting a gift for a wife or a mistress.

Lucien quickly surveyed the counter near his target and saw a red velvet reticule with an enormous gold tassel hanging from the bottom. He pointed toward it. "That would be the perfect gift, er, well—for my mother." He heard Monty groaning behind him in disgust. "Monty, you look as if you might faint. Why don't you sit down," Lucien said under his breath.

Monty obeyed without protest. Sitting on a dainty, pink-upholstered chair, he pressed his fingertips to his temples, a long-suffering look on his face. Lucien went to stand next to Miss Valentine. She was as tall as he. He turned his head just as she did, and their eyes met. Something slammed into his chest as if he'd been shot, and he saw her jerk back a moment later. Blood rushed to his face as some strange sweetness flooded his chest. He *never* blushed.

She blushed as well, and her eyes ignited with emotion, whatever that emotion was, as she looked at him. Fanning herself rapidly with the fan she'd picked up from the array on the counter, she looked away.

"That fan does not suit you," he said. "The color is all wrong."

She started as if he'd pinched her, and her gaze darted back to his face. "Did I ask for your opinion, sir?"

Lucien shook his head, cursing himself for the comment that had jumped unbidden out of his mouth. "Reds and pinks are more your colors, and certain blues. Yellow is unflattering."

"Thank you for the unsolicited advice," she said coolly.

He had really put his foot in it now, so he might as well go all the way. "That yellow she's pondering," he said, pointing at the bolt of fabric the chaperone held up, "is all wrong for you. Your skin would fade away against the yellow."

"Who says it's for me? Your gall is beyond the pale, sir." She gave him a withering stare. "Besides, I don't believe we have been introduced, and I've no desire—"

He bowed, knowing that every second brought him farther from success, which was just as well. "I'm Lucien Montclair."

He noticed the minute flinch as he mentioned his name. At

this moment it bothered him to have a reputation—something that had never been a bother before. She inclined her head, but didn't respond. By society's rules, he'd made a great faux pas by introducing himself, but he'd never worried about such things.

"And you are Miss Valentine."

She flinched again, and her voice couldn't have been haughtier. "How did you know?"

"By *your* reputation. Like me, you are somewhat well known, and I saw you flinch when I introduced myself."

She turned red again, and her eyes flashed. He noted that they were very beautiful and very deep, the surrounding lashes thick and luscious. "I flinched because of your uncouth manners!"

He could drown in those eyes. "I apologize if I've horrified you, but as I said, that shade of yellow is not your color, Miss Valentine."

"You're getting off the subject, Mr. Montclair. To my knowledge, I don't have a reputation."

Damn it. He was really floundering now, and Monty was rolling his eyes at him and chuckling silently. It was too late to rescue this conversation, and he rarely lied to people. "It has been said you're someone too high in the instep to find a husband." Then he burned his bridges completely. " 'Tis common knowledge that your fiancé jilted you at the altar—very unfortunate indeed. I understand if you're bitter, but I'd say he's the one who lost the most—"

"I've never!" Her gasp was sharp, and her face paled. "You're excessively vile, Mr. Montclair." Her gaze darted to her chaperone, who had not noticed their heated exchange. Aunt Elvie riffled through a stack of fabric bolts, her back turned toward them. "Of all the uncivilized behavior." She flung the fan onto the counter. "Do you want to know what the world says about *you,* Mr. Montclair?"

He shrugged. "I already know. I'm considered a useless rakehell and a gambler, and my cronies are no better."

That cut off her flow of recriminations, and a frown appeared between her fine eyebrows. "That's nothing to be proud of."

He silently agreed, but he needed no one to berate him. He didn't understand why he'd been so direct with her. He usually treated the ladies with courtesy, but it was as if he needed to destroy any chances he had at winning the stupid wager. He surely would now, which was just as well. He had no desire to hurt Miss Valentine.

"I sleep well at night," he replied.

"Well, you shouldn't. It's not gentlemanly to break hearts all over London just to get your own way."

"Have I broken hearts? But I've never been in love, and I don't think any woman has given her heart to me. I've no interest in the word *love.*"

"Then you're even more empty than I suspected at first," she said, and lifted her chin into the air. "You are only an empty shell of a man. You dally with innocents for the moment, then throw them away."

"Innocents? Never. I prefer only the married and adventurous women," he defended himself.

"That's despicable, Mr. Montclair," she said, her voice dripping with disgust.

"I'm honest, Miss Valentine." He leaned his elbow on the counter, and the clerk, who had tried repeatedly to show him the velvet reticule, finally put it down with a look of exasperation.

Miss Valentine threw a glance at the article. "I daresay you're shopping for your mistress."

"Or for my mother. She likes odd fripperies, and Christmas is coming quickly."

"You're jesting, surely. That reticule is not for a lady."

He threw a quick glance at the velvet and cursed his choice, but what did it matter? He had already ruined any chances with Miss Valentine, and now he didn't care. But he admitted that the conversation was the most arousing he'd participated in for a long time.

"Are you suggesting my mother is not a lady? She's the daughter of a viscount and a stickler for propriety."

She blushed once more, and he knew she must hate him at this moment. "She must be very disappointed to be related to you, Mr. Montclair. *I* would be embarrassed to be related to you in any way."

"I see. I daresay you're shocked beyond belief at my behavior."

"I'm shocked, but not at all surprised." Miss Valentine threw a glance at her chaperone. "After all, rescue is only steps away."

"But you haven't called out to her, or left my presence. Nor have you shown any signs of having a fit of the vapors."

She shook her head, but didn't say anything. She fingered some of the other fans, but didn't pick one. He noticed that her fingers trembled, but her bearing was proud. There was vulnerability about her lips—now set into a thin line—which endeared her to him. He didn't understand why she'd been on the shelf for so long. He found her rather fetching in her own way.

"That bright blue one with the bird designs would suit you well indeed," he suggested. "It's dramatic and different. Or that red-and-gold fan."

"Only a hussy would carry a fan like that," she protested.

"You *are* a snob, aren't you, Miss Valentine?"

"And you're unbelievably rude and impossible, Mr. Montclair. I'm out of patience with you."

He laughed. "I must seem very annoying. I apologize, but I have a reputation to uphold."

"You are addlebrained," she said. Her eyes blazed with fire, and he sensed that Miss Valentine had a passionate heart that the gossips had forgotten to mention.

Her anger brought life to her face, and he felt strangely drawn to her. He wondered what she would look like in the throes of lovemaking. He had to admit her eyes had both intelligence and wisdom, more than you would expect from an inexperienced young woman.

"And you're excessively outspoken, Miss Valentine."

She glared at him. "I never asked for your comments in the first place or expected you to pay attention to me. You say I'm outspoken, but you're beyond rude. You've made me positively ill with disgust." She began to cough, which brought her chaperone across the room. The large-bosomed and plump woman dressed in dark gray gave him a gimlet stare, no doubt pushing all blame on him for her charge's discomfort.

Lucien bowed. "I daresay your charge is developing a chest cold."

"Sir?" the older woman said, and levered her eyeglass to her eye. She looked at him from top to bottom, and a curious gleam lit her eyes.

"I apologize. I'm trying to choose a gift for my mother. Christmas, y'see." He pulled away discreetly, then motioned to Monty and they fled out of the shop.

"Phew," Monty said, as they got into Lucien's coach parked around the corner. "I've never heard more balderdash dripping from your tongue, Lucien."

"I surely ruined any chance at successfully wooing Miss Valentine, and frankly, I don't care. Freddy can keep his paltry thousand pounds, or whoever wins it." He glanced at Monty's green face. "I suspect it won't be you."

Monty groaned, massaging his head. "But why did you deliberately insult Miss Valentine? I've never heard you in such a taking before."

"She rubbed me the wrong way, awakening the devil on my shoulder, but you have to admit she gave as good as she got." He laughed at the memory. "I find her quite fascinating, truth be told."

"Don't tell me she managed to touch your callous heart? As you well know, Miss Valentine *is* poor, and is expected to make an advantageous match."

"Well, it won't be with me." His words sounded hollow to

his own ears, and he realized that if he ever married it would be to someone like Miss Valentine who dared to challenge him. She showed a great deal of courage, and he had sensed that she disliked her position immensely.

Angela fumed as she joined the maid waiting in the carriage. She'd never, ever been so angry as when she stepped out of the modiste shop. He had thought nothing of introducing himself and throwing insults at her. *The conceited fribble.* It galled her terribly that he was handsome and confident, his eyes a cool, devilish blue, his jaw terribly firm, nose hatefully patrician, his shoulders disgustingly powerful, and to top it all, his demeanor revoltingly insolent. How could he approach her and speak to her as if she was some kind of . . . some kind of doxy? He had, and part of her had found it terribly exciting. How could she?

"What is bothering you?" asked Aunt Elvie. "You are literally glowering. I have never seen such a display of temper on your part, which surprises me no end. You literally flounced out of the shop and into the carriage."

"I've never flounced in my life, Aunt. How can you accuse me of such immature behavior?"

"Was that gentleman addressing you when I approached?"

"Gentleman? You mean the coxcomb looking for gifts for his . . . er, mistress?"

Aunt Elvie gasped and pressed her gloved hand to her mouth. "And he *spoke* with you?"

Angela's heart constricted as if a knife had penetrated it. "Yes, and a lengthy conversation it was." *Where were you when I needed you?* she asked silently.

"What would he want with you?" Aunt Elvie asked without sympathizing with her discomfort at all.

The old lady had such a low opinion of her. Angela sighed. "I don't exactly know."

"Oh, dear, what if someone witnessed the exchange? It'll

be all over town as fast as the gossips can catch their breath. Who was he? Obviously doesn't move in our circles."

"Everyone shuns him, no doubt. He's Lucien Montclair, one of the worst rakes in London."

Aunt Elvie moaned and rocked back and forth, but then a gleam entered her eyes. "Lord Flagston's grandson? Montclair will be an earl eventually, and he's quite plump in the pocket."

"Sapskull," Angela said under her breath. "Wretch. Lummox."

"He showed a marked interest in you?"

"Definitely not," Angela replied icily. "Besides, I would never condescend to give him further attention."

"How can you be so cold, Angela? Montclair is an eligible bachelor, and no one has been able to snare him. You could—"

"They are fortunate to escape the attention of such a man."

"Harsh words for a young lady without prospects," Aunt Elvie said, her nose quivering with displeasure.

"Should I consider a man who treats me with disrespect?" Angela stared at her aunt in disbelief.

"Let me remind you he has a large portion and a title coming to him, and you can't turn up your nose at opportunity when it strikes. If he showed an interest—"

"That's neither here nor there. On principle, I would never consider someone so arrogant and cold." She took a deep breath, feeling the pressure of her aunt's expectations. "We're not that desperate."

"We are."

The words hung between them like a sword suspended on gossamer thread.

"You would *sell* me to the highest bidder, Aunt Elvie?" Tears burned in Angela's eyes and she had to look away.

"How dare you accuse me of such a thing?" Aunt Elvie's voice grated on Angela's ears. "I brought you here to London from that dismal abode in Yorkshire where you lived with Henry, and I presented you to the *ton,* and now you defy me?" She slapped the seat beside her.

"Uncle Henry never berated me, and I like the North Country."

"Don't gainsay me!"

"I never do, Aunt Elvie."

Aunt Elvie trained her gaze out the window of the carriage. "Anyway, he ought to sell this pile in London and set us up in style, but will he ever? No, the roof will fall over our heads first, and he'll give any surplus funds to the orphanage."

"You're exaggerating, surely."

Aunt Elvie eyes blazed. "Your problem, Angela, is that you're much too outspoken and independent. No true gentleman will speak with you more than once, and with your coloring . . . well, the whole business is unfortunate. I've suffered as much as you have these last three years."

Angela's heart squeezed with pain at her aunt's words. She knew she had little to recommend herself, but she had intelligence and a talent for music. Life had been quite tolerable before she came to London. Uncle Henry was an old curmudgeon and every other word out of his mouth was a complaint, but she'd learned to handle him. And the people had liked her in Yorkshire; she was one of them: honest and plainspoken. She had nothing in common with the glittery world of the *haute monde*.

"We're invited to a dinner party this evening, and you must look your very best. Come Christmas, you're going back to Yorkshire, and then I'll wash my hands of you."

That would be a blessing, Angela thought. This last Season in London had been a painful experience to say the least. Not only had Uncle Henry refused to open his purse to pay for more than two new dresses, he'd also rejected any pleas for funds to hire a French maid who could fashion Angela's hair into the latest style. Even before she came to London, Angela's chances to improve her appearance had been foiled, so when Aunt Elvie demanded that she'd "look her best," it was rather an empty command.

"At least Uncle Henry doesn't scrutinize my appearance at breakfast every morning and find fault with it," she said quietly.

"What's that? Speak up, young lady. I'm quite out of patience with you."

"Nothing, Aunt Elvie. Just thinking aloud."

"'Tis all that thinking that frightens away all those eligible gentlemen. Intelligence won't attract suitors."

"A gentleman of sound reason might prefer a woman who can think for herself."

"Pah! Of all the silly notions, your comment quite takes my breath away." She fanned her red face, and stared hard at Angela. "You've humiliated me more than I can say this Season with your frank speech. That's what kept us from gaining vouchers for Almack's. The patronesses were quite shocked when you offered your opinion about the current politics. They branded you a bluestocking, and then there was the matter of your unfortunate past. Tom Finley did you a great disservice when he fled to the Continent on your wedding day."

Angela groaned inwardly, but she didn't show how much her aunt's words hurt her. The world was closing in on her. Either she found someone to marry, or she would have no choice but to return to Yorkshire and live in genteel poverty. She might take a post as a governess, but her relatives would never speak with her again if she did, which was just as well. The thought sparked some hope.

She glanced out the window at the dismal rain blanketing London. Everything was as gray around her as she was inside.

Chapter Three

The dinner party at Mrs. Fenton's began in a sedate manner with a glass of sherry in the parlor. Angela wore one of her two elegant dresses, a cream, Empire-style, silk dress with silver fringe around the modest neckline and the short, puffed sleeves. A silver shawl hung around her shoulders and she wore long, white gloves and a strand of pearls—finery borrowed from Aunt Elvie.

Her hair had been fashioned into a crown of curls on top of her head, and a bandeau of silver fabric held them in place. She longed to have the short, Grecian curls that were all the rage, but her aunt blankly refused to allow her such frivolities. But perhaps if Angela presented her with the finished result, who knows . . . *After all, I am of age, so she can't stop me.*

"You look splendid," Major Helms, one of the invited guests, said to Angela as he looked up into her eyes.

He was rotund and almost seventy-five, and on the lookout for a young wife. She could always marry him, she thought, but he had nothing to recommend himself, neither name nor fortune. And she didn't trust him. He always tried to touch her body when she least expected it.

"Thank you, Major." She fanned herself with her blue fan, and glanced around the room. Five elderly people stood by the fireplace sipping sherry with a young lady named Letitia Wells. Angela had heard that Letitia was poor, and that was not all.

Miss Wells's dress had been poorly chosen, an unflattering,

garish pink that flared like a sail around her short, plump body. She looked unhappy but resolute as she sipped her sherry.

Aunt Elvie had gone to great lengths to secure an invitation, though all the unwed males of good lineage were over fifty. When two young popinjays arrived, it was clear they were hangers-on from the fringes of society. Aunt Elvie must be desperate, Angela thought, worry and defeat churning in her stomach.

Love was never an issue in these matters, alas, only duty.

They were walking in to dinner when two other gentlemen joined the party, and Angela's heart almost stopped when she recognized the two men from the modiste shop in Bond Street. Mr. Montclair looked handsome and worldly in a black evening coat, knee breeches, and an immaculately starched and folded neck cloth. He carried himself with great style and confidence. His friend looked pale of face and somewhat bilious, and wore an expression of pain. He was another handsome and burly gentleman who looked out of place in these sedate surroundings.

She blushed and admonished herself for blushing. Her breath hung caught in her throat as Mr. Montclair looked at her. That strange jolt she'd experienced the first time they'd glanced into each other's eyes struck her again, and she fought to find another breath. She gripped the back of a wing chair and willed her heart to stop pounding so hard, but it wouldn't obey.

"You," she whispered.

A small smiled played over his lips, and recognition flashed in his eyes. He lifted his eyebrows a fraction. "Miss Valentine, how very fortunate I am," he greeted, and bowed over her hand.

"Fortunate? I don't see—"

"Oh," cooed Aunt Elvie, and surged forward as she noticed the new arrivals. "You must be the young gentleman my niece met at the modiste shop in Bond Street."

Liar, Angela thought, feeling embarrassed for her aunt. *Not so young and not a gentleman.*

Aunt Elvie held out both her hands and Mr. Montclair took them as if she were a long lost, beloved friend of his and squeezed them in a hearty fashion. Drat the man!

"How delightful to see you again . . ."

"Lady Figdon, Angela's aunt. Then there's my husband Henry, of course, but he never leaves Yorkshire. We're enchanted to see you again, Mr. Montclair."

The gentleman who had entered with Mr. Montclair looked disgusted. He knew the truth, too, Angela thought. His bold, blue gaze met hers, and she looked away. Mr. Montclair introduced him as Montague Blaine, another man with a poor reputation but a pot of money, she thought. Mr. Blaine stood tall and massive as a barn, his hair curled and pomaded in the latest style. He had a kind but weary expression, she thought.

Mr. Montclair looked around the room to each guest. She had forgotten how handsome his face was, and how quick his blue eyes could be. His hands looked large and capable as he kissed her aunt's fingertips with practiced nonchalance. *The bounder,* Angela thought, and swore she would stay away from him all evening. He wasn't going to enjoy himself at her expense.

But that idea was thwarted as she discovered that their hostess had placed him beside her at the dinner table. If she'd only known, she'd have pleaded a headache. Angela fumed as she looked into his smiling face. Thank God a footman held out her chair, or *he* would've done it, and it would've been difficult to accept the courtesy.

"Miss Valentine, you looked annoyed when I arrived," Mr. Montclair said. "Did I say something improper?"

"How very presumptuous of you to think that anything you say would matter to me, Mr. Montclair."

On the other side of the table, Mr. Blaine coughed as if shocked by her statement, and Letty Wells sitting beside him, smiled at Angela as if delighted with the cynical exchange.

"Everything *you* say matters to *me,*" Mr. Montclair said, his expression mercurial as if he were enjoying his position.

"Why would it?" she challenged, her hand trembling as she toyed with the stem of her glass. "If you're expecting to entertain yourself at my expense, you'll find yourself deeply disappointed."

"I find something to entertain myself everywhere if I care to look," he said with a shrug. "But I don't expect you to entertain me, Miss Valentine."

She yearned to throw her napkin at him, but he must've seen her intent and leaned back in his chair lest she fulfill her unspoken threat. Not that she ever would make such an unladylike gesture. He wasn't worth the effort, and he would only laugh at her, a thought she couldn't abide.

"I'm surprised to see you gentlemen in such sedate surroundings," she said, schooling her voice to be calm. "We must be dull company."

"Not at all," he said, and she felt the proverbial rug slowly being pulled from under her.

"I don't believe that," Angela replied.

Aunt Elvie smiled encouragingly from the other end of the table, and Angela was grateful that her aunt wasn't sitting anywhere near, or she would've suffered a fainting spell in an instant.

"What would you know about my taste in entertainment?" he drawled.

To Angela's surprise, Letty Wells spoke up. "My cousin tells me all the sordid details of the escapades of gentlemen, and it shocks me to learn . . . well, the truth."

"Gambling and drinking are rather bad habits," Angela said, fueling the fire.

"And foul," Miss Wells said.

Mr. Blaine looked uncomfortable, and he gave Miss Wells a sideways glance filled with trepidation, as if she frightened him more than he cared to admit. Miss Wells might be formidable, but Angela didn't think she was unkind. She'd never noticed Miss Wells speak out for herself. The young woman always hung back in gatherings, an observer.

"Ladies cannot understand the thrill of gentlemen's escapades," Mr. Montclair said, but his voice held little conviction.

"Your protest is not credible, Mr. Montclair. Such pastimes would become tiresome quickly," Angela said. "They carry no substance."

His eyes narrowed. "I see. Well, I don't have to convince anyone, and you don't really know what you're talking about, Miss Valentine." He touched the back of her chair and leaned closer.

She shied away, knowing he would have to behave with everyone watching, yet she sensed that he would not hesitate to take advantage of her if given a chance. The thought disturbed her no end, and that treacherous heat rose in her face. She wondered what it would be like to be whisked behind a tree and kissed by those sensuous lips of his. They curled upward in a most charming fashion.

"That's as may be, but anyone can see that too much brandy will bring on the most severe headache," she said.

Mr. Blaine groaned softly across the table and looked down on his plate with a hangdog expression.

"I can't find anything favorable to say about that," Angela continued. "And gambling is only a thrill for the moment. There are some who kill themselves after losing fortunes at cards."

She braced herself for the scathing reply sure to come, but the footmen carried in platters of quail stuffed with prunes and nuts; boiled ox tongue in a wine sauce; beef, mutton, and an array of green beans, potatoes, and peas cooked in butter. The servants moved around the table in silence, and the hostess held forth about the latest gathering she'd attended where they were served sour wine and stale cakes. "It was a most trying evening."

"How uncouth," Angela's chaperone twittered. "I daresay it's very trying when you're forced to eat and drink, pretending there's nothing wrong with the food."

"I was shocked. The way that Mr. Frederick Longman was paying court to Miss Agatha Ponsonby, you'd think he'd come across a diamond of the first water. The poor Miss Ponsonby was so taken she almost fainted away toward the end of the evening. He was very solicitous and held her hand in a most endearing manner as she reclined on a settee, but I ask you, was he acting in a gentlemanly fashion? I don't think so," she said, her voice turning peevish. "He was pushing himself on poor Miss Ponsonby, who has never had so much attention during all of her Seasons in London. Everyone knows she's been . . . well, on the shelf . . . for a long time."

"It's a very unfortunate business," said one of the old gentlemen without preamble. "Very unfortunate."

"She's a dear lady who doesn't need attention from the likes of Freddy Longman," one of the other gentlemen said, and looked askance at Mr. Montclair and Mr. Blaine. "I shall warn him off if her grandfather doesn't."

"I don't know if I agree," Lady Figdon said. "You'd have to be grateful that someone pays attention to an . . . er, young woman like that. When you're desperate like Miss Ponsonby, you can't be too . . . well, choosy, or she'll be wearing a cap before too long, and then all will know she's given up."

Angela pinched her lips at her aunt's speech, knowing only too well that she might share Miss Ponsonby's fate before long. "Miss Ponsonby is a very intelligent and kind woman," Angela defended her unpopular friend. "Just like me, she has a fondness for the pianoforte and for books on antiquities."

"That's nothing to be proud of," Aunt Elvie said, mortifying Angela even more. "That will just frighten off eligible—"

"Dear Aunt, your wineglass is going to topple any second," Angela interrupted, deeply embarrassed that her aunt would voice such a sentiment in public.

Her aunt stared at her wineglass that stood perfectly planted on the table. "I don't understand, Angela," she said in confusion.

"It looks stable to me." She smiled brightly at Mr. Montclair. "I'm delighted that we have some young gentlemen attending here tonight. It's refreshing indeed."

Angela cringed once more, and wished to wring her aunt's neck. Her newfound friend across the table stared heavenward, and Angela knew the pointed comment had bothered Miss Wells, too.

"We're delighted to be here," Mr. Montclair said, and Mr. Blaine groaned again.

Angela suspected he was in some kind of pain.

"It was hard to wangle an invitation from Mrs. Fenton, but fortunately she's an old friend of my mother, so here we are," continued Mr. Montclair.

"Really? Be honest now, why would you want to attend this particular dinner party?" Angela whispered to him. "There can't be any kind of attraction for a man of your tastes, or Mr. Blaine's."

"On the contrary, Miss Valentine," he said with a suave smile. "I knew you'd been invited, and I wanted to see you again."

She sensed a large plumper. "I suppose I have to take your word for it, but I don't trust you're wholly truthful."

His gaze challenged her. "And why not?" He put down his fork after cutting up a slice of mutton, and lifted his wineglass. "I'm serious."

His long, sensitive fingers caught her attention. "I sense this is no more than a lark for you, Mr. Montclair. After all, this is the first time I've seen you attend a society party anywhere."

"We probably arrive long after you've left the gathering. We keep late hours, don't we, Monty?"

Mr. Blaine nodded. "Very late, Lucien."

Angela didn't think it was something to be proud of, but she couldn't very well state that. It was highly suspect that Mr. Montclair had singled her out. He'd never shown any interest the few times they had crossed paths before. In fact, he'd never given her a second glance.

She remembered colliding with him once at the Opera, but he had barely apologized, let alone looked at her. She narrowed her gaze and scrutinized his face for clues, but he only smiled at her, showing only pleasure. His blue gaze revealed nothing but delight.

"Just when my life was becoming unbearably—" he began.

"I don't trust you," she said *sotto voce,* and concentrated on the pile of food on her plate. She had no idea what she was eating, and she felt his gaze upon her.

"That's unfortunate," he said, "but not something we can't overcome if we work at it."

"Overcome? What do you mean? I have no intention of continuing this conversation."

"You'll have to if you don't want to create a scene right here, Miss Valentine."

"A scene? Why in the world would I do that? I never have and never will. Besides, nothing transpiring here is worthy of upheaval."

"I'm enjoying this sparring, and I hope you see the humorous side of our confrontation, Miss Valentine. I find your views invigorating."

"You're doing it too brown, Mr. Montclair."

"We will have to work on the trust between us. I might be frank at times, but I'm not a complete ogre."

"That's from your point of view," Angela said, and dabbed at her lips with her napkin. "You'll find no favors with me."

"Why would you dismiss me out of hand without even trying to discover if you like me?"

"I don't want to like you—after that unfortunate first meeting in Bond Street," she said under her breath. "This whole situation is outlandish. Since I don't have a feather to fly with, it's not possible that you're interested in some kind of monetary reward. You're quite settled in that department. I know my appearance has never inspired poets, so why would they inspire you? I'm quite comfortable with who I am, and I have accepted that I can never compete with a diamond of the first water, but that's all fine and well. So, without having to actually point out the obvious, which I did anyway, there's absolutely nothing that would draw your attention to me." She straightened her back and stared him squarely in the eye. She inhaled a deep breath. "As I said, I'm content, and I don't need your false admiration."

He nodded. "That was quite a lecture and I admire you for it. I daresay you could add 'uncommon frankness' to those qualities. Listening to someone who dares to speak the truth is very refreshing."

"Refreshing? I have done nothing but cut you down since you first opened your mouth in Bond Street."

"I enjoy some vigorous fencing. In fact, what I do like about you is that you don't shrink back, and your conversation shows—besides bluntness—intelligence and great self-control. You speak with experience and wisdom, and you are to be admired for that. You have great inner beauty."

"I look at my life without blinders. One can't remain blind to the truth. If one lies to oneself, one lives forever in ignorance."

He nodded. "It's a great strength that you're honest with yourself."

She looked for any hint of mockery, but detected none. "Without that, what kind of life would I have? I might pretend that I am something I'm not and be wholly miserable. Like you, perhaps?"

He smiled, his expression unreadable.

"It's difficult to decipher if you're condescending, or if you're serious, Mr. Montclair. I don't like it."

"What would I gain by belittling you, Miss Valentine?"

"Secret mirth that you can share with your cronies later."

"Blunt to a fault," he said with a sigh. "You paint a very dreary picture of me, but I assure you I have no need to share this conversation with anyone. And I assure you my cronies have no interest in my conversations."

"My picture is close to the truth, no doubt." She threw a

glance along the table and her aunt winked to her and smiled broadly as if the wine had loosened up some muscles that rarely moved on her face. She must think they were having a scintillating conversation that would lead to an offer for Angela's hand by the end of the evening.

"Harsh and without compassion," he muttered. "Cool and contained, yet passionate on a level where the passion never burns out. Unforgiving."

"What? I don't understand your assessment, Mr. Montclair."

"I find you fascinating, and I apologize for any cutting observation I might have uttered before. I find your company uplifting."

"I doubt you know the meaning of the word, sir. You can't call your kind of existence uplifting and full of compassion for others. Yours is a life without purpose, a piece of driftwood floating down the river without the slightest concern for where you're going."

"You don't know much about my existence except for the face I show to the world," he defended himself, but she sensed she'd touched a chord.

"I daresay your memoirs would fill an excessively slim volume. It would contain all about the horse races you attended, and the wages you entered, and the other kinds of gambling you enjoyed."

"Now you're being cruel as well."

She pushed the beef aside and set down her fork, as all of her appetite had gone. "What do you expect? You put yourself into my path, and you've done nothing but aggravate me. I have no encouragement to give you, and it's unfortunate that you should put yourself into this position, as I have no interest in you. I don't want to be rude or considered ill-tempered, but, Mr. Montclair, I've had enough of you."

He laughed, a sound of delight rather than hollow defeat, and she stared in amazement. What was wrong with him? He should be furious by now. She blushed and tried to look everywhere but at him.

"You're the most invigorating female I've met in a long time. I abhor vapid sweetness in a woman, and it seems to be all the rage among the ladies to display no substance between the ears whatsoever. It quickly becomes tedious. I know from experience that such insipidness will tend to lead to hypochondria or other failings in later years."

"I agree with that, yet I'm appalled at your poor view of us females."

He thought for a moment. "I have a lot of experience, and I believe it's about the roles we play. Some gentlemen like to play the popinjay."

"Oh," she teased. "I thought you had a bone to pick with the entire female species."

"Not at all. I support anyone who dares to show mettle."

"That's good. I'm surprised we're in accord on one matter—or you're just trying to divert me from my earlier opinion that you're aiming to worm your way into my good graces. It won't work."

"Suspicion is not an attractive trait, Miss Valentine, and you don't have to repeat yourself. I took note of your caution."

"It's always wise to err on the side of caution."

"Anyhow, why are you so set against my advances? What have I done so wrong that I've earned your utter scorn?" He was leaning toward her, his gaze roving down her neck and further. She felt the heat, and wished the dinner were over so she could flee to the terrace, or, better yet, home. Not that Aunt Elvie would bestir herself. She seemed to enjoy the company.

"We don't need to go over that again. Simply stated, I'm not attracted."

"You're hurting me beyond speech, Miss Valentine."

"That's utter rubbish," she said and inched away from his proximity. "Your hide is too thick." *If only the dinner were over.*

She glanced at Letty Wells, who simpered over something Mr. Blaine said into her ear, and wished her newfound friend would stand strong against his assault. It was clear to Angela that the gentlemen had no serious goal with their dalliance, and she didn't want Miss Wells to get hurt.

She narrowed her gaze and tried to decipher Mr. Blaine's motives, sensing some hidden duplicity. Whatever the gentlemen were about, they acted in a subtly predatory fashion, which made her nervous.

Chapter Four

After dinner, Angela stood with Miss Wells on the terrace, fanning herself. The evening was cool, but she couldn't soothe the heat under her skin, and she sensed her companion's agitation.

"Letitia, I apologize if I'm prying, but what did Mr. Blaine say to you?"

"That he's highly attracted to me, and that he'd like to . . . er, well, kiss me."

"What? Of all the uncouth—"

"He's very kind, and I've a mind to let him—kiss me, that is. I've always wondered what it's like."

"He's only toying with you, Letitia. I don't want to be the bearer of bad news, but he'll break your heart if you let him."

"Really?"

Angela nodded. "Yes."

Letitia looked unsure, and she chewed on her bottom lip. The unfortunate pink of her gown positively glowed in the many lights from the chandeliers inside and the lanterns on the terrace. "Do you think so, Angela? He seemed rather forceful."

"He has a lot of experience with—er, ladies," Angela said.

"Oh."

Angela wanted to ask why Letty thought Mr. Blaine was interested in kissing her, but her newfound friend might take the question wrong. If it had been someone other than a notorious rake, Angela could accept his motive, but Mr. Blaine had no need for a woman like Letty Wells, or herself, in his life.

"You truly believe he's only pulling the wool over my eyes?"

Angela nodded and told Letty about her own experience with Mr. Montclair. "I'll never trust him."

"He's so very handsome," Letty said with a sigh. "And charming, and eloquent. You ought to consider yourself fortunate—"

"Fiddlesticks. He's not serious. Like you, I have a very small portion, and everyone knows about that." She patted her friend's arm. "If we were plump in the pocket, we would be deluged with suitors, but you know they've been few and far between."

Letty sighed.

"I wish there was something we could do to put these men in their place." Angela tossed ideas about in her mind and discarded them just as quickly.

"I have a cousin who frequents the gentlemen's clubs. I could ask him to find out why these men are pursuing us," Letty said, flapping her fan vigorously. The red of her face clashed abominably with the pink of her gown. Then she smiled, and Angela thought she had a very attractive smile, and her kind blue eyes sparkled like diamonds.

"The worst part is that my aunt thinks there's hope for a future with Mr. Montclair," Angela said. "She'll never stop harping on it now."

"I know." Letty shook her head as if used to such cavalier treatment by unfeeling relatives. "You'd think they'd have more circumspection."

"If I'm correct and our two gentlemen have devilry on their mind, I'm determined to fight back."

"I'll send you a note just as soon as I know anything."

Two days later, Angela received a note from Letty Wells.

Angela—I hope you don't mind me using your first name—you were right. I found out from my cousin that five friends—a dissolute group indeed—are vying for the attentions of certain young ladies, including you and me. The Misses Ponsonby, Mottingrow, and Knoll have also been singled out, because sadly we are the least affluent and the most unfortunate in appearance of all the haute monde. The gentlemen are trying to make fools of us! Furthermore, the man who first brings one of us to the dance floor at Mrs. Barton's ball wins the wager.

Angela could see tear stains smudging the ink, and the missive had been wrinkled and straightened out again. Letty's state of agitation was clear from the very paper. Pinching her lips together in anger, Angela swore revenge.

Later in the morning, she gathered her pelisse, hat, and gloves, and asked her maid to accompany her to Green Street, where Letty was staying with an older sister.

The butler showed her in at once. Letty reclined on a sofa, her legs covered with a blanket, and a dish of bonbons on her lap. A black cat vied for her attention, but Letty kept eating bonbons and drying her tears with a very wrinkled handkerchief. Judging by her puffy face, Angela surmised her friend had been crying all morning.

"We have to strike back," Angela said, just as soon as she'd sat down. "And beat them at their own game. We can't allow them to use us as pawns."

Letty nodded and looked miserable. She wouldn't invent anything constructive, Angela thought. "What shall we do?"

Letty shook her head. "I don't know. Shoot them?"

Angela laughed dismissively, though she admitted it wouldn't be a bad notion. "We can call them out at dawn."

"A duel? Excellent," Letty said. "But I don't have the faintest notion of how to wield a sword or a pistol." Her forehead creased in thought, and she dried her eyes. "What would be the best revenge?"

"If they are out to make us fall in love with them, we ought to make them fall in love with us, and then cruelly jilt them."

"They are never going to fall in love with us," Letty said with a miserable sniff. "Look at me, I weigh five stones too much. The modistes flee when they see me coming."

"And I'm by far too tall and lack any sense of style, and my hair is a disaster."

"It costs a fortune to be fashionable," Letty said, "and I shall never lose this excessive weight." She pinched her ample middle.

"But are you willing to do it?" Angela felt a stir of excitement.

Letty nodded, her blond ringlets bouncing. "Yes. I'm desperate, and I'll starve myself with tea and dry biscuits to find a husband, if only to get away from my sister. She's a worse nag than my mother ever was." She pushed away the plate of bonbons, throwing a last, lingering look on the delectable chocolate. "What else could we do?"

"I shall talk to my Uncle Henry. If he thought he would get me off his hands, my chances at getting some money from him would be greatly improved. Aunt Elvie would confirm that Mr. Montclair is pursuing me. She doesn't know it's a hoax. I'd like to start by cutting off my hair."

Letty clapped her hands together. "That's a splendid idea."

"Short Grecian locks."

Letty squealed. "You would look very lovely in short hair."

"And slim, you shall have all the eligible bachelors at your feet, Letty," Angela said, patting her friend's hand. "You have a great character that you've been hiding."

Letty looked misty-eyed with longing. She lifted her legs down and sat up straight on the sofa. "This past Season has been extremely dull, and I have suffered snubs and barbs. There's nothing that I'd like to do more than to show the world that I'm a person no matter what size I am."

"Yes, that's understandable. We shan't waste any time preparing, and if the others want to join us, we'll welcome them. I'll write immediately to the ladies involved and explain this dreadful wager. All they have to do is to reject any offer to dance with the men involved in the wager at Mrs. Barton's ball."

In another part of town, and ten hours later, the gentlemen met at Watier's to discuss their progress. Everyone had something positive to report. Only Lucien felt any sense of regret, as he had no intention of completing his challenge. He'd found that Miss Valentine was a delightful woman who didn't hesitate to stand up for herself. He sensed a depth in her that he longed to explore, and he wished he'd met her under different circumstances. Despite their confrontations, he found himself spellbound, and his heart beat faster every time he thought about her. *That* he could not explain.

Angela Valentine had been right when she challenged him about the lack of purpose in his life. It had struck a nerve that had bothered him since the dinner party.

She didn't lie to herself; he'd lied to himself most of his life.

He had to see her again.

"I'd say Miss Wells has a beautiful smile and very lively eyes," Monty said as he was drinking at Lucien's elbow. "And a great sense of humor."

"She does, and Miss Valentine has wit and charm that compels me to know her better. We brought out the worst in each other, yet underneath I sense there's a lode of gold to explore."

"How we go on about the virtues of these ladies. We must be deuced addled if we can see qualities that no one else noticed."

Lucien nodded and heaved a deep sigh. "We are corkbrained, to be sure, but perhaps no one has taken the time to look behind the façade of these ladies. I only expected insipidness and an instant prostration of gratitude at my feet, but found a tigress hiding behind that tall, haughty exterior. Miss Valentine brought a wind of fresh air into my life."

"Miss Wells has a different character altogether, sweetness and delight."

"We sound like besotted moonlings, Monty. It's not like us."

"Well, they say that when Cupid strikes, he aims straight for the heart."

"Cupid? Balderdash. Some romantic fool invented that fat cherub."

A furious gust of wind shook the building, and blew out the candle on the table. Both men looked around.

"Odd, to be sure," Lucien said. "I never realized Watier's was this drafty."

Monty glanced toward the door in fear. "Very strange."

"However, I don't believe in that romantic drivel, and I have no intention of pursuing Miss Valentine after the wager." He didn't quite convince himself.

"I will surely win the gamble," Monty said, with great confidence.

The five gentlemen on the prowl found that their prey had gone to ground. No matter what gatherings they attended, there was no sign of the young ladies.

It was as if the earth had opened up and swallowed them. Whatever plans of seduction they'd harbored were for naught, and they called a meeting at Watier's two weeks later to plan a new strategy just as Christmas was about to arrive. However, at one of the duller dances all of the young ladies were present, though only Lucien went by to greet the hostess, as she was an old friend of the family.

He had just straightened after placing a kiss on Lady Penwick's hand, when he saw Angela Valentine. She looked different. Her hair lay in expertly cut, gleaming curls around her head, accentuating her slim neck, and her white gown had shimmering embellishments that concealed the angular shape of her body, and a shawl of the same material lent sparkle to her smile and eyes. She looked beautiful. The hair arrangement brought forth the delicate structure of her face, transforming it.

Beside her stood Letitia Wells. She, too, looked different in a modest, light green gown that hung in perfect folds around her plump body and made her seem taller. He couldn't exactly put his finger on the change, other than that her face looked slimmer, and her hair sported the same elegant Grecian cut as that of her friend. In these last two weeks, the ladies had acquired style and aplomb. How unexpected. He saw the other three dancing in the ballroom beyond.

Wait until he told Monty and the others.

He gave Miss Valentine a hesitant smile, and she nodded graciously, her smile dazzling. His heart thumped faster, and he found himself strangely foolish. Heat crept up his neck.

"Miss Valentine," he greeted, and kissed her hand. Just to touch her made his blood race. "Miss Wells." He greeted Letty with a warm smile. "You both look remarkably elegant." This time, he meant every word, and he could read in their faces that they were pleased. "A stunning change, and I'm delighted. When did this transformation happen?"

"Between pianoforte recitals and attending boring tea parties," Miss Valentine said, a small smile playing at the corners of her lips.

She had gained a deeper sparkle, and he couldn't take his eyes off her. "I'm speechless," he muttered. He indicated her dancing card with a nod. "Are you available for any of the dances, or is your card full?"

She gave the card a cursory glance. "I daresay I can spare the next to last dance for you."

"And also the last?" He waited eagerly for her reply.

"The Duke of Engelstone has claimed that privilege. Besides, I would never consider dancing twice with you, Mr. Montclair."

"Whyever not?"

"It's unseemly. I've no intention of creating rumors of any kind, and two dances in one evening will do just that."

Her words perturbed him more than he liked to admit. She refused him, yet gave him a warmly inviting smile, and for a moment he associated himself with a worm on a fishing hook. The sensation was novel to him, and he sought for a reply. "I never thought you cared a fig for what people say, Miss Valentine."

"Only where my reputation is at stake."

"Of course. I didn't ask you to do anything scandalous."

"As in flashing my ankle for all to see?"

Miss Wells gasped and put her hand to her mouth. Hiding a giggle, she accepted an invitation for a dance from a rather robust gentleman of mature years. Lucien watched her move away and noticed that she looked smaller all around.

"Something nefarious is going on," he said to Miss Valentine. "You're changing right in front of my eyes."

"It is time that something did change, and we decided to fight back. For much too long, we've been the laughingstock of the *ton,* the plain and the plump, the ones on the shelf, the bluestockings, and those without funds. But we refused to think of ourselves as undesirable any longer."

"Well done. Your spirit will have every gentleman at your feet." He found the idea intolerable. "You show great courage, Miss Valentine."

She smiled and flapped her fan. "Since we're old . . . enemies, why don't you call me Angela?"

"Enemies? That's surely an exaggeration."

"I doubt that we can hold a civil conversation . . . er, Lucien. Enemies throw insults at each other, and since the first moment we laid eyes on each other, we have fought with every sentence."

"Sparred."

"Fought. I shan't argue with you further, and I beg of you to keep your comments to yourself when we dance. I enjoy dancing and I won't allow you to ruin my pleasure with callous comments."

"We'll make a striking couple on the dance floor."

"Until the music stops." Her eyes flashed.

"Why can't we just keep a civil conversation?" he asked. "We're communicating in naught but veiled barbs and threats."

"You began this debacle. I never asked to be introduced to you, and I never was, so in my opinion, you're still a stranger."

"You cannot tell me that after all this time. Sincerely, I don't feel any animosity toward you, only curiosity."

"The curiosity you feel toward the dwarves at Astley's Amphitheatre?"

"No." Filled with exasperation, he shook his head. "You have to be the most stubborn female I've ever encountered. Let's lay down the swords."

She paused. "Very well."

They stood in tense, fragile silence staring out over the quiet garden. A bird darted by and the breeze played in the tree leaves. Angela longed to sit on a bench and contemplate this evening's events, but her inner tension would not allow her such peace. She was about to abandon her spot when the music came to a halt.

The next dance was his—a waltz. She didn't know if she could handle the challenge of feeling his arms around her. But when he bowed and said, "I believe this is mine," she had to comply, however reluctantly.

Tucking her hand into the crook of his elbow, he pulled her onto the shining dance floor. With the other couples they waited for the music to start. His hand crept around her waist and she placed one hand in his and the other on his shoulder. Her heartbeat betrayed her agitation. She knew her tongue wouldn't obey her if she opened her mouth to speak.

The music started. With a slow smile, he led her into the midst of the dancing couples and she discovered he was an excellent dancer. Due to his easy flow, it was effortless to follow, and she quite enjoyed the feeling of his strength. He looked into her eyes as if reading her every thought, and she felt totally vulnerable. In the light of the chandeliers, he must be aware of her acute embarrassment.

"You're very light, an exceptional dancer," he said, and whirled her around until she laughed.

Dizzy, she replied, "I hate to admit it, but you are as well."

"Yes? Thank you." He laughed, and the sound spellbound her.

Everything about him had caught her interest and she hated herself for it. She wasn't going to let some rake get the better of her! *Remember the wager,* she told herself.

She forced herself to look away from his eyes. *Remember the callousness that these men represent. They're ruthless.* She cringed at the thought, and it pained her that Lucien would be one of them.

"Angela, you look very preoccupied all of a sudden." He made a swirl across the floor, and she had to follow.

"I forget what is important sometimes," she murmured, more to herself than to him.

"Enjoy life and what it offers."

"Or use it to satisfy your own plans."

"That is a very strange sentiment. I don't understand."

"I'm talking to myself." She was acutely aware of his warm hand on her back, and she could smell the scent of his shaving soap on his skin.

"I've found newfound vigor in my life. I've decided to concentrate on my inheritance and help my grandfather with the estate. It's time."

"A solid plan, no doubt." She heard the music arriving at the end of the piece, and she longed to tear herself free, but he held on. To her surprise, he whisked her out onto the terrace and down the steps onto the dark path. He stopped, still holding her arm and looked toward the sky.

"Look at the stars."

She obeyed, too shaken to resist. Stars glittered against the infinite darkness.

"We are rather insignificant, don't you agree? As you look into eternity, there's no argument left to support our tiny selves. Whatever we find so important means so little when you look at the immensity of the sky."

"Yes." She found the sentiment surprisingly deep coming from someone who spent his time in idle pursuits. It was as if he could read her thoughts and he laughed.

"You looked startled. I do have some serious interests in my life. Astronomy is one. The mystery of the universe in which we live has always fascinated me, and I've been fortunate to study under some scholars on the subject." He gave another laugh. "I enjoy shocking you."

Before she could reply, he'd swept her into his arms and his mouth found hers in a deep kiss. Never had she been untethered from the ground and thrown up among the very stars he had been talking about. His mouth moved gently, yet hungrily across hers, and she moaned against him, her body losing all substance.

She vaguely realized she was pushing against him, but he was so much stronger, and he had no qualms about pressing her closer to himself. This is what it would be like to be swept off into a raging sea of passion. She had no control; she could only cling to him.

And then they reached some kind of inner shore, and the raging quieted down. He lifted his face from hers, his breath harsh and quick against her mouth. She clung to his shoulders until her head stopped spinning.

"Are you still angry with me?" he whispered.

Chapter Five

"I'm still angry," she said, her voice trembling. She was tossed on a sea of conflicting emotions. "This was a dastardly move on your part, and wholly unacceptable. What if someone saw us?"

"No one did. They're dancing the last dance, and we're concealed behind this tree in a dark garden." He indicated the tree that grew before the terrace. "How can you be angry after this wonderful moment? I'm elated." He looked into her eyes and appeared to be eager to kiss her again.

His eyes did shine and his grin was wide, but was it because of his belief that victory was near, or did he honestly feel something for her? "You're wielding your seductive powers without shame. Did you have all this planned for tonight?" She pulled away from him when she could find the strength to do it. Throwing a tense glance toward the terrace, she whispered, "You're shameless, aren't you?"

"Absolutely, but I couldn't help myself, and you didn't try to stop me. You looked so tempting tonight, and I fear I lost my head. I couldn't resist the temptation."

She couldn't shake her suspicion, and the knowledge of the wager poked its thorn into her mind. "No chance of that. I suspect you're very levelheaded. You had this 'gesture' planned from the moment you saw me tonight."

"Perhaps you'll never believe me, but truly, I hadn't planned to kiss you, Angela, but I don't regret it at all."

"That is rather obvious." Tears choked her throat, and as if he could feel her agitation, he held her face with both hands.

"You've swept me away, Angela. I don't know why I never noticed you before."

"You obviously weren't looking."

He took her hand, and she wanted to run back to the house, but couldn't resist him, for which she berated herself. His proximity made her weak and indecisive. *She had to remember the wager,* she kept repeating. It stood between them, and nullified everything he said and did, but her curiosity could not be stilled. He maneuvered her toward the house and held her behind a curtain by an open window where warmth from the fireplaces streamed toward them.

"I might catch a chill," she murmured as he pulled her closer.

He wrapped his arms around her, and she could feel his heart hammering madly against her chest. It wasn't lying to her. It was as agitated as her own, and she felt his quick breath against her hair.

"I've come to the conclusion that I need to start my life anew. By your directness, you've helped me to open my eyes, Angela. I'm finally ready to face my responsibilities. Grandfather was elated when he heard about my plans, and said it was about time I changed. It has been long in coming, and he's right. I've taken the good things in life for granted, but everything could easily be taken away if I don't shoulder the care of what my ancestors built."

"You're right, and in this I do believe you. There's always a time where the old ways have to go. Times of change have come upon me as well," she said into his shoulder. She had to pull away, but couldn't.

"What do you mean?"

"I'm going back to Yorkshire. My Uncle Henry has one great, redeeming quality. All his life he's worked at bettering the life of children, and I've helped him in the past. I was quite happy doing that until they invented the harebrained idea that I should have a Season in London. It set me up for heartache and disappointment. It didn't matter that I was at peace with my previous life, and then there was always the matter of the finances."

"Ah! That's the truth." He held her shoulders and looked into her eyes. "I don't understand why someone didn't see your sterling qualities, or notice your lovely eyes and sweet lips."

"I didn't really invite anyone, and after my fiancé . . . well, left me, no one showed an interest." Her voice trembled. "I was blamed for the whole and became a social outcast from then on—as you were quick to point out."

"Small-minded people lose great opportunities." He sighed. "I'm not going to be one of them." He caressed her neck and frissons of pleasure went down her back. "I long to know you better, Angela. There's a lot more, and I need to know everything about you. And I deeply apologize for my rude comments in the past."

She teetered on the verge of excitement, but couldn't quite allow herself. She feared rejection, but more so to be the victim of a cruel joke. Until he divulged the truth about the wager and claimed he would have no further part of it, she could not move forward. Another truth was that she couldn't trust him—not so much due to his past, but that he was callous enough to enter a wager that could only hurt her friends' feelings. She pulled away from him.

"I wish I could say that we could explore each other's hearts and minds, but I have to decline. I don't trust you and your motives, and that has to be the end of it." She contemplated whether to confront him with her knowledge of the wager, but decided against it. He would get his comeuppance in due time. "You will have to prove yourself in depth, Lucien."

"I see." He rubbed his chin and an expression of frustration came over his face.

"And I don't care what you *say*. I need to see positive action."

"Hmm, you have a point there. I shall endeavor to show that I've changed."

She waited, breathless, for his declaration that he was part of a cruel joke, but he never spoke. Disappointment washed through her. "I don't know what suddenly brought you across my path. I can't quite understand what lies at the bottom of this." She let the statement hang, but he didn't offer any explanation, and it lowered her mood further.

"I daresay there's nothing else to say at this point," she whispered, as she didn't trust her voice to carry much further. "Good night." She hoisted the hem of her gown and walked toward the open terrace door.

"No, wait! Don't reject me off hand, Angela."

She turned a deaf ear to his plea. She determined that her curls lay smooth and stepped into the room. She looked for Letty, but she was nowhere to be found, and her aunt was talking to a dowager, which was a blessing.

She hurried to the room upstairs that had been set aside for the young ladies to freshen up and sat down in front of the mirror. Was she this wild-eyed woman with swollen lips? she wondered, and looked away in confusion. What had he done to her? Her world would never be the same, and she had let him kiss her. She had responded with equal passion, and that worried her even more.

Tears flooded to her eyes, and she wiped them away with an impatient swipe of her hand. Drat the man! Life had barely been acceptable before this, but whatever peace she'd had was now gone.

The door opened behind her, and she recognized Letty's face before she tried to hide her face behind her handkerchief.

"What's the matter, Angela? I noticed that you ran upstairs. You look devastated."

"I'm crushed, I'm humiliated, and I'm filled with unspeakable confusion."

Letty kneeled beside her friend and gave her a hug. "Oh dear, what happened?"

In halting words, Angela told the story, her voice breaking as she came to the incident of the kiss.

"The uncouth man!" Letty cried out. "Does he have any decency at all?"

"Perhaps some, but probably not." Angela cleared her throat. "What bothered me the most is that I enjoyed his kiss immensely."

"What?" Letty looked aghast. "You couldn't."

"Yes. He's an expert. None of those dry pecks I'm used to from friends. His was a full-blown assault on my senses."

Letty gasped. "I've never felt that kind of attack." Her eyes took on a dreamy look. "I wouldn't mind experiencing that someday."

"Yes, but not with any of the gentlemen here." Angela moaned into her handkerchief. "What am I to do? I refuse to let him win some silly bet with his cronies, and I refuse to let him take command of my senses."

"Of course. We shall think of something. He's a beastly worm, and I, for one, will tell him so next time I clap eyes on him."

"He'll only laugh at you. This is not your usual type of gentleman who cringes every time you snap your fan shut. I'm disgusted at myself for my weakness, and part of me is crying out for revenge."

"I believe our strategy worked. The man could not stop himself from kissing you. After all the work we did on our appearance, you're bound to turn heads, and not just his." Her eyes brightened. "Mayhap this is a new beginning for us."

"He could have held back if he'd wanted to. I believe he's very much in control of himself, and that he possibly planned this whole thing despite his claims to innocence."

"He couldn't have known you would be here."

"Yes, he could—if he cared to find out. My whereabouts are no secret, and he must've wondered what happened to all of the ladies involved in the wager."

"Calm yourself, Angela. Everything will be resolved. We stand together, and you know we have one advantage. We're privy to the bet."

"Dastardly scoundrels," Angela said between gritted teeth. She wiped her eyes dry and took some deep breaths. "We'll fight back, just as planned. We shall show them at Mrs. Barton's ball."

The next morning, Angela still agonized over the past events. She had not slept a wink, but she suspected that Lucien had slept soundly, not giving his actions a second thought. To him it was probably commonplace to kiss damsels, be they gentlewomen or not. She suspected they belonged in the second category, because no lady in her right mind would let him take advantage of her. "Except I," she whispered.

"I could've shouted for help, and he would've been taken to task for his behavior," she said to her pillow, but she hadn't. That fact disturbed her no end. "He won this round."

At his lodgings on Conduit Street, Lucien had risen after a turbulent night of fitful sleep and colorful dreams, but his head felt clear. He had drunk no claret or brandy last night, and it made for a beautiful morning. Drinking coffee in his dining room, he studied the newssheets, but he couldn't concentrate. Before his inner eye stood the transformed Angela, and he'd realized how much beauty she had. The kiss had been the most arousing he'd tasted in a long time, perhaps ever, and it bothered him that the whole reason he'd kissed her was to find out how she tasted. Well, it wasn't the whole truth. He was genuinely attracted to the dark-eyed woman.

He sensed she had a passion that matched his own, and it worried him. With her there would be no discreet arrangements. She would expect to lead him into Parson's Mousetrap before he got any further. That's how it was supposed to be, and he could only respect the convention of this, but he was torn. He had no desire to marry, but she had stirred emotions in him he didn't know he had. Perhaps marriage wasn't such a bad idea now that he'd decided to dedicate himself more to his estate and to the people who depended on him. Angela would brighten up Flagston Hall—that is, if he could win her heart.

He glanced out the window where the sun was shining weakly. It had rained earlier, but now the sun brought hope for a better day. He had arranged to meet Monty at one of the clubs later in the afternoon to hear about any developments in the tiresome wager. Lucien had decided to bow out of it. If he hoped to get closer to Angela, he couldn't make her the object of his cronies' jests.

It was about time to go home to Flagston Hall in Humberside for Christmas, and he would end this whole charade before he left. He didn't look forward to spending time with his mother, who currently had—what she thought was—inflammation of the lungs, and a broken hip. But according to Grandfather, she walked quite briskly through the rambling estate when no one was looking. He refused to give her any pity, only encouraged her to live as if nothing bothered her, but she didn't want to listen. Her sister would arrive for a visit at Christmas and between the two of them, he would have his hands full.

He put down his newssheet, and decided to pay Angela a formal visit at eleven and apologize for last night's events—that is, if he could get her alone for one moment. Her chaperone would simper over him and not give them a moment's peace, but he'd have to deal with Lady Figdon with brisk efficiency.

To his surprise, she left him alone with Angela with the excuse that she had to write an urgent note. Lady Figdon had simpered plenty when he arrived, but she'd eyed him with a shrewdness he never suspected that she possessed.

Angela's eyes looked haunted, and her face pale. She was reluctant to speak with him, let alone spend any time in his presence. She looked lovely in a bright blue gown that brought out her dark hair and eyes, and a Persian shawl that hung gracefully over her shoulders.

"I came to apologize for last night," he said softly. "It was despicable that I would take advantage of you."

She glanced at him suspiciously. "I'll never know if you're serious. You could just have decided to come here and gloat."

"Absolutely not! I realize you're a lady, and I behaved in an abominable fashion. On the other hand, I can't say I regretted the action. I wouldn't mind taking up where we left off last."

"Of all the nerve." She glared at him with those glorious eyes, but her words held no sting. He didn't like her pallor, but perhaps she hadn't slept well last night, either.

She gestured toward a chair. "You might as well sit down, but none of the chairs are comfortable."

He was delighted to obey. At least she didn't demand that he leave. "I know you hail from Yorkshire, which is not far from Humberside and my home. I hope that you'll allow me to visit you during the Christmas celebrations." He waited for her to light up with expectation, but she remained untouched, even subdued. It looked as if he'd made scant progress last night; he'd been so sure she'd enjoyed his advances.

"I doubt you'd be welcome," she said hesitantly, as if searching for the right words.

"Your aunt seems to accept me. Did I say something to offend you? My sole desire is to get to know you better."

She looked as if she didn't believe him. In fact, she was changing right in front of his eyes; her eyes took on a thunderous expression.

"What's the matter?" he asked, when she didn't reply.

"I doubt that this 'friendship' will progress," she said in a tight voice. "I appreciate your offer to get better acquainted, but it's not to be."

"Whyever not?" Her change in mood unnerved him. "I've tried to redeem myself with you. We didn't exactly have a brilliant start."

She shrugged. "Be that as it may, I don't want to waste my morning hours bickering with you, so I accept your apology. Now you can go."

He looked around the room, where everything hung faded and lifeless. "I don't understand the sudden, cold breeze coming from you. Last night you were quite approachable, and now you're back to that standoffish position."

"Don't you know it's a lady's prerogative if she wants to change her mind? I don't see any kind of future for this situation."

"But you haven't allowed me to show my better qualities. There's so much you don't know about me, or I about you. We made a promising start, so why ruin it?"

"You'll have no support from my family, Mr. Montclair. My aunt was taken by utter surprise when Jennings, the butler, brought in your card. Instead of leaving us alone, she should be asking you all kinds of uncomfortable questions right now."

He chuckled. "I must have brought on a wave of confusion, but I doubt Lady Figdon would think of questioning my motives. After all, I'm of impeccable lineage."

"That's not enough. Aunt Elvie would need to know about your plans for the future, your reason for visiting us in this fashion, and what your intentions are. But when all's said and done, Uncle Henry in Yorkshire should be the one to ask you those questions, but he never comes to London. I daresay my aunt has sadly failed in her duties."

"Hmm, well—"

"I know you have no intention of coming up to scratch. Why would you suddenly go from a gentleman shunning marriage to someone who's eager for courtship? This must be a farce, and I don't know why you bother to show your face here."

"Because I wanted to see you—it's that simple."

"You can't have veered off your chosen path that drastically."

He frowned, confused. "Please explain."

"Your path of dissipation and usage of other people to further your goals."

"Yes, I have taken another path. You're the only lady who has ever sparked an interest from me, and that's the truth."

His expression of bewilderment fueled her anger. Surely he remembered the wager. She debated with herself if she should divulge the information that she knew about it. "All I can say is that you're not trustworthy—never were and never will be, and I'm sorry to have to say that. It's a cold fact."

"You know me better now, Angela. Why believe the worst of me? Why believe I'm incapable of change?"

"I've watched you and your cronies over time—none of you has married and you've viewed Society with a disdainful eye. Since you know about my dismal Seasons in London, you have to understand that I refuse to make a spectacle of myself anymore, and I refuse to become the object of your attention. It will ultimately lead to more disappointment."

He sighed. "It doesn't have to end in that manner."

"Why I speak to you about this, I don't know. You can't really understand the pain of it all, and I'm not the only victim. Several of my sisters in misfortune are targets for contempt."

"That's most unfortunate."

"Stop your false commiseration. You should remain speechless as you're as guilty as your cronies for contemptuous behavior," she said angrily.

His eyes narrowed, and she sensed their conversation was heading for a patch of thin ice. "You're speaking strangely, Angela."

The words about the wager hung on her lips, but she couldn't utter them. She would have to curb her desire until the Barton ball, so that they could all snub the men and treat them with the scorn they deserved. She took a deep breath. "I think this conversation is finished. You'll gain nothing for this morning's visit."

She stood, and he had to do the same. He had nothing more to say. She noticed he'd gone pale, and a flame had ignited in the depths of his eyes. "Please just leave now, Lucien."

"I realize you're upset, and I'm not sure why. My intentions are honorable, and I plan to approach your Uncle Henry at my earliest convenience," he said.

She nodded, her whole body tense with the effort of keeping her temper under control. The nerve of the man! How could he stand there with an innocent expression on his face and speak of a future with her? It was outside of enough.

"If you don't remove your presence from this house within thirty seconds, I'll have the footmen throw you out."

He bowed stiffly. "If that's your attitude, I shall depart, but I want you to know that you're making a grave mistake."

"Your words mean nothing to me. You're always going to move on to the next conquest. I hear what you're saying, but as for living honestly, you haven't an inkling."

At this point, anger burned in his eyes. "You're right, but it's never too late to learn. You have pointed out the obvious and I've taken your words to heart. You're not much different. You're trying to fulfill your obligation to find a husband who will provide a comfortable life for you. Is that mission worthier than my plan to mend my ways?"

"No," she had to admit. "Due to financial circumstances I've been forced to think along those lines, but as I've stated before, I shall concentrate on improving the state of the orphanage that my uncle started some years ago outside of York. My life shall not be wasted with trifling pursuits."

She pointed toward the door. "More than thirty seconds have passed, and you're still here."

"That's because you keep talking," he said, with a sudden laugh.

She felt a peculiar need to laugh as well. "Someone has to point out the truth, and I'll never be one of your conquests. I have explicitly made that clear to you. Good morning, Mr. Montclair."

He bowed, his gaze sliding away. After he'd left, she fell onto the sofa, her whole being deflated. This had not been an easy task. She had to accomplish another step to end the silly wager. When her strength returned, she wrote notes to all of the ladies who were targets, suggesting that after the Barton ball, they put an article in a London newssheet to defame the rakes who had been involved. That would definitely put an end to their pursuit and it would save the ladies' reputations.

They all sent positive replies and Angela drafted an article that she sent around for comments, and everyone replied with excitement over the bold revenge. The world would shun the rakes—at least temporarily—once this became public knowledge.

Chapter Six

Angela traveled back to Yorkshire with Aunt Elvie shortly before Christmas. The weather turned bitter and gray for the holidays, and the sun didn't show its golden face for weeks. As the days moved into January after a dreary Christmas season, she felt restless and eager to welcome brighter days. She didn't hear from Lucien, but since he harked from the neighboring county, she discovered through the servants' gossip that he'd had a riding accident that had bruised his ribs and disfigured his face on a tree branch.

She had indeed won a kind of revenge, but the knowledge gave her no satisfaction. She corresponded with Letty Wells, who said she'd heard from Montague Blaine—strangely enough, he was still pursuing Letty—that Lucien was secluding himself at his grandfather's estate, Flagston Hall. No one had seen him since the accident.

Like a dog with his tail between his legs, he'd slunk out of sight. It irked her that he lived close enough for her to visit. Not that she would, of course. She secretly admitted that she missed him, but through the servants she discovered that he was up and about again two weeks later. His handsome face was marred, though, and the servants thought it had been a great waste that Mr. Montclair was no longer the most handsome man in the North Country.

Pah, Angela thought to herself. Perhaps he'd now be able to look beyond the tip of his own nose. Unable to clear her mind of him, she tied her bonnet strings under her chin, pulled on a heavy wool cloak, and set out to see how the children at the orphanage had fared since yesterday.

She discovered that an anonymous donor had given enough to provide new clothes, plenty of food, and myriad carved wooden toys and stuffed dolls for the children. A large deposit of coal had arrived to keep the young ones warm. They were rosy-faced and bright-eyed, and Angela spent a pleasant day playing with them. Uncle Henry's coffers had been depleted of late, and the orphanage had eked out an existence in the last year. The donation was a great blessing, and she'd soon find out who the donor was.

The Yorkshire farmers were a tightfisted and contrary lot, and Angela doubted that the funds had come from them. Perhaps Lord Applewood was the benefactor. The elderly earl was quite wealthy, and kind to boot.

She spent more and more time at the orphanage, but no one discovered the name of the secret patron.

Two weeks later she was invited to attend a small dinner party with her aunt and uncle at Longfell Manor, Squire Fenwick's home. The gentleman farmer was a distant cousin of hers, but due to severe weather, the family rarely came together in the winter. A thin sheet of snow lay on the frozen ground, the roads hard and clear. It was only an hour drive to the manor, and Angela looked forward to the break in the routine. She couldn't wait for spring to arrive so she could oversee the planting of the garden.

On the day of the dinner party, she dressed in a wine-red wool gown with a high collar and long sleeves. Over that she wore an embroidered and fringed gray shawl that lent warmth to her back and shoulders. Pearl drops hung from her ears, and, sadly, her hair had started to grow back into riotous curls, which would have to be pruned at her earliest convenience. She wore half-boots and a thick cloak as she and her family stepped into the coach and took to the road to Longfell Manor.

Her aunt looked somber in dark green wool with a feathered turban, and her uncle always wore brown wool clothes, blending nicely with the Yorkshire soil. They stared morosely out the window, where a bleak sun had finally dared to peek from behind the clouds. The light dappled the shadows of the trees lining the road. It flickered across the coach, and raised Angela's spirits. Soon it would disappear and bring the day to an end—too soon, in fact. She disliked the darkness of the long winter months.

The gathering was a godsend. She looked forward to seeing Cousin Fenwick and his wife, and their son, Theo, who was up from Oxford.

Longfell Manor stood stately on a knoll on the moor. Mountains loomed in the distance, and the snow glistened in the crevices of the rock. The tall, gray stone mansion with its white-painted window frames reminded her of a stern dowager who held no illusions.

Oil lamps lit the windows, and she noticed two other carriages in the stable yard. Evidently, they had invited other guests, probably the prosy Parson Thompson of Longfell.

"The mutton will be stringy and flavorless, and the beef dry," Uncle Henry mumbled.

"Uncle, just remember that Cousin Fenwick has a superb wine cellar. He's bound to bring out an excellent bottle."

Uncle Henry brightened. "By God, you're right, gel. A good port will soften any annoyance that might lurk over the meal."

"I find their cook acceptable," Aunt Elvie said. "There's always plenty on their table." She craned her neck to stare at the other coaches. "I wonder who they invited. I pray it's not one of those tedious Murrey spinsters from the village."

Angela sighed. This could turn out to be a very tiresome afternoon and evening. A footman handed her down, and Nelson, the butler, greeted her at the door. The warmth of the house invited her, and she kissed her cousin on the cheek. He looked as healthy and prosperous as ever, and his blue eyes glowed with pleasure at seeing her.

"Henrietta will be so happy to see you, Angela," he said, as his wife hurried forward to greet them. She was dressed in an unbecoming bright green satin dress and a black spencer that did not flatter her form. She kissed Angela on both cheeks and went to greet the others.

"I have a new guest here," Henrietta said with great pleasure.

Angela glanced into the library, where two gentlemen were sipping wine, and immediately recognized Lucien Montclair. Her heartbeat ran havoc in her chest, and tears pressed to her eyes. Of all the gall! Of course, Henrietta didn't know about Angela's disastrous past with Lucien. In these remote parts one didn't hear the latest *on dits*. Perhaps she would hear something three months after the fact.

Lucien didn't smile, but he gave her a courteous bow.

She put her hand to her heart and drew a deep breath. If only she could flee, but she couldn't leave without her aunt and uncle. She nodded in return, but her face burned with embarrassment. Why did his presence disturb her so much? She ought to be neutral to his charms by now, but her heart spoke a different language.

Henrietta bore down on her and trilled, "I have some younger people here tonight for you, Angela. I didn't want you to be bored." She took Angela's arm and pulled her into the library. "This is dear Miss Valentine." She introduced Lucien and another gentleman, a Montclair cousin named Alan, a personable young man with a friendly and open smile. He'd come up from Oxford with Theo. He bowed and kissed her hand.

"A pleasure to meet you, Miss Valentine. I always thought this area was rather quiet, but I see that it's not."

Angela smiled at the compliment. He was kind as well, and it had been a while since she felt kindness directed at her. Henrietta introduced her to Lucien. Clearly, she had not found out what had transpired in London. Lucien's face held a pallor that shocked Angela. A thin red scar crossed his left cheek from eyebrow to lip, a mark that diminished his attractiveness, yet his eyes hadn't changed. Mercurial, they searched her face, and she tried to smile when she only wanted to cry. Her hand trembled in his warm grip.

"Good afternoon, Miss Valentine," he said smoothly. "It's a delight to meet you."

At least he didn't make any references to their past acquaintance. "Mr. Montclair, a pleasure I'm sure," she murmured.

Then everything crashed around her as Aunt Elvie surged forward, both hands outstretched. "Mr. Montclair! What an unexpected and pleasant surprise."

Henrietta looked from one to the other. "They know each other?"

Lucien nodded. "I met Miss Valentine in London, but our association was cut short due to unforeseen circumstances. However, I'm happy to encounter her here unexpectedly, so far away from the city."

"She's a welcome guest here, and it's a blessing we see you more often, too, Lucien," Henrietta said. "You spent most of your time in London."

"My London days are over," he said, giving Angela a meaningful glance.

Why did she care where he spent his time? Surely it didn't matter to her what he said. Their acquaintance was over, and since he was here now she could be civil, or completely ignore him.

The butler served glasses of sherry, and Angela clutched hers tightly, though it tasted like mud.

"I realize you had a serious accident, Lucien," Henrietta said, "but that shouldn't remove you from the social rounds."

"Believe me, I don't long for the social gatherings any longer."

For the murky gambling dens, more likely, Angela thought.

"You can't closet yourself at Flagston Hall forever, Lucien," Henrietta admonished. "I understand nothing is the same since the accident, but you have to come alive."

He reddened with embarrassment. "Do you always say what's on your mind, Henrietta?"

"I'm of the belief that there's nothing to hide—especially among friends and family."

"Let all the skeletons out of the closet?" Lucien's lips curved upward at the corners, and Angela remembered how attractive his smile had been. Now it had an element of a grimace due to the scar. In a sense, it made him more human, and she liked the change.

"If you have any," Henrietta said brightly.

"I have plenty," Lucien said, "but I'm afraid they would shock you if I let them out."

Henrietta laughed and Aunt Elvie gasped as if already shocked. Angela felt only annoyance at his charm. He sent her a veiled glance and she looked away. If only she could still her racing heart.

They went in to dinner, served unfashionably early in the country, and to her chagrin Angela found out that Henrietta had placed her between Lucien and Alan. Theo sat on the opposite side, his freckled face wearing a teasing expression. She would have a word with the bounder when she had the chance. Lately, she hadn't been very charitable toward men.

She felt Lucien's gaze on her, and she stared stubbornly across the table where Theo was teasing Aunt Elvie.

"I've changed a lot since we last spoke," Lucien said, *sotto voce.*

"Yes, you lost your 'face,' " Angela replied. "But I daresay you lost that long before the accident."

"You're right," he said quietly.

"I shan't speak with you unless you address topics like the weather," she said under her breath.

"I was just searching for the right words to describe the latest snowstorm." His gaze followed a footman carrying a sauce tureen toward the other end of the table.

She waited, almost holding her breath.

With a sigh, he turned toward her. "It was wrong to pursue you as I did in London, and I apologize. To expect that you would welcome my advances was outright ignorant, but I sustained a foolish hope."

"Foolish it was," she said.

He laughed. "I can count on you to support my observations. You'll be the first to find faults. I can't change what happened in my past, but I've learned, and I assure you, it has been a painful experience."

"You're alluding to the accident?"

"And the realization what my past behavior did to the people involved. I honestly thought they didn't care. I didn't realize that I trampled hearts left and right."

"Not that you would stop and look behind you," she replied, her mouth dry as dust. She drank some more wine, and allowed the footmen to serve her slices of beef with a dab of brown sauce. People talked along the table, and Aunt Elvie stared at her with a silly grin on her face. She probably believed they had renewed their romantic intentions and were now involved in a conversation of the heart. And perhaps they were.

"You're right, but I don't regret my past. Life has been interesting, to say the least, and I'm now spending my days studying the ledgers. My grandfather is an eager teacher."

"I feel for him," she said, and he laughed.

"His patience is wearing thin, but I'm learning. To my surprise I find the studies interesting, and I can't wait to put some of my theories into practice."

"I'm certain the farmers are quavering in their boots."

He laughed once more. "That they are, and they are difficult to convince. They don't want to try anything newfangled."

"They are stubborn and take great pride in it," she said. She smiled. "I can almost hear their comments. Why we would change something that already works, et cetera."

"You're right on that score. They don't like change and they employ the same farm practices as they have for hundreds of years. I'm eager to try out some new machines to lighten their burden."

"They will fight you tooth and nail."

"I like the challenge." He sighed. "I so enjoy it when you smile, Angela. I sense the exhilarating tension that runs between us. It has since that time I encountered you at the modiste shop in Bond Street. Why deny it?"

He was right. Was this another opportunity to face the truth? This confrontation always happened in his presence, and it unsettled her.

Her hand trembled as she lifted her napkin to her lips and dabbed at the corners. "I don't know . . . I can't acknowledge it, and I still don't trust you. I don't need upheaval in my life now. It's a relief to be back in Yorkshire. I'm devoting myself to good works." She remembered she had something positive to share with him. "By the way, an anonymous donor is supporting the orphanage, and the children had a wonderful Christmas season."

"I donated those things," he said, and speared orange disks of boiled carrots with his fork.

She almost choked on a piece of tough beef, and had to stop everything to allow the food to travel down her throat. He glanced at her, concerned.

"Do you need—?"

She shook her head, and sipped some wine. Her throat cleared and she drank some more. The room started taking on a rosy glow as the wine took hold of her senses. "You're the anonymous donor?"

"Yes. I can see you're not too pleased."

"Why the anonymity?"

He thought for a moment. "I daresay you would've rejected the funds if you knew the source."

She suspected he was right, and she was disgusted with herself. She took a deep breath and admitted, "I might have, yet I'm very grateful for your generosity. You made the children's lives brighter. They had a wonderful Christmas, thanks to you."

He smiled, and something lifted in her heart. It wasn't so

difficult to be pleasant after all. Was it possible that they could let bygones be bygones? She had to forgive him, but she feared he hadn't changed. If she allowed him any closer, he was bound to step on her heart.

Fear gripped her. She couldn't take that step; she couldn't expose herself to more heartache.

"I appreciate your thoughtfulness concerning the orphanage, and if you want to continue to support us, contact the bank in York. They'll take care of everything."

"I'd like to be more involved. The thought of playing with the children seems rather livelier than interacting with the bank manager in York."

"I can't see you taking time with the children."

"Why not?" He finished his slice of beef just as the footman brought a platter of ham to their attention.

She didn't know what to say.

"I really want to know why you would get such a notion, Angela."

"I surmise you have no experience with children, and even less patience. By custom, you gentleman rarely involve yourselves with the rearing of children."

He thought for a moment. "You're right, but I don't mind learning more. One day I might have children of my own."

The thought of his future children stirred her emotions, and she found herself filled with longing for a family. She wished things were different; she wished he had an impeccable past and honorable intentions toward her. She wished she would be the mother of his children, but that was impossible.

He put his hand to his cheek, and she sensed his discomfort. It made him every bit more human.

"Does it ache?" As he nodded, she whispered, "How did the accident happen?"

His face twisted in pain, and she knew he'd gone through a difficult time. "I'd been breaking in a colt—great horseflesh, yet too skittish. I had taken him for a ride, and he bolted as a flock of grouse rose out of the grass. Before I had a chance to control him, he skirted an oak with low-hanging branches and wiped me out of the saddle. I sprained my ribs, and cut my face."

"I'm sorry to hear that."

"Penance for my sins, don't you agree?" His mouth quirked in a wry smile. "My face will never return to its former . . . shape." His eyes had darkened with embarrassment. "I've learned to accept that."

"I suspect you took your, er . . . elegance for granted."

He nodded, but didn't say anything.

This admission made him more human than ever before. She softened for a moment but steeled herself against the softness in her heart.

"I had a missive from Monty Blaine. He's about to ask for Miss Wells's hand in marriage. According to him, she has changed completely."

Angela smiled inwardly. How wonderful that Letty had continued on the fashionable course that they had planned together. "Letty is beautiful."

"Yes . . . but I rather like the tall, angular type," he said under his breath. "I prefer dark hair and dark eyes."

She blushed, and her aunt tittered as she noticed Angela's discomfort. Angela sent her a furious glance, one that Theo caught. He lifted his arms as if to shield himself. His freckles moved as he laughed. "A beet could not be redder," he teased. "What did you say, Lucien, to stir her anger?"

"Desist, Theo," she said, but he only continued to laugh.

"I daresay he touched a tender spot," Theo continued, and Aunt Elvie looked very excited. She could probably hear the wedding bells already.

" 'Tis rather a talent to find a weak spot in Angela's armor," Aunt Elvie said, her words making Angela cringe.

"Not at all," Lucien said. "She's quite soft if you know how to look."

Theo slapped the tabletop. "By Jupiter, I believe Angela has found a true champion. It's about time."

The whole table silenced and all eyes were directed at her. Her mortification went deep. All attention then went toward Lucien, who squirmed beside her. Were they all expecting wedding bells now?

"Why did you say that?" she whispered to him. "I'll never squash the rumors now. You know how they love to gossip."

He looked at her, his gaze intent. "Perhaps it wouldn't be such a bad idea to, well, pursue our friendship. Who knows where it will lead?"

She didn't believe she'd heard him right.

Chapter Seven

Lucien stared out the window in his library at Flagston Hall. The snow lay thin but hardened on the ground, and as January moved into February, the cold had an iron grip on the region. Frustration filled him as he considered going on a ride, but the ground presented difficulties for the horses, so he had to postpone that idea.

But perhaps he could take a drive in the coach. His ribs ached, and his face felt tight as he worked the muscles that had been damaged when he fell from the colt. Every morning he looked in the mirror and rejected the face that stared back at him. The fall that had transformed his life forever, still made him cringe in horror at his image. He had told Angela that he'd learned to live with it, but he'd lied. Perhaps he would get used to it in time, but the injury had dented his confidence. He'd found that his sense of worth had been based on a shallow yet boggy foundation within.

He had fought the realization, and had been forced to look deeply for a reason other than his wealth and his countenance, which had always been handsome.

But who was Lucien? He sensed he stood on the verge of new knowledge.

A letter from Freddy Longman came in the mail that morning, and Lucien knew it held a reminder of the challenge ahead—one that Lucien had no intention of contributing to after all that had happened.

He read:

Lucien, old fellow, we miss you in London and expect to see you shortly to challenge the wager during the St. Valentine's celebrations. Mrs. Barton will have a conniption when she finds us all attending, and whoever manages a dance at the Barton ball will be a thousand pounds plumper in the pocket. We're meeting at Watier's the night before the ball, and I expect you to be there. I know your accident has put a damper on everything, but you need your friends to cheer you up. Y'r obedient friend, Freddy.

Lucien tossed the letter on the desk. He wasn't going to take any part in the Barton ball, yet part of him wanted to see his friends again. He worried about the teasing his face would receive from them, but it didn't matter. He needed a break in the routine.

Instead of going on a drive locally, he asked his valet, Tompkins, to pack for London. Two hours later, the coach headed south on the Great Northern Road.

The men gathered at Watier's on the night before St. Valentine's Day. Freddy was deeply in his cups, and Monty's face glowed with the brandy he'd consumed. Eddy had already finished off two bottles of claret, and Vincent was on his third, bleary-eyed and pasty-faced, Lucien thought. He drank a glass of claret and realized how changed he felt since he'd last sat at this table. The accident had showed him truths that he'd never paid attention to in the past. His grandfather had turned out to be a great fount of wisdom and support, something he'd never noticed before, due to his sporadic visits to Flagston Hall. He also felt that the crust around his heart was slowly crumbling.

He still enjoyed his friends; none of them really meant any harm with their pranks, but it was time to grow up, he thought.

"What are your plans for gaining entry to the ball, gents?"

Freddy called out, his voice just on the verge of slurring. "How do you plan to get onto the grounds?"

"We're not telling you our plans so that you can steal them, Freddy. I suppose your feeble mind has not come forth with a plan of action," Monty said. "I'll win, because I'm already in Miss Wells's good graces. I'm going to ask for her hand in marriage."

"I suppose you've confided our wager to her and she'll be waiting by some window to let you in," Vincent said, his hand trembling around the glass.

"And play you, my friends, foul?" Monty shook his head in disgust. "That would be unforgivable."

Eddy turned to Lucien. "With that face of yours, you won't have a chance. And last I heard, Miss Valentine hates you. Everyone will cower in fright when they see you, and she'll faint dead away."

"She's not the fainting type." Lucien had planned to bow out of the wager, but with all these callous challenges flying at him, he changed his mind. "I'll find my way into Mrs. Barton's ballroom, have no fear." Lucien gave a wry smile, *and Miss Valentine will dance with me*. "My face won't make a difference, and it matters not if the damsels decide to have fits of vapor."

"You show false bravado, Lucien, but I admire you for it," Monty said.

"How are your courtships going? What about the Misses Ponsonby, Knoll, and Mottingrow?"

Vincent snorted, his eyes crossing. "To win the wager, all we have to do is manage one dance at Mrs. Barton's. I doubt that it's worth it, but I could use a thousand pounds."

Eddy said. "I've been overcome with nightmares that I would have to face my conquest at the altar—against my will."

Vincent groaned in agreement and started on his fourth bottle. "But did you notice that something happened to the ladies after we placed the wager? It was as if all of them became more attractive, wore prettier dresses, and cared about their appearance. Gentlemen began to pay them more attention. The whole thing is very strange."

"Yes," Monty said, "it's almost as if they knew about the bet."

"They can't have," Lucien said. "Miss Valentine would've cut my head off if she knew."

They all nodded in agreement.

Vincent said, "You're not drinking, Lucien."

"I've lost my desire," Lucien replied.

Nobody commented on that.

"The wager is a rather silly one," Lucien continued. "I discovered as I pursued Miss Valentine that she's a very decent woman, and I'm hoping to continue our friendship after the wager is over—that is, if she doesn't explode with anger first as she realizes what we've been doing."

"You can't be serious?" Freddy said, his bloodshot eyes wide. "Your children will be beanpoles."

"That is, if she'll have me. I ought to bow out of the bet to impress her, but this is my last prank, and no female shall dictate my life." He had bowed and scraped enough to her.

" 'Pon rep," Freddy said, his nose quivering. "She won't have you, despite your brilliant mind. When she sees your face . . . I'd say she'd reject you." A gleam entered his eyes, and Lucien immediately saw where Freddy's thoughts were going.

"No, absolutely not! I'll not be the object of another one of your wagers, Freddy." He gripped his friend by the coat lapels. "Do you understand?"

"Damme, there's no reason to get into high dudgeon." Freddy put up his hands as if to ward him off. "I daresay Miss Valentine is a sore spot with you."

"More than you'll ever know," Lucien said.

Freddy sat silent, studying him. "By Jupiter, I believe Cupid's arrow has struck you, Montclair."

"Perhaps. It's not an unpleasant feeling, but rather frustrating."

"I've scouted the grounds around Mrs. Barton's in Greenwich," Eddy said. "There's only one huge wall to scale, and that's the only detail I divulge as you have to do your own investigation."

Everyone looked at him as if he'd grown two heads. "Eddy, I'm not about to climb a brick wall in my silk knee breeches. They're bound to rip," Vincent said.

"We'll contrive, and remember, I have the advantage as Miss Wells actually *likes me,*" Monty said.

"Oh, why don't you shout this to the heavens," Freddy said in disgust.

Lucien stood. "Let the best man win. I'm leaving so I can go on the attack with a clear head tomorrow."

His cronies chided him, but he left, and the cool night air had never smelled so fresh. He lifted his aching face to the skies and inhaled deeply.

Mrs. Barton's house in Greenwich had somehow become the favored spot to celebrate St. Valentine's Day. She had obscure connections to dukes and earls, but her lineage was modest, and Mr. Barton, rest his soul, had only had an immense fortune to bolster his success in society. It had gone a long way toward acceptance into the highest circles, and Mrs. Barton had the reputation for being the greatest stickler of all.

Lucien approached the estate from the back and after scaling the wall, he scouted for his competitors in the bushes. He found both Eddy and Vincent with flasks in the boxwood hedge behind the terrace. They were already three sheets to the wind and giggled over shared jokes.

"You're not hard to spot," Lucien said.

"No room for you, Lucien. Find your own shrubs."

"I've no intention of muddying myself further. My evening shoes are quite muddy as it is."

He glanced up toward the ballroom, lit up like a sunny afternoon with chandeliers and candelabras in every niche and on every table. The room was packed with dancers, and he caught glimpses of the women involved in the wager. Satin gowns of all colors danced past, and precious gems glittered in the light. He looked for Angela and saw her dancing with a portly gentleman, and she was laughing at something he'd said.

She looked beautiful.

A stab of jealousy gripped Lucien, but he pushed it away. How ridiculous to feel anything, he thought. She had no real interest in him, which she'd pointed out so many times, so he might as well go out in style.

"What are you waiting for?" he asked the others.

"A waltz," they said, giggling.

"Where are the others? They must be hiding somewhere."

"Haven't seen them," Eddy said, upending the flask in his mouth.

Lucien skirted the bushes and walked along the side of the mansion toward the front. He looked for Monty and Freddy, but didn't see them. They might already be inside, hiding in a cupboard or under a piece of furniture.

He would be bolder than that. He would just walk right into the ballroom, find Angela, and wrest her from whoever had bespoken the dance.

He walked up the front steps behind a party of heavily cloaked guests still arriving at the mansion. Unnoticed, he slipped behind the butler and melted behind a tall urn holding a large bouquet of flowers. The hostess had been speaking with someone in the throng at the door and hadn't noticed.

He viewed the hallway and the stairs leading to the ballroom upstairs. At the moment, they were empty, and he decided to make a dash for it. Taking the steps two at a time, no one stopped him in outrage.

He was familiar with most of the guests, but they would know he wasn't welcome at Mrs. Barton's—she always complained heartily about the extravagances of the young bucks of London, Lucien's group in particular.

He stood behind a marble bust of one of the Barton forefathers and looked into the opulent ballroom. Gold-and-light-yellow damask panels, fishbone patterned parquet, mirrors, and masses of flowers made up the interior, and his gaze sought Angela. She was dancing with another gentleman now, a tall, slender man with a serious expression. Laughing, she looked so different from the Angela he remembered of old. She wore a gossamer-light, shimmering white dress that showed off her beautiful neck, and her hair had been cut and brushed until the curls shone. Her lips were red and inviting, and his arms ached with a longing to hold her. It was clear other gentlemen had noticed her as well.

He realized he'd fallen in love with her, and he didn't want other gentlemen to hold her. He contemplated backing out of the wager even now, but she would discover the truth whether he was there or not.

Freddy was advancing up the stairs quickly. "Montclair, you're going to lose," he called out as he stepped into thc ballroom.

Squaring his jaw, Lucien decided to step forward as the new dance began. Surprise was the best strategy. Angela would perhaps protest, but convention demanded that she not cause a scene.

Mrs. Barton might swoon but he'd take the risk, and he would have to face the possibility that Angela would never speak with him again. He hesitated, but sensed he'd already gone too far down the wrong alley with her.

The strains of a waltz began and across the room, Monty was climbing through the window right behind Miss Wells. Perhaps they had a plan of their own. Monty bowed before her as couples gathered on the floor.

Lucien had to act immediately and as a gentleman moved toward Angela, Lucien stepped in front of her.

She gasped, her eyes widening and her mouth dropping open. Wearing a hesitant air, the other gentleman stepped aside.

"Good evening, Angela. May I have this dance?"

She fluttered her fan, and then slapped it shut, her chin setting in a stubborn line. She raised her voice so that the whole ballroom could hear. "Absolutely not!"

"You can't refuse me," he pleaded.

"I can."

He cringed at her loud voice, and realized his stupidity.

People began to speak in loud voices around them, but Lucien watched in a haze, wholly focused on the woman before him. This bet was the most ill-advised action he'd ever taken, but it was too late now.

He wanted Angela Valentine.

He slowly noticed that women were screaming as Eddy staggered through the door, thoroughly drunk. Freddy linked his arm to Eddy's and the two men sang at the top of their lungs. They called for their ladies, who rejected them in loud voices and slapped their faces.

Vincent climbed through the window and approached Rosamunde Knoll, who hid behind her chaperone. "I don't want to dance with you!" she cried, enraged, as he tried to pull her onto the dance floor.

The chaperone swung her reticule against the side of his face, and he staggered back with a yelp.

Angela stepped forward to the middle of the room and asked for everyone's attention by raising her arms. The outraged chatter stopped.

"Gracious hostess, dear guests," she began. "Some of my friends and I have been the recipients of a cruel joke—a nefarious wager, in fact, that these gentlemen instigated. The Misses Wells, Mottingrow, Ponsonby, Knoll, and myself were considered some of the most undesired ladies on these men's list. They had plans to embarrass us tonight in front of everyone, but we have been fortunate to know about the wager, and we've been prepared."

Everyone gasped at her blunt words. She looked pale but determined, and Lucien wondered how she'd discovered the wager. Her aunt had fainted at the back of the room, and other guests waved a vinaigrette under her nose.

"Behold these uncaring gentlemen and treat them to the same ridicule they had planned for us."

The other guests murmured in approval, and Freddy, Eddy, and Monty found themselves immediately with bruised faces and bleeding noses. Vincent had fled, but they heard him squeal downstairs, and Angela pushed Lucien toward a group of approaching male guests who proceeded to knock him down. He lay in great pain and watched the goings-on through a pink haze. He deserved every bit of this, he thought, humiliation digging deep within.

Mrs. Barton stepped forward and commanded the room, condemnation written all over her face. "This is the most nefarious scandal!" She pointed at each intruder in turn. "I demand that you leave this instant, and the whole world will soon hear about your unforgivable transgression."

Footmen gathered to escort the offenders outside, and Lucien felt a deep sense of defeat, on several levels. He cared wildly about Angela Valentine, and he'd been so sure she would dance with him. He felt shame about his involvement. If the women hadn't know about the wager, it would have just been a gathering he and his friends had entered uninvited, but it had turned into a farce.

This would be the end of any chance to win Angela's approval, and he found he cared very much about that.

Her eyes burned into him as he walked toward the door, and he swallowed hard. She came to stand in front of him. "No one wins in this, yet my friends and I won unexpected dignity, which we didn't have before we found out about the wager," she said for everyone to hear. "You gave us the incentive we needed to improve our lives."

He wanted to sink through the floor as everyone cheered. The footmen had escorted the laughing Freddy and Eddy out the door, and he knew he would be next. The only one who seemed untouched was Monty. He and Miss Wells exchanged loving glances. In a sense, Monty won the bet, and he gained love. *How come he could succeed where I could not?* Lucien thought.

Even as the footmen approached, Lucien looked at Angela, hoping she saw the longing in his eyes. "I love you," he whispered, knowing she could not hear him over the din. He bowed to the outraged Mrs. Barton and left the room.

The next morning, after a sleepless night, Angela sent the article she'd written when she found out about the wager to *The Times*.

The disrespect and lack of conscience among gentlemen of fashion is rampant in London.

The victims of a distasteful wager found out that Vincent, Lord Ecton, Mr. Frederick Longman, Mr. Montague Blaine, Mr. Edward Miles, and Mr. Lucien Montclair placed money at Watier's club on who would be the first to win a dance at the fashionable Mrs. Barton's St. Valentine's ball with the "most unattractive" unmarried young lady of the Season. Five names of highly respected ladies were pulled out of a hat, and unwanted attention toward these defenseless ladies was initiated, plans that were to culminate at the Barton ball. It is the opinion of the author that such unsavory behavior should not go unpunished, and we, as the offended group of victims, demand a public apology for such ill-mannered and arrogant behavior. The world should question the dubious quality of these men's morals, and it is unconscionable that these gentlemen are to become the future backbone of England. They have no backbone, and this is the sad truth about the future leaders of our country. The virtues of the ladies involved were never considered, and the distress these so-called gentlemen caused demands amends.

* * *

Angela waited breathlessly for a printed apology, which arrived for the world to see two days later. She cried with relief when she saw that the author was Lucien. He wrote:

> *What started out as an innocent prank quickly turned into a distasteful spectacle that should never have happened. I apologize for myself and my brothers for any pain we may have caused the esteemed ladies in question. We should consider ourselves fortunate if they would turn a benign eye upon our publicly shamed selves and find forgiveness in their hearts.*

Lucien's grandfather would be livid. Lucien's admission spread balm on her senses, as she knew that he had found the courage to stand up for what was right. He and his cronies would be barred from all the great houses in London, but she doubted if they cared. She would have to be satisfied with the apology. She would have to put this episode behind her and move on to the next stage of her life.

If only Lucien hadn't mouthed the words "I love you" at the Barton ball. This very act had taken her by such surprise, and kept her sleepless at night. Their relationship could've been so different if they had begun on a different note, but he would never have noticed her in the past.

Three days later, she received a letter in the mail with a nicely written personal apology from him, and she discovered that the other ladies had, too. He stood up to the outcry of outrage that followed in the newssheet.

He had whispered, "I love you." All she heard in her head was those repeated words, and curiosity grew within her. Why had he even gone to the effort of mouthing something that *difficult* to her? She didn't want to feel any more pain, and she doubted his motives. He'd had no reason to say those words.

Why did she spend so much time thinking about him? She was foolish again, just as she'd been when the unmentionable Mr. Bolton had bolted to the Continent.

She stood by her drafty bedroom window at the mansion in London, and she shivered. The drafts grew wider every winter here, and the furniture grew more mold, not to mention drabness in every tuck and fold. She would end up like these ramshackle chairs if she weren't careful.

She pulled the wool collar of her dark green gown closer around her neck, and pulled at the points of her tight sleeves. Her hands felt icy and stiff, and her feet ached with the cold sweeping along the old floors.

The worst blow had been Aunt Elvie. After waking up from the swoon at Mrs. Barton's, she'd berated Angela all the way home. "Like a man, you stood and addressed everyone. I'll never be able to live down the humiliation," she'd cried into her handkerchief.

"Someone had to stand up for those who were insulted."

Aunt Elvie's chins wobbled. "You destroyed any chance those poor ladies had of making an advantageous marriage."

The fact of her aunt turning against her had burdened Angela ever since, and there had been more swooning and a verbal explosion when her aunt had discovered the article in the newssheet. "We are now condemned to Yorkshire for all eternity," she'd shrieked.

Angela had nothing to say, as nothing could soothe her aunt's raw sensibilities.

The days sequestered in the mansion in London without company pulled every ounce of patience from her. She tried to convince her aunt they had to travel back to Yorkshire, but the weather had turned treacherous.

A week after the St. Valentine's celebrations, the sun peeked from behind the clouds, cheering every heart in London. Angela was putting on her gloves to go outside for a walk, when someone knocked on the front door.

The butler opened it, letting in a blast of cold air. On the threshold stood Lucien in a many-caped coat. He halted his step as his gaze fell on her, and he took off his hat.

The words to shun him hung on her tongue, but she couldn't quite get them out.

"Can I speak with you, Miss Valentine?" he asked.

The servants looked disapproving, but she nodded, leading the way into the gloomy library that smelled of dust and moldy books. She turned toward him. "What do you want? I thought I made it perfectly clear that I never wanted to see you again."

"It's not that simple, Angela. We began something, but . . . but I want more than that. I want to find the tender side of you. I want to spend a life finding and enjoying all your little quirks. I long for a woman to share my life, and I want a family. Ever since I kissed you that first time, I've been yearning for you."

She wanted to say something cutting, but nothing came out. Instead she felt the tears pressing hot and urgent on the inside of her eyelids. He sighed and stepped close, pushing away a wayward curl from her forehead. Without a word, he pulled her into his arms and held her gently.

"It can't have been that bad," he murmured against her hair. "Just think of all the feathers that were ruffled at Mrs. Barton's. They haven't been ruffled for so long, we did the people a great service."

She was going to push him away, but couldn't. His arms embraced her with warmth and strength, and she'd never realized how much she needed him. No one had ever felt so good and so *at home.* She had been starved for affection and never realized it until it was freely given.

"You are beautiful and loving," he murmured against her hair.

She sighed. "I want to believe you, but—"

"Shh, let me show you. Give me a chance to court you correctly. Help me to find the other side of me," he begged. "You helped me open the door to that person, and I'm eager to discover more about Lucien Montclair."

"You can't be serious," she replied dreamily as he rained kisses over her face.

"I've never been more serious, Angela. I may have entered a stupid wager that would culminate on St. Valentine's Day, but you are the true gift of love."

"Are you claiming that Cupid's arrow pierced your heart?" She looked into his blue eyes that weren't cool any more. They were soft and warm.

"Well, if you'd asked me two months ago, I would've laughed at you, but I have to admit that something struck me rather hard the first time I saw you."

She smiled. "In your opinion, what was it?"

He brushed back a stray hair from her ear. "I'd say it was love. For the first time ever, love struck my heart, and it opened up. I've never been more surprised. And what about you? Are you still angry?"

"I've forgiven you, strangely enough. I should be disgusted with you, outraged at your behavior, but I think my heart was assaulted as well with that strange feeling."

"You think it's love?"

"Perhaps."

He held her very close. "I love you so much," he whispered against her hair. "I have to approach Uncle Henry with my intentions, but I cannot wait. I'd like to know—" he took a deep breath "—if you'd be willing to become my wife?"

Her breath lodged in her throat, and her heart pounded. Part of her wanted to protest, but her heart shouted, *"Yes!* Yes, I'd like to become your wife."

His mouth found hers anew, and sweetness coursed through every part of her being. She wagged her finger under his nose when he lifted his face from hers. "No more wagers."

"They are over for good." He held her face between his hands. "I want to spend the rest of my life exploring the depth of the love I feel for you."

She read the truth in his eyes, and her heart made a somersault. "I love you, too, Lucien . . . you scoundrel."

MY WICKED VALENTINE

Kate Huntington

To Bob Chwedyk, my valentine of twenty years, with all my love.

Chapter One

November 1817
India

"Is something wrong, Antonio? You are solemn today," Caroline Benningham remarked when the handsome, urbane Count Antonio Zarcone called for her at her hotel.

Antonio was a wicked flirt, and it was odd to see him without the playfully mocking expression that was habitual to him. She found it quite disconcerting.

"It is a day to be solemn," he said, regarding her from soulful, dark eyes. He touched the corner of her mouth with a gentle forefinger, but he didn't kiss her as she half expected. "I will remember this day for the rest of my life."

With his usual gallantry he ushered her out into the sunshine to help her onto a fine white Arabian mare and to mount his own white Arabian stallion. As he led the way from the hotel, his servant followed at a discreet distance on horseback with an enormous basket attached to his saddle containing, she assumed, a sumptuous *petit dějeuner.*

Oh, dear.

When she realized that they were on the street that led to the Taj Mahal, the most romantic edifice in the world, her heart pounded within her breast.

He had called on her nearly every day since they had come to India on the same ship, she to chaperon a young friend and he to seek amusement in foreign climes, which seemed to be his primary purpose in life.

Caroline just knew that Count Antonio Zarcone, the most deliciously wicked man in the world, was going to propose marriage to her today in the shadow of the exquisite monument a king had built to his enduring passion for his queen.

And she would have to refuse him, even though it would break her heart to do so.

Antonio was so sophisticated that he made her feel fresh and new, even though she was well established on the shady side of thirty and had been married once before. Before him, all the gentlemen of her acquaintance paled to insignificance.

When Antonio was near, her blood sang in her veins, her voice was always on the point of song, her lips perpetually burst into laughter. This past month in India as the object of his gallantry was the happiest of her life.

But he was a rake, and a selfish rake at that. Caroline's infatuation with Antonio did not blind her to his faults.

His was a breed with which Caroline had much sad experience. She had married Giles, her first husband, in defiance of her father's expressed wish because he stirred her girlish passions like no other. He had been unfaithful to her before the ink was dry on their marriage lines.

No. Not again.

She adored Antonio. No man had ever made her laugh as much, or long so much for something that she knew would be very, very bad for her.

Antonio probably believed he loved her. He would know that she loved him. She was as inept as a starry-eyed schoolgirl when it came to hiding her true feelings for him.

She frantically tried to think of some way to dash his hopes as gently as possible.

Then the sensually shaped dome of the Taj Mahal loomed ahead, and the count gracefully dismounted. He held his hands out for her with a sweet smile on his face, and she slid into them, closing her eyes to savor the sensation of his arms coming around her.

It was, perhaps, for the last time. After this he might never want to touch her again.

She was already mourning him in her heart as she watched the count's servant spread their meal on a linen tablecloth laid on the ground. Plump, red grapes. Strawberries and cream. *Pâté de foie gras*. A crisp baguette of bread. A rare vintage of champagne, for Antonio had educated her about such things, cooled in a silver bucket filled with snow brought from the mountains.

All of her favorites.

Oh, Antonio!

The count nodded to the servant in approval and dismissal, and the servant retreated to a discreet distance to take charge of the animals.

"Antonio, I—"

He placed one hand to her lips.

"My beautiful Caroline, I must speak," he said. "You must know how much I adore you."

She took a deep breath.

"You have been most . . . kind," she said, and she could have bitten her tongue for sounding so missish. She wouldn't have blamed him for laughing at her, but he did not.

"I would be much more than kind to you," he said. There was the hint of a smile in his eyes. He took a ripe strawberry, dipped it into the cream and held it to her lips. She opened her mouth for it, and after she swallowed, he gave her a gentle kiss.

He took her hand and solicitously guided her to sit on the embroidered cushions the servant had spread on the ground for their comfort. The count sat beside her and reached for the bottle in the silver bucket.

"Some champagne?" he asked, as he expertly popped the cork and poured the silver liquid into a crystal glass for her.

"Please," she said. Perhaps the wine would settle her fluttering stomach.

Be strong, Caroline, she told herself. *You must refuse him. Even if it breaks your heart.*

She had no illusions that it would break *his* heart if she refused him.

It was well known that Count Antonio Zarcone had no heart. He might be quite cast down for a week or two, but so charming a man could have his pick of ladies. They fell into his arms like ripe apples from a tree in autumn.

Caroline took such a large, fortifying sip of the wine that it set her to coughing, and the count patted her on the back until she regained control of herself. Her eyes were watering.

"You are nervous," he said indulgently. "I do not blame you, for you must have sensed what I am about to ask you."

"Please, Antonio," she said, despising herself for the weakness of her voice. "You must not—"

"I cannot be silent a moment longer," he said passionately as he grasped her hands and raised them to his lips. "My darling, my adorable Caroline. You must and will be mine! I have made all the arrangements. We will leave tomorrow for my villa in Rome, where we will spend our days basking in the sunshine and our nights making passionate love in the moonlight."

"I am sorry, Antonio," she said. "But I cannot—"

She blinked and sat up straight. She pushed his hands away.

"*What* did you say?" she demanded. There was nothing weak about her voice now.

"I am asking you to be my love," he said, smiling indulgently at her.

"Your *mistress*, you mean," she said tartly.

It was his turn to blink.

"Yes. Of course," he said, sounding puzzled. "What did you think?"

His eyes widened as enlightenment dawned.

"Oh, my poor, poor dear," he said so sympathetically that

Caroline longed to rip his face off with her nails. He put his arm around her shoulders as if in consolation, but she shook him off. "Did you think I intended to propose marriage to you?"

"Never mind," she said, teeth clenched. She wanted to die of mortification.

"I do beg your pardon," he said. "I meant no insult."

"You meant no insult? You have just offered me a slip on the shoulder, you beast!"

"I have asked you to live with me in my villa, and be my love," he said with great dignity. "No other woman has ever been so honored."

"Honored! You have asked me to be your *trollop*! Did you think I would be *grateful* for that? I should have known that a widow rather long in tooth would not be good enough to marry the illustrious Count Antonio Zarcone! No doubt you will find yourself a nice, nubile *young* wife for that honor and ruin her life for her!"

"My dear Caroline, you are distraught," he said, as he laid a placating hand over hers.

"For your information, I would have refused you!" she shouted. She snarled at him when he tried to shush her. Other tourists strolled nearby and turned to stare at them.

Antonio's mouth opened and closed like that of a landed fish. It gave Caroline a mean sense of satisfaction.

"Refused me?" he repeated in shocked disbelief.

"Yes," she cried. "I would not marry you if you were the last man on earth!"

With that, she scrambled to her feet, picked up the bottle of champagne, and poured the remainder of the wine over his head.

Then, while he was still sputtering with the shock, she walked over to the Arabian mare, mounted clumsily, for her hands were shaking, and rode away with tears of rage coursing down her cheeks.

* * *

What a woman, Antonio thought admiringly as he watched her neat, erect figure retreat on horseback down the hill. *How magnificent she looks when she is angry!*

Antonio laughed out loud, and his cringing servant stared at him in astonishment. Droplets of champagne flew from his hair as he shook his head to clear the wine from his stinging eyes.

No other woman of his acquaintance would have dared treat him so.

He waved off the fussy ministrations of his servant, who was attempting to mop his face with a linen serviette.

So, she would not marry him if he were the last man on earth.

He did not blame her for saying this to him.

In truth, he respected her for it.

He honored her for it.

But he did not believe it for a moment.

She was an aristocratic woman from the phlegmatic race of the English. It behooved her not to surrender her virtue lightly, even if she did mean to surrender it eventually. Antonio, of all people, knew how this game was played. He blamed himself for the misunderstanding between them, but how could he have known this worldly woman had expected him to propose marriage? No doubt she was regretting her rash behavior, even now.

Marriage was not for such as she. Caroline valued her independence as much as he valued his own. What he had suggested was a perfect arrangement, and, contrary to what she apparently believed, he *had* honored her by proposing it. Although he had enjoyed scores of mistresses, he had always set them apart in separate establishments like pretty toys confined in sturdy boxes so he could get them out any time he wished to play with them, and return them whenever he tired of them. They didn't share his real life, not in the way he meant for Caroline to share it.

Was he to believe that Caroline longed for a stodgy, conventional marriage and a brood of children? She would be bored senseless within the twelvemonth, as would he.

Instead, they would tour the world together, enjoying its beauty. He already knew she loved to travel, and she truly appreciated all the hedonistic little luxuries at his command.

Antonio wanted to show her the pyramids. And the beauties of Amsterdam. And the ornate four-poster bed at his primary palace in Naples, in which he had been born. It had been designed and built for one of the Medicis.

He would be magnanimous, he decided. He would give her another chance to accept his proposition.

And she would be grateful.

So grateful.

His breath quickened in the anticipation of his very great pleasure in permitting his passionate Caroline to demonstrate her gratitude to him for the privilege of being asked to be his love.

Antonio waited a day for her temper to cool off. Then another two days for her to miss him. For good measure, he added three more days, just to make her worry that he might not deign to forgive her.

He did not spend those long days without her in vain. He dispatched a letter with instructions to his servants in Rome to prepare his villa for Caroline's reception. He purchased a ruby the size of a hen's egg and had it mounted into a heavy gold setting as a ring to seal the bargain.

On the seventh day, he realized he could not do without his Caroline for another moment, so he anointed his person with bay rum, dressed in his finest clothes, tucked the ruby ring into an ornate chest of silver, bought an enormous bouquet of jasmine, that most sensual of blossoms, in the marketplace, and sauntered off to make Caroline the happiest of women.

When he called at the hotel, however, he found her gone. She had left a letter for him.

I have gone to England. Do not bother to follow. If you call upon me, I will not be at home. I never want to see you again as long as I live.

Antonio grinned.

This curt message did not fool him in the least. A child could see that his Caroline intended to lead him on a merry chase. Of course, she expected him to follow.

He was a trifle disappointed, it must be admitted. He had quite looked forward to sweeping her off her feet to his villa. And winter was a miserable time to be in England.

No matter.

She wanted to be coaxed out of her sulks, did she? Antonio was an expert at soothing feminine tempers.

He had no doubt that he could tame the impetuous Caroline to his hand, and their coming together would be all the more passionate for it.

Chapter Two

February 14
St. Valentine's Day

What a symbolic day for Count Zarcone to arrive in London, prepared to make Caroline Benningham his love.

That was about all the weary Antonio could say for the place. It was just past dawn when the private carriage he had hired pulled up in front of the Clarendon Hotel, but the sky was weeping gray instead of rosy-fingered, as a proper dawn ought to be. The air was damp, and the wind was cold.

Only a juiceless, phlegmatic Englishman could love such a dreary place. The sooner he took Caroline and himself away from it, the better.

After he had availed himself of the steaming bathwater brought by the obsequious staff of the hotel and arrayed himself in freshly pressed clothes, he sauntered forth to mount his campaign to recapture the lovely Caroline's heart.

Caroline had just come down to the parlor, fresh from her maid's ministrations, when the first volley in Antonio's merry war arrived.

"Ma'am, look what has come for you!" her parlor maid said, wide-eyed, as she regarded the enormous bouquet of exotic lilies in her arms. Instead of the usual small, elegant white card that, as a rule, accompanied such tributes, the flowers arrived with a large, gilt-edged Valentine of stiff vellum trimmed three times around with elegant lace—imported from France, Caroline observed, or she knew nothing of female adornment.

She had never seen anything like it.

Caroline knew of only one person extravagant enough to trim a St. Valentine's Day greeting in a length of expensive lace with which any fashionable lady would be proud to adorn the bodice of her best ball gown.

Caroline gritted her teeth, for Count Antonio Zarcone, her *bête noire,* was about to swagger back into her life.

My Wicked Valentine, the missive began in ornate script, *how I have missed your laughing eyes, your delightful wit, your graceful figure that makes mortal men praise the Divine Sculptor for the perfection of His art. Your hair is a damask curtain, dark as night; silk to the touch of my adoring fingers. Your lips, sweeter and more lush than the red grapes that grow in my vineyards. Cruel Beauty, you were wicked to run away from a love such as ours. The fault was partly mine for failing to convince you of my devotion. May these flowers plead my case. Adored one, in my eyes you are one of these blooms from a hotter world than that of your pallid England. Your pale countrywomen are the common roses that grow in every garden; your beauty, your radiance is of a more vivid kind and deserves a better fate. Not for you, their ordinary lives. Fly away with me, and let me worship you in the way you deserve.*

It was signed, *Your Antonio.*

My Antonio, indeed!

"Throw them out," Caroline said, hardening her heart.

"Ma'am?" the maid said, staring at her.

"Throw those flowers out."

"But, ma'am—"

Caroline then pulled the expensive lace from the card and tore the stiff vellum into pieces.

"Ma'am, ma'am! What are you doing?" cried the girl.

"Here," Caroline said, handing the parlor maid the lace, even though she knew her personal maid had a better right to it. "Take it. Save it for your wedding dress, for I am certain you will wish to marry someday."

"Oh, thank you, ma'am," the girl said, as she bobbed a little curtsy. Her eyes were moist with tears. It was a most extravagant gift. "And the flowers, miss?"

"Throw them away, as I have said. I do not want to see them again." When the girl lingered, she added pointedly, "That will be all."

"Yes, ma'am," the girl said. She fled, clutching the precious lace and the enormous bouquet of flowers.

Caroline put a hand to her pounding heart.

Be strong, she told herself. She took the torn pieces of the vellum, put them on the listlessly burning fire of the fireplace, and watched them burn.

She had been invited to a Valentine Ball at the home of her friend, Lady Diana Arnside, for that evening, so Caroline did not intend to pay afternoon calls that day. Instead, she and her young houseguest, Penelope Chalmers, sipped tea in the parlor and received a few callers. They were alone at one point later in the afternoon, no doubt because the other ladies of her acquaintance were at home preparatory to adorning themselves for the ball. They had just decided to play a hand of cards when the butler came to announce a caller.

As soon as Caroline saw the ornate, gilt-edged visiting card proffered on the butler's silver tray, her heart clutched. A cursory examination of the card confirmed her suspicion. It was *his*.

"Are you feeling quite the thing?" Penelope asked her in concern. "Your face is quite flushed."

"Count Zarcone is in town," Caroline said bitterly. She turned to her butler. "Inform the count that I am not at home."

"Very good, ma'am," the butler said. He bowed and left the room.

"That dreadful man," Penelope said darkly. "He is quite in my black books for forcing us to leave India. It has done nothing but rain and snow since we arrived in England."

"It was necessary, my dear," Caroline said, feeling guilty. She knew very well that what Penelope missed most about India was a certain vastly ineligible young artist, and that if her guardian had the slightest suspicion that an attachment had been formed between the two young people, he would remove Penelope from Caroline's household without delay.

"I know," Penelope said with a sigh. "But the crossing was dreadful. It has been so dispiriting here, especially during the time the court was still in mourning for poor Princess Charlotte's death."

"And you miss Mr. Rivers," Caroline said knowingly.

Penelope's soft, pink lips trembled.

"Yes," she admitted. "But he does not feel the same about me."

Caroline doubted that very much. Bernard Rivers, a picturesquely sunburned young artist who had not a penny to his name beyond what came to him with the labor of his two hands, worshipped Penelope. A child could see it. But he had set her at a distance, for she was a considerable heiress and far too young to form a serious attachment besides. Her guardian would never permit her to marry him, even though he was so talented and his portraits were so popular that he was sure to achieve the distinction of being the youngest man ever to be admitted as a member of The Royal Academy.

A mere artist, no matter how respectable his birth, was no match for the wealthy Miss Penelope Chalmers.

"Does Count Zarcone know about—" began Penelope.

"No," Caroline said firmly. "And you are not to tell him. If he finds out, he will do something quite dreadful to spoil it all."

"My lips are sealed," Penelope declared. "Shall we go upstairs to dress?"

Caroline looked at the handsome mantel clock.

"Yes," she said, smiling. "I must look my best tonight."

* * *

She had refused to see him.

Antonio could not believe it. He had been so sure she would throw herself into his arms and beg for deliverance from the interminable English gloom. Instead, she had her butler show him the door.

His Caroline was even more vexed with him than he had thought.

No matter.

He would soon batter down all her defenses. His victory would be all the sweeter for having been hard won.

It did not take long to learn that everyone who was anyone in London would attend Lord Arnside and Lady Diana's St. Valentine's Day Ball this evening. Gaining entrance might be a bit tricky because he did not have an invitation, but, armed with a huge bouquet of flowers, he had no doubt his hostess would make allowances for a foreign gentleman of polished address and manners who just happened to find himself in London on the holiday.

Dressed elegantly in black, Antonio sauntered off to the ball, assured of his welcome.

Penelope Chalmers put her hand on Lady Diana's arm and pointed toward the doorway.

"What on earth is *he* doing here?" she asked.

Lady Diana turned to see what had caused her young friend's pretty face to wear such a forbidding frown.

"Good heavens, it's Count Zarcone," she exclaimed. "I do hope Nicholas will not make a scene. The last time they saw one another they nearly came to blows."

The count had made the very grave error of attempting to make Diana the object of his gallantry before her marriage to Lord Arnside, who took violent exception to this. It was quite a relief when the count had transferred his attentions to

Diana's friend, Caroline Benningham. Well, if he was here to cut up Caroline's peace, Diana would put a stop to it at once!

"Count Zarcone," Diana said sweetly when he sauntered over to her to present his compliments. He kissed her hand, and then Penelope's. "How nice to see you—and if you dare to annoy Caroline this evening, I shall have the footmen throw you into the street."

"My dear Lady Diana," he said, not in the least put out of countenance by this threat. He had a soft spot for a beautiful, spirited woman. Moreover, he had quite a penchant for blondes before he became intrigued by his raven-tressed Caroline. "How can you accuse me of such a thing? I seek only to renew the acquaintance of old friends."

"By all means, do so," Lady Diana said. "A single gentleman is always welcome at a ball. I shall expect you to do your duty by all the ladies present, mind."

"With the greatest of pleasure," he said.

"You may start with me," Penelope said purposefully as she took his arm and practically dragged him to the dance floor where a waltz was in progress.

"Miss Chalmers," he said, when he had put his arm to her waist, taken her hand, and waited for the beat to guide her into the whirling company of dancers. "Whatever have I done to put such a forbidding expression on your face?"

"You have ruined everything, is all," she said, practically baring her teeth at him. "If you had not insulted Caroline beyond all bearing, I would still be in India and not in all this cold and damp."

"I sympathize, my dear young lady," he said. "I find London especially dreary in the winter. And I feel sure a certain young man finds India sadly flat without you."

"I will thank you to leave Mr. Rivers out of this," she snapped. "Caroline does not want to see you."

"She does not mean it," he said kindly.

"Oh, I feel certain she does," Penelope said with a smile that quite unsettled him.

The dance ended and Antonio bowed to her. He took her hand and scanned the crowded dance floor for Caroline. Then he saw her. She was smiling up into the eyes of a distinguished-looking gentleman who appeared to be some years her senior. She gave his hands a firm squeeze in both of hers when he whispered something in her ear that made her eyes shine with delight. She was wearing a magnificent gown of scarlet satin. Antonio loved her best in strong, passionate colors. She was a refreshingly exotic bloom in this pastel sea of milk-and-water misses.

Caroline's companion walked straight to Lord Arnside, their host, and said something to him that made him clap the older man on the shoulder with approbation.

Antonio relinquished Penelope into the hands of the shy young gentleman who was to serve as her partner for the country dance and purposefully made his way to Caroline.

He could not wait to lay his heart at her feet. The gardens would not be tolerable in such beastly weather, but surely the two of them could find a little parlor somewhere in the house where they could be quite alone.

"Go away," Caroline said with a fierce smile frozen on her face when he made his bow before her. "At once."

"Caroline, my sweet. Surely you are not going to punish me just because my ardor overcame my judgment and—"

"Quiet now," she said, turning her back on him to face Lord Arnside and the older man. She shrugged Antonio off when he put his hands on her shoulders.

The rest of the guests had fallen obediently into silence at a gesture from their host.

"Your attention, please, ladies and gentlemen," Lord Arnside's pleasant baritone voice echoed through the room. "I wish to make an announcement. I have just learned from Lord Mandelton that he has proposed to a lady among us, and that she has accepted him. What could be more appropriate than for them to announce their engagement at a St. Valentine's Day Ball?"

The ladies made little exclamations of excitement and

the gentlemen applauded. So, this explained the little scene between Lord Mandelton and his Caroline. She was congratulating him upon his engagement.

"Caroline," Antonio persisted, annoyed. What cared he whom Lord Mandelton was about to marry?

"Be silent," Caroline said through her teeth.

"I give you," Lord Arnside said with a sweeping gesture into the crowd, "the future Lady Mandelton, Mrs. Caroline Benningham!"

Caroline started walking in the direction of the two smiling gentlemen. Antonio seized her hand.

"Caroline, you must not do this thing!" he said, absolutely horrified.

She shook him off and sailed away.

Antonio watched, ashen-faced, as she gracefully walked up to this Lord Mandelton and allowed him to kiss her hand. Then the orchestra struck up a second waltz, and the gentleman gracefully swept Caroline onto the floor as all the female guests sighed with rapture at the sheer romance of it all.

Chapter Three

"My God, Caroline, what have you done?" Antonio said under his breath when his host and hostess came to flank him. To bystanders they most likely presented the appearance of merely doing their social duty by one of their more distinguished guests, but Lord Arnside's muscular hand was like a steel band on Antonio's arm.

"She is about to make an extremely desirable match," Lady Diana said with a determined smile on her face, "and all of us who are her friends can only be excessively pleased for her."

Antonio's eyes narrowed as he looked from Lady Diana's sweet face to her husband's determined one. He knew quite well that Lord Arnside held a grudge against him for flirting with his wife before they were married and would be delighted to pound him to a bloody pulp at the least provocation. Antonio was certainly in the mood to give him the opportunity to try. The men were well matched in height, girth, and strength, although Antonio had nearly a decade in age over the viscount.

"That will be quite enough of that," Lady Diana said sternly as she quickly stepped between the two glowering men. Her gloved hands gripped their arms with a strength that belied their slender grace. "Count Zarcone, if you do *anything* to upset Caroline, I shall be extremely vexed with you."

"And *I* shall be extremely vexed with you," said Lord

Arnside softly, "which you will find very unpleasant, I promise you."

"Stop it, Nicholas," Lady Diana snapped. "I will not have the two of you making a scene in my ballroom."

"I offer her the world, and she accepts this . . . Englishman," Antonio said with a gesture of disgust toward the waltzing couple.

"Lord Mandelton's reputation is of the very highest," Lady Diana said. "His fortune is excellent, his breeding is impeccable, and he has a kind heart. He will make her very happy."

"He will bore her senseless within a week of their marriage. My Caroline, married to a cold, correct Englishman? Every feeling revolts!"

"He will never give her a moment's anxiety," Lady Diana said complacently.

"Or a moment's true joy," Antonio countered.

He started forward as the dance ended. Lord Arnside's arm tightened on his.

"A glass of wine with me in the card room or the door," he said. "Which will it be?"

"The wine, of course," Antonio said as he extricated his arm from Arnside's with a tug that almost caused the younger man to stagger. Antonio brushed the arm of his coat with fastidious fingers and gave Arnside a smile that showed all of his teeth. "Never let it be said that I am not a civilized man."

Caroline, by that time surrounded by a bevy of giggling women eager to present their wishes for her future happiness, watched the count and Lord Arnside leave the ballroom in apparent amity. She caught her lower lip between her teeth to keep it from trembling.

"I trust these are tears of happiness, my love?" asked Lord Mandelton, who at that moment appeared at her elbow.

"Of course," she said, smiling mistily up at him.

Lord Mandelton's gentle courtliness had been balm to her troubled soul after her ill-fated flirtation with the flamboyant Count Zarcone. Lord Mandelton brought her delicate nosegays. He danced with her at parties, which was rather flattering, considering that more than one matron had been quick to tell Caroline that he had danced very rarely since the death of his first wife seventeen years ago. He asked nothing of Caroline that she was not willing to give.

How could she refuse such a chivalrous and handsome gentleman when he paid her the honor of asking her to take his name and share his life?

Lord Mandelton did not make her pulses race, but he seemed to delight in her conversation. He treated her as if she were the most precious, most desirable woman on the earth. And he honored her by introducing her to all his family and friends. For the first time since before her ill-fated marriage to Giles Benningham, Caroline was surrounded in a positive glow of acceptance from a legion of well-wishers. Ladies who had once considered the notorious Caroline Benningham quite beneath their notice suddenly bombarded her with invitations and seemed breathless with eagerness to hear her wedding plans.

All of Caroline's friends were absolutely delighted for her. It was an unbelievable triumph to carry off such a matrimonial prize from beneath the very noses of ladies who had long despaired of Lord Mandelton taking a second wife.

Now she would be settled down with a good man at an excellent address in Mayfair during the Season, and at his ancestral home playing lady of the manor during the rest of the year.

Her position in society was now assured. No longer need she fear dwindling into a lonely old age and being pitied by those few who remembered her at all.

"My dear," said Lord Mandelton, cupping her chin gently with one gloved hand at the end of the dance. "You look troubled. Is it that man?"

Caroline and Lord Mandelton had no secrets between them. He knew very well that she had fled back to London from India because of some man, and others were eager to supply his name.

She smiled at him.

"No, of course not," she said. "He is behind me."

"Indeed," Lord Mandelton murmured as Count Zarcone approached them. He raised one eyebrow when the count bowed to him. Caroline whirled around in dismay.

"Lord Mandelton, may I offer you my congratulations?" the count said audaciously. "Permit me to introduce myself. I am—"

"I know who you are," Lord Mandelton interrupted coolly. "Mrs. Benningham has told me everything about you."

Antonio sincerely doubted it.

"Then you must know we are quite old friends. I assume you have no objection to a dance between us for old time's sake."

"That is for Caroline to decide," Lord Mandelton replied. Antonio felt a stab of jealousy at the man's use of Caroline's Christian name.

"Mrs. Benningham?" Antonio asked, extending his hand in invitation.

Chin lifted, she placed her own into it.

"Of course," she said.

Under her breath, she added as he escorted her to the dance floor, "I am not afraid of you."

"*Brava, bellissima*," he said as he placed his arm around her waist and enjoyed the fragrance of her perfume. Caroline did not anoint her person with ordinary rose or orange blossom scent. Instead, she wore the perfume of exotic lilies procured at exorbitant expense from one of London's most exclusive shops. To make the mystery of Caroline even more intriguing, one could not detect her perfume until one was quite close.

"I am going to marry him, you know," she said, sounding determined.

"Caroline, Caroline," Antonio said. "If this truly is what you want, I could not be more pleased for you."

"Rubbish," she scoffed. "He is a good man. He loves me."

"How could he not?" Antonio said warmly. "You are infinitely worthy of love. But I ask you, my darling. Does he love you as I do?"

"I should hope not!" she snapped. "Your so-called *love*, Count Zarcone, is a shallow thing. You would abandon me as soon as a younger, more beautiful woman captured your fleeting attention."

"There are many younger, more beautiful women than you, my dear Caroline. They are as nothing to me."

"Rubbish," she said again. "You only want me because I have escaped from your snare. The spell is broken, Count Zarcone. You no longer have power over me. Your hateful proposition killed any feeling I might have had for you."

"Then why are you trembling in my arms?" he asked softly.

"I am trembling from anger," she said as she stiffened her back and strained against his confining hands.

"I stand corrected. Caroline, you are making a grave mistake. You are doing it from pique because you are angry with me, of course. My passion overcame my judgment, and I—"

"My engagement to Lord Mandelton has *nothing* to do with *you*," Caroline said curtly. "I will thank you to stop annoying me with your attentions."

"You do not mean that," he said, taken aback. He had been certain that a moment's private speech with Caroline would convince her to abandon this mad plan of marrying that Englishman and return to his arms.

"I certainly *do* mean it," she insisted. The dance ended at that moment. "Now, return me to my fiancé."

"How can I do so," he said, "when my arms refuse to release you?"

"I would advise them to do so," she said, smiling sweetly, "or, if I am not mistaken, Lord Arnside will engage to break them. He is glaring quite fiercely at you."

Antonio sighed.

He had no doubt it was true.

"My dear Caroline, I hope you do not think I would lower myself to engaging in a vulgar brawl with my host at a party," he said with great dignity. He was not afraid of Lord Arnside. Far from it. But he would retreat, as the saying went, to fight another day.

"I think you capable of anything," she said. "Here is Lord Mandelton come to collect me."

The older gentleman smiled blandly at Antonio and took possession of Caroline's arm. He raised his eyebrows at Antonio when he retained his hold on her waist. Reluctantly, Antonio released her.

"Your servant, Count Zarcone," Lord Mandelton said pleasantly as he escorted Caroline away from him.

"Count Zarcone, you do not have a partner," said his hostess as she took his arm. Antonio realized he had been staring after Caroline, no doubt with his heart in his eyes like a callow fool.

"Do you offer yourself, my lady?" he asked, regaining his aplomb.

"Certainly, if you wish it," she said, smiling at him. There was genuine humor in her lovely blue eyes. And not a little sympathy.

"You probably believe Lord Mandelton is the best man for her," he told Caroline's best friend, "but you are wrong."

"Her mind is made up," Lady Diana said. "The best thing for you to do is accept it. So kind a woman was made for marriage and a loving family. She will make Lord Mandelton a delightful wife."

"I have no doubt of it," Antonio growled. "But he will make her a bad husband."

"Count Zarcone," she said earnestly. "Please believe I say this for your own good as well as hers. Nothing good will come of your interference in Caroline's future happiness. Giles Benningham made her completely miserable."

"You dare compare me to that . . . fellow," Antonio said, catching himself in time from using a term for Caroline's late husband that must not be uttered in a lady's presence.

"I did not know him," Lady Diana admitted. "I was in the

schoolroom when poor Caroline was widowed. But he was a hardened rake, and he broke her heart. Everyone knows this. It is why she has never married again in all these years."

"And yet, she is willing to marry *him*," Antonio said bitterly.

"There is only one explanation. She is in love."

Antonio let it pass. No doubt Lady Diana believed this.

For himself, Antonio was highly skeptical.

Does the peacock fall in love with the sparrow?

Does the lioness fall in love with the ordinary mouser?

No.

Caroline had not fallen in love with Lord Mandelton.

She was running away from love.

His.

"I have no intention of ruining Caroline's happiness," Antonio declared.

On the contrary, he intended to ensure it. The only man truly capable of making Caroline happy was Antonio himself.

"Good," Lady Diana said with satisfaction. "I told Nicholas you would be reasonable once I explained the matter to you. Now, may I present Mrs. Phillips to you as an extremely desirable partner for the next dance?"

"You may, my dear Lady Diana," he said, giving her graceful fingers a light squeeze.

He turned to the attractive widow Lady Arnside indicated with a bow and an invitation to perform the country dance.

He took the simpering widow's hand and watched Caroline and Lord Mandelton bask in the congratulations of a small group of well-wishers as the orchestra struck up the opening chords of the dance.

Patience, he told himself.

He had lost the battle, but he would win the war.

Chapter Four

Caroline, fresh from her maid's ministrations, had just donned her coat in preparation for making afternoon calls with Penelope Chalmers when her maid brought her an extravagant bouquet of bright red bougainvillea. These gorgeous tropical flowers were not easily obtainable in London in the middle of winter. They reminded Caroline of hot, sultry nights beneath the Indian moon, and the scent of spices in the air.

"How beautiful they are," Penelope said. "How I miss India!"

Only one person could have sent them.

"Is the gentleman waiting?" Caroline asked crisply.

"Yes, ma'am," said the maid, cringing a little in the face of Caroline's almost feral smile. "He said he would wait upon the doorstep."

Antonio pretending humility. The gall of the man!

Caroline snatched the flowers from the maid, marched to the front door, and tugged it open.

The count had his back to her, facing into the street. When he heard the door open, he turned, looking eager.

He was dressed magnificently, though appropriately, for day in light-colored pantaloons and a dark coat. His neck cloth was a work of art. He carried a curly brimmed beaver hat in his hand, and his dark hair had been tamed with Russian oil. His brown eyes crinkled at the corners at the sight of her, and his full, sensual lips relaxed into a smile.

He opened his mouth to speak, but Caroline, with all her strength, threw the exotic blossoms so they sailed over his head and onto the step behind him. The pretty paper in which the flowers had been contained split and spilled their expensive cargo all over the ground.

Caroline turned at once and stalked back into the house, which forced Penelope, who obviously had followed her and watched the little drama from the open door, to retreat backwards.

Then Caroline slammed the door and rested against it, breathing hard, as if she had averted a calamity.

"Caroline, that was quite possibly the rudest thing I've ever seen in my life," said Penelope with some admiration. "I should think that would leave him in no doubt of your wishes."

"That vexatious man!" Caroline said, stamping her foot with temper, which was completely unlike her. "Now we cannot leave the house until he goes away, for he is capable of standing on the doorstep all afternoon, waiting for us to emerge."

"You could send your butler and two of your footmen outside to order him to leave."

"Excellent idea," Caroline said. "And if he refuses to go, I shall set the watch on him. I refuse to be a prisoner in my own house."

"That is the spirit," said Penelope.

Caroline gave the proper order, and she and Penelope went into the parlor to wait until it was safe to leave. The butler returned to tell them that the count apparently had decided to move on, for he no longer waited on the doorstep, and Caroline found herself irrationally annoyed by this. Matching wits with Antonio was always exhilarating. She had worked herself up for a fight, and now she felt sadly deflated.

At that moment, Lord Mandelton appeared in the parlor's doorway and politely stepped aside so his seventeen-year-old daughter, Serena, could enter the room ahead of him. As usual, the girl had a glower on her face.

"My dear Caroline, it appears that one of your admirers has taken to strewing flower petals in your path from the look of your front door," Lord Mandelton said humorously. He gave Caroline a straight look. "Shall I call him out?"

Obviously he was in no doubt of her admirer's identity.

"Certainly not," Caroline said, eyes flashing. "I would not have you soil your hands on him."

"You relieve my mind," he said ruefully. "I have never fought a duel in my life, and I would be sure to botch the business. But I would not be remiss in defending the honor of my bride."

"It is what I value most about you," she said as she put her arm in his. "Your common sense in refusing to indulge in follies such as duels. It pleased Count Zarcone to make me the object of his gallantry when we were in India, as I already have told you. But his attentions are fleeting and will no doubt light on some other lady if we ignore him."

"Precisely my own opinion," Lord Mandelton said, "although, personally, I would not be so willing to give you up. I have waited for the perfect woman for too long."

The perfect woman.

Caroline didn't miss his daughter's sneer of derision. Caroline reflected that the girl would vow never to sneer again if she could see how the unpleasant expression marred an otherwise pretty countenance.

Caroline knew very well that Lord Mandelton's horrified friends and relations had been eager to point out her imperfections to him. Serena, especially, had been determined to dissuade him from putting Caroline in the place occupied in spirit heretofore by her late, much-lamented mother, who, by dying in giving birth to Serena at a heartbreakingly young age, had achieved the status of sainthood in the minds of her husband and children.

It was a proof of Lord Mandelton's infatuation with Caroline that he did not listen to those who would blacken her reputation. On the contrary, he informed all and sundry that those who criticized his future wife in public would no longer be welcome in his home, and this included Serena.

"But, my dear," Lord Mandelton continued, "I perceive you are on the point of leaving the house."

"Penelope and I were about to pay afternoon calls, but we need not," Caroline said, smiling. "It will do us good to stay home one afternoon."

"Nonsense," Lord Mandelton said. "It is a beautiful day. I have no intention of interfering with your plans—at least not until we are married, at which time I will reserve the privilege of monopolizing all of your time. Serena and I will accompany you, if we may. I should like to become better acquainted with your friends."

Serena gave her father a look of shocked disbelief. Caroline knew very well that she suspected Caroline's friends were composed of lecherous rakes and vulgar demi-reps.

It was untrue, of course. Caroline's conduct had been above reproach for the past several years, and, even before that, she had never consorted with the dregs of society.

"Yes, perhaps if we are very fortunate, we will see your *dear* friend, Count Zarcone," the girl said with venomous sweetness.

No doubt the count's jealous behavior last night had been noted by all the *ton*, and had set the gossips' tongues wagging.

Lord Mandelton gave his daughter a look that caused her to blush and look down at her hands.

"Shall we agree," he said pleasantly, "to consider that remark unsaid, Serena? Mrs. Benningham has made it clear that she has no wish to receive that man's attentions. It is not her fault that he persists. I hope I have taught you better than to listen to idle gossip fabricated by malicious tongues to malign the innocent."

"One cannot help hearing it," the girl said. She gave Caroline a look that would curdle milk. "It is everywhere."

"Obviously, my girl, you would benefit by some time spent in the quiet of your own home of an evening instead of gadding about to parties. Apparently you have fallen in with undesirable company."

Serena made a sound highly suggestive of a fish suddenly thrown out of its bowl and onto the floor.

"I have fallen in with undesirable company!" she exclaimed. "What about *her*?"

"That will do, Serena!" Lord Mandelton snapped. "You will apologize at once to Mrs. Benningham and Miss Chalmers, and then I will escort you to the carriage."

"I did not wish to come, anyway," she grumbled.

When he simply looked at her, she gave a long-suffering sigh.

"Oh, very well," she said. "Please forgive me, Mrs. Benningham. Miss Chalmers, I am most sorry."

It was insincere at best, but Caroline gave a stiff inclination of her head in acceptance.

Lord Mandelton's jaw was hardened as he offered his arm to his daughter.

"I shall return in a moment, Caroline, Miss Chalmers. Pray excuse me."

"What possessed you to make such a spectacle of yourself before my fiancée?" Lord Mandelton said in tight-lipped fury as he escorted his daughter to the carriage.

"I cannot bear the thought of having that woman put in my mother's place," she said. Her pretty face crumpled, and she did her best to squeeze a tear from her eye. Fortunately, she was angry enough to make a proper job of it.

Her father was unmoved.

"Do not play off your tricks on me, Serena," he said sternly, "for I know your tears are false and manipulative. In this regard, Mrs. Benningham is your moral superior, for she is above such tricks. She has never said a word against *you*, for all that you have given her every provocation. You are a spoiled, selfish brat, and I have made you so. But you will honor my wife in her own house, or I shall send you to stay with your grandmother for the approaching Season instead of bringing you to London."

"You would not," she said, face ashen. "Send me to Tunbridge Wells with all the invalids? Grandmother never leaves the house! She receives no company except for old ladies!"

"Good. Perhaps they will teach you sense," he said as he handed her into the carriage. He turned to the coachman. "Take Miss Serena home. If she asks you to take her anywhere else, or if she orders the carriage for herself later in the day, she is to be denied."

Ignoring Serena's pleas to reconsider such a strict punishment, he turned on his heel and strode back into the house.

"Now then," he said, smiling at Caroline and Penelope. "Shall we go, ladies?"

"My lord, I hope you were not too harsh with the girl," Caroline said. She could still see the vestiges of temper in his face despite his mild tone. "She is young, and I am certain that accepting a stepmother at her age is difficult."

"Serena's behavior was unpardonable, yet you have pardoned her," he said, softening. "You are a woman in a million."

He kissed her hands, first one and then the other, and she smiled up at him with hope in her heart.

"You do me too much honor, my lord," she said earnestly.

"That, my dear Caroline," he said, quite restored to good humor, "is quite impossible."

Chapter Five

It was February 15, the date upon which, from ancient times, the festival of the Lupercalia was traditionally observed in Rome. The Christians, when they civilized Rome, or so they thought of it, turned the raucous pagan festival that honored the fertility god Lupercus into a celebration of the pathetically bland domesticity they mistook for love, and did the world a great disservice thereby, in Antonio's opinion.

Thus was born the Christian holiday of St. Valentine's Day, named after a saint who died ignominiously at the hands of his enemies. The holiday now was celebrated a day early, and all its pagan overtones were obliterated.

Oh, that the Lupercalia had come to this—a celebration of marriage and martyrdom.

Pitiful. Absolutely pitiful.

In ancient times, the pursuit of passion was honored. A man and a woman came together for pleasure, and in so doing populated the earth with joyful abandon.

The Lupercalia was a celebration of freedom.

Leave it to the modern world to ruin something so simple and honest, and link it with marriage, the most confining and unsatisfactory of arrangements between a man and a woman, Antonio thought in disgust as he rode his newly purchased black stallion through the park, looking for his Caroline.

Oh, the depths to which he had sunk!

Before he fell in love with Caroline, Antonio would have laughed in the face of anyone who suggested that he would willingly participate in such a boring activity as the promenade in Hyde Park, when he could be lolling about his suite, recruiting his strength for the pleasures of the evening, instead, or inspecting the wares of various art and antiquities dealers in search of treasures. Antonio was an indefatigable collector of ancient art and a worshipper of beauty in all its forms.

If he were going to spend the afternoon on horseback, it should be in racing his animal to test its mettle or getting from one place to another as speedily as possible. Or in joining the hunt in the brisk morning air with the dogs barking and the prey running in terror before him.

There should be sport in riding on horseback.

There should be exhilaration in it.

Instead, he plodded along at a snail's pace, and the tip of his nose was numb with cold.

Lord, how he hated this miserable English climate! The pale orb of the sun was shining in what passed for good weather here, but Antonio longed for Italy, where he had expected to spend the winter ensconced in his sumptuous villa under the Roman sun, drinking lovely, cool wine with his beautiful Caroline.

As if that alone weren't enough to put him in a black mood, he had received the report on Lord Mandelton's past that he had commissioned from his man of business. His man had dug into every nook and cranny of Lord Mandelton's financial transactions and interviewed the gentleman's neighbors, looking for dirt.

Surely the man had committed *some* indiscretion in his life—something that Antonio could produce for Caroline's delectation to prove to her that her precious fiancé was no paragon. Lord Mandelton had been long without a wife, so it would not be surprising that he had a mistress or two tucked away somewhere.

But, no.

Lord Mandelton was a perfect gentleman. He had remained true to his wife during her lifetime and enshrined her memory in his heart ever since, if his acquaintances were to be believed. Never, since the day his wife drew her last breath, had he looked at a woman save for Caroline.

He was an exemplary father and had been a devoted husband. He had served in Parliament and was generally known in government circles as an intelligent and honest man. No one in London had an unkind word to say about the excellent Lord Mandelton.

Antonio's lip curled.

It was unnatural for a man to be so virtuous!

He clenched the reins, careful to confine his horse to mincing among the carriages so he would not offend the sensibilities of the English by trampling any of the dawdlers along the path. Several of his acquaintances drew abreast of him to chat and extend invitations to their parties, which he accepted with every appearance of pleasure. He could hardly afford to spurn any gathering, for he knew the hateful Lord Mandelton was accepted everywhere, and he would not turn down an opportunity to meet Caroline in society.

He raised his hat to the ladies who caught his eye and smiled, but his heart was not in it.

The only woman he truly wanted to see was Caroline, and he had just begun to fear that she would not appear when he saw her at some distance. She was accompanied by Miss Chalmers and the thrice-cursed Lord Mandelton.

How lovely she looked, with her dark eyes sparkling and her lustrous hair crowned by a hat fashioned of blond straw and red silk roses. Her promenade gown was green and closed at the high neck with red silk frogs to match the roses in her hat. Beside her, Miss Chalmers in her pale yellow ensemble and Lord Mandelton in a coat of dull brown, were insignificant.

Could she not see that she did not belong here?

In England, she was an exotic bird set among the pigeons.

While Antonio stared at Caroline, mesmerized, a pretty blond girl walking with another girl and a plainly dressed older woman who was obviously a servant, gasped and nearly walked into Antonio's horse. He reached down to catch her elbow to prevent this.

"Do not let them see me!" the girl exclaimed as she disengaged her arm from his grasp and ran to the other side of the horse. Her companions attempted to shield her as well.

Amused, Antonio stopped his horse and obligingly served as a screen.

"In hiding, are you, little one?" he asked.

"Yes, from my father," the girl said, indicating the group that had commanded Antonio's interest.

"Your father is Lord Mandelton?" he asked, regarding the girl with greater interest. She was a pretty thing by English standards, but far too demure for his tastes. What appeal had cornflower-blue eyes when one had basked in the glory of Caroline's passionate dark ones? The girl's lips were pink, where Caroline's were vibrant coral. How sad that Caroline had ruined him for all other females—he, who was once a connoisseur of feminine beauty in all its delicious forms?

"Yes, and he must not see me. He ordered me to go home, and he ordered the coachman not to let me have the carriage today. But I had to come here, to keep an eye on him with that *hussy*!"

Antonio raised his eyebrows. She was speaking of Caroline, of course, and Antonio ignored the fact that if a man had spoken so, he would have impaled him on the point of his sword for insulting his chosen lady.

It seemed there was rebellion in the paragon's house.

How delightful.

"I am Count Antonio Zarcone, at your service, my dear young lady," he said.

Her pink mouth dropped open.

"You!" she exclaimed, raising one delicate hand to her throat in horror.

Her companions regarded him with wide eyes, for all the world as if he might descend from his horse and devour them.

Some respect. At last.

"At your service," he repeated solemnly.

"Are you not very, very wicked?" she asked. There was speculation in her eyes, but no fear.

"Very," he confirmed.

She tilted her head, which caused the pink ribbons on her chip hat to flutter becomingly.

She was the picture of sweet innocence, but her eyes were shrewd and unblinking.

"My name is Serena Mandelton and my father has made a very grave error in judgment," she said, indicating Caroline. "Will you help me extricate him from it?"

Lupercus, I thank you.

"It would be my very great pleasure, little one," he said, showing all his teeth.

Later that afternoon, Antonio presented himself at the lending library and waited patiently among the stacks of ancient volumes. He had just taken down a leather-bound copy of one of Virgil's works that, by some oversight, he did not happen to own when Miss Mandelton approached him, looking carefully about her.

"Miss Mandelton," he whispered.

She quickly caught his arm and towed him behind a stack of books.

"Do you think anyone saw us together?" she asked anxiously.

"No," he said, raising his eyebrows. "At the risk of being crude, might I suggest that it is much more scandalous to be discovered alone with a man in hiding than it is to be seen conversing with him in a relatively public place? Will you not permit me to escort you to Gunter's and purchase an ice for you so we may converse in comfort?"

"Are you *mad*?" she exclaimed. "My reputation would be ruined if I were seen in public with you!"

Antonio frowned.

"Oh, that was terribly rude, was it not?" she said quickly. "I do apologize."

"You would not be the first young lady to meet me by prearrangement and then pretend not to know me in company."

She gave him a look that suggested that it had never occurred to her that a rake's feelings could be hurt.

"Oh, dear," she said softly. "This is starting very badly. But I *cannot* be seen in Gunter's with you."

"As you wish," he said with a sigh. "What service may I perform for you?"

"I want you to help me stop my father's marriage to that creature!"

"That *creature* is the woman I love," Antonio said.

"I'm sorry," she said, chewing her lower lip. "I hate her. I can't help it. She will make him miserable. I just know it."

"Let us agree, then, that the marriage cannot go forward," Antonio said, restraining himself with some difficulty from turning on his heel and walking away from the tedious little creature.

And she had the gall to call *him* wicked!

"Yes," she said, looking more cheerful. "We must think of something that will expose her to my father as the scandalous woman she is."

Scandalous? Antonio had never known *Caroline* to meet a man in secret to plot the downfall of another woman who had done her no harm. No. She had simply gone about her life, pursuing her own interests with complete honesty. She never made a secret of her objectives or hid her attachments to her friends simply because society might not consider these persons acceptable.

That apparently made her scandalous in this society.

"Do you know where they will be tonight?" he asked.

"At Lady Marsdon's ball."

"Excellent. I received an invitation from Lady Marsdon just this morning," he said. "You may leave all to me. Before the evening is over, your father and, indeed, all of London will be privy to the worst of Caroline's past indiscretions."

"How very fortunate," Miss Mandelton said. Clearly she had not thought that a man with his reputation would be invited to such a respectable hostess's house.

In truth, before he met his Caroline, Antonio would have put an invitation to what promised to be an excruciatingly dull and proper event on the fire without hesitation.

"I will see you tonight, then," he said absently.

"You must not approach me in public," she said.

"Naturally not," he said dryly.

Chapter Six

Caroline was extremely vexed to see him in Lady Marsdon's reception room before the ball.

"Do you want to leave, my dear?" Lord Mandelton, as always her devoted escort, asked quietly.

"Certainly not," she said, moving forward with resolution. Never let it be said that she had fled a party from sheer cowardice simply because her hostess had seen fit to invite Count Antonio Zarcone.

The handsome count was quite the sensation in a dull London winter. Since Parliament had convened, many of the politicians' wives and families had felt obligated to accompany them to the capital. But it was some months from the start of the Season, and no one of real interest would be here until then.

A foreign rake with a reputation for being a hit with ladies of all degrees of gentility was sure to be welcome in any ballroom.

It was nothing to her, Caroline told herself firmly, whether or not he chose to honor Lady Marsdon with his presence. She wished him luck in finding another woman upon whom to shower his fleeting attentions.

The receiving line had advanced to the point where the count had reached his hostess, and Lady Marsdon was listening raptly to whatever he was saying as she plied her fan over her flushed face. It was not warm by any means, but Caroline knew from experience that Count Zarcone's smiles and gallant attentions had the power of raising the temperature of any lady's blood by several degrees.

Caroline considered for a moment that Antonio might be paying court to Lady Marsdon. They were of an age, and Lady Marsdon certainly was attractive.

But, no.

Despite his supposed wickedness, Antonio never pursued married women. It was quite the only redeeming quality he had, in Caroline's opinion. She, too, never dallied with married persons. That was one indiscretion that Caroline would never commit.

"Oh, my dear! Such a triumph," Lady Marsdon confided to Caroline when Lord Mandelton's party had reached her. "I had little hope that Count Zarcone would honor us with his presence, although you may be certain I sent him a card straightway when I heard he was in town. Such a charming gentleman! And so kind to honor my house on such short notice. I am persuaded that half the tales one hears of his wickedness can be attributed to idle chatter and poor-spiritedness."

Caroline, who had reason to believe that at least some of them were true, responded with a polite smile.

All the time, she could feel that girl's eyes boring into the back of her head.

Having to live with Serena Mandelton until the girl could find a husband was the only drawback Caroline anticipated in her marriage to Lord Mandelton.

How such a kind, compassionate gentleman had managed to produce such a selfish, malicious child was a mystery to Caroline. His other children, all married and with families of their own, had been polite but chilly when their father presented them to Caroline, but only Serena had dared make her dislike of her father's fiancée so obvious.

As a rule, Caroline got on well with young people when their parents would permit them to get within twenty paces of her. Pity she did not get on with Serena. She would have enjoyed having a surrogate daughter to shop with and take about to parties, much as she did with Penelope Chalmers, but she had no illusions that she would ever enjoy such a friendship with her fiancé's youngest daughter.

After Lord Mandelton's party entered the ballroom, Caroline's heart nearly stopped for a moment when she saw Antonio approach.

"The dreadful man is coming this way," Serena said, looking panicked.

Her father raised his brows in surprise at her and was about to say something when Count Zarcone bowed, unsmiling, to him and Caroline, but singled out Penelope to ask her to dance. He ignored Serena completely.

Penelope smiled and nodded her agreement, then left the group on his arm for the dance floor. As she left, she cast Caroline a look of apology. Truly, it would have been excessively rude of her not to accept him as a partner.

"Well, what do you make of that?" Serena said, putting her hands on her hips. "I am appalled that he would have the audacity to come up to us like that, a man with his reputation."

She bent a malicious look on Caroline.

"What are you about, Mrs. Benningham, to let your ward dance with him?"

"Miss Chalmers is not my ward," Caroline pointed out. "And she has been out in society for some years. If she chooses to dance with Count Zarcone, it is certainly no business of ours."

Yours, she meant.

Serena's thin lips tightened at this mild set-down.

As Serena watched Penelope Chalmers laugh at something the count said, she began to wish she had not insisted so vehemently that he must not approach her in public. The other women, it was clear, envied Miss Chalmers her partner.

When the dance was over, the count returned Miss Chalmers to Mrs. Benningham's side. Serena smiled and tried to catch his eye, but the irritating man ignored her.

How vexatious of the count to take her at her word. Did his mind have to be so literal?

"I do not suppose you would grant me the honor of a dance for old time's sake," he said wistfully to Mrs. Benningham.

"Hardly," she said with a laugh. "But I thank you for asking."

His dark eyes warmed for a moment. Then he bowed again and moved on.

"Impudent fellow," muttered Lord Mandelton. "It is not too late for me to call him out."

He looked to be only half joking.

"I pray you will not," Mrs. Benningham said with a pretty laugh. She, at least, was choosing to treat it as a joke. "We were good friends once, as I have told you, so I can hardly take exception to being asked to dance by him on occasion."

"If he had asked *me* to dance," Serena said, following the count with her eyes, "I would have sent him about his business with his ears ringing, and no mistake!"

"Then it is fortunate that he has not," Lord Mandelton said dryly. "Mrs. Benningham shows good sense in not calling attention to herself by making a scene that would be sure to delight the gossips."

Thus reprimanded, Serena stuck out her bottom lip and pouted until their hostess approached with a young man in tow who asked her to dance.

"At the risk of being redundant, my dear, I must once again apologize for my daughter's bad manners," Lord Mandelton said with a sigh as he took Caroline's elbow and ushered her to a chair at the side of the ballroom.

"Whatever for?" she asked, genuinely surprised. "I do not believe she said anything particularly unkind."

"Not compared to some of the other remarks she has made in your presence," he said ruefully. "It makes it all the more embarrassing that her rudeness tonight should pass as mild behavior in your eyes."

"She is young," Caroline said, putting her hand over Lord Mandelton's. "She has heard the gossip about Count Zarcone and judged him unfairly."

"The fault is mine and not hers," Lord Mandelton said.

"When Serena's mother died giving birth to her, I became too attached to her. I should have married when she was yet a child, I know. She would have had a mother to teach her properly. I know nothing of girls, although I *did* try. But after my wife died, I could not bring myself to marry another. I indulged her, more than any of my other children, and the result is what you now see."

"She is young, and may yet learn wisdom," Caroline said again.

"I would be pleased," he said, squeezing her hand, "if she would learn it from you."

"Whyever would the girl listen to me?" Caroline asked in surprise. "I am merely the dreadful woman who intends to marry her father."

"Your young friend Miss Chalmers dotes upon you, and the girls are much of an age."

"Miss Chalmers does not see me as a rival for the affections of a much beloved father. Believe me, if you had asked one of the very patronesses of Almack's to marry you, Miss Mandelton would be just as displeased with your choice."

Lord Mandelton raised his eyebrows.

"Is that what you think this is? Mere jealousy because her father is about to take a wife?"

"Of course I do," Caroline said warmly. "And it is perfectly natural under the circumstances. It is no wonder that a daughter with such an indulgent father would be reluctant to share him with another."

Lord Mandelton looked overcome for a moment.

"Oh, my dear Caroline," he said, clasping both her hands in his. "I do not know what I have done to deserve such an understanding fiancée. Do you think I do not know that a lesser woman would be clamoring to send Serena to boarding school?"

"She is rather too old for that," Caroline said.

"True," Lord Mandelton said grimly, "but she is not too

old to be sent to her grandmother in Tunbridge Wells if she fails to pay proper respect to my wife, and so I have told her."

"You could not have told her such a thing!" Caroline exclaimed, truly alarmed. "Surely you would never do so! Displace the poor child from her own home? Tear her away from the father she loves so devotedly? I would never permit you to make such a sacrifice for my sake, for I know you love her dearly. No wonder the poor girl hates me, if you have made such a threat."

He threw up his hands.

"I *told* you I know nothing of girls!"

"Well, you have done well enough until now," Caroline said soothingly as she pointed out Serena, laughing up into her partner's eyes. "She is healthy, she is well educated, and she is beautifully turned out. Look how gracefully she dances. She will do you credit yet, mark my words."

"Yes, she is pretty enough," Lord Mandelton said grudgingly. "But without a kind heart, a pretty face is valueless."

He gave another sigh.

"I wish she were more like you," he said.

"My lord, I beg of you!" she said, laughing. "Do not tell her so. If you do, I shall expect to find spiders dropped into my tea!"

Reluctantly, he laughed along with her.

"My darling Caroline, I do not deserve you," he said vehemently.

"Oh, I am certain that somewhere in your past you have committed some sin that would entitle you to such a fate," she said. "Ah, I see they are going to have the country dance next. At the risk of seeming forward, my lord, would you dance with me? I long for some exercise."

"I should be delighted, my dear," he said.

Lord Mandelton's legs were not as young as they once were, and he would have much preferred to remain seated, but when Caroline smiled at him like that, he could refuse her nothing. He hoped that his joints would not creak so loudly that she could hear them above the music!

Count Zarcone was already standing in one of the sets with a ravishing young woman whose face was flushed with excitement. His figure was as slim as an arrow.

Perhaps, after all, Lord Mandelton thought ruefully, he should give in to the advice of his tailor and allow himself to be fitted for a corset.

As Lord Mandelton escorted Caroline to the dance floor, he was surprised to see a fleeting look of naked misery on Count Zarcone's face as he watched them from the corner of his eye.

So the man was still in love with her. Well, Lord Mandelton could hardly blame him, for he was in love with her himself.

Lord Mandelton hardened his heart. He had no pity to spare for Count Zarcone's anguish in losing Caroline.

He needed her too much.

Chapter Seven

Antonio bowed politely to his partner and affected to be deaf to her hints for him to procure a glass of wine for her.

It was time to do his worst.

A qualm of conscience assailed him as he walked to stand quite near the group where Lord Mandelton and Caroline were conversing with a member of the House of Lords and his wife, a lady known to be one of the greatest busybodies in London society.

Perfect.

It was a simple matter to gather a crowd around him. He had merely to smile at Lady Marsdon, and that lady, ever the gracious hostess, approached him at once. Not in her ballroom was any guest left to stand alone, bereft of conversation.

"My dears, may I present you to Count Zarcone?" Lady Marsdon said to the two ladies who saw the direction of her steps and hastened to join her.

"So pleased," one of the ladies said to Antonio. He smiled and kissed her hand. Then he kissed the hand of the other lady, who breathed an inarticulate greeting.

"Count Zarcone," said his hostess by way of introducing a topic of conversation, "is just arrived in London from India, although he makes his home in Italy. Rome, if I am not mistaken, Count Zarcone?"

"Yes, I do have a villa in Rome, but my main palace is in Naples," the count said with one eye on Caroline, who had stiffened at the sound of his voice.

"Naples! How exciting!" the first lady said. "I was there with my husband just last summer, visiting the ruins of Pompeii. So fascinating!"

"Yes, indeed they are. My palace is quite accessible to the ruins. It crests a hill near the Tyrrhenian Sea. A most felicitous aspect, would you not agree, Mrs. Benningham?"

It gave him great satisfaction to see Caroline jump, as if startled. She stared at him with wide eyes, struck to silence.

He grinned.

"But I forget," he said suavely. "It was quite the middle of the night when you visited my palace, was it not? I am afraid it was rather too dark for you to take any particular notice of the setting."

Antonio had never in his life set out to deliberately embarrass a lady, for it clashed with his admittedly flexible sense of honor.

The look of betrayal on Caroline's face made him feel like a cad, but he did this, he told himself firmly, for her own good. She remained silent with head bowed. Lord Mandelton, looking concerned, put a hand on her shoulder and glared at Antonio.

A flurry of excited whispering around them told Antonio he had achieved his end.

The tale of Caroline paying a visit to Antonio at his palace in Naples in the middle of the night would have made the rounds of every house in London before dawn.

At that moment, Lady Diana stepped through the crowd of unabashed eavesdroppers and faced him.

"Very true," she said coolly. "It was quite a boring party, and so we left the palace early."

"You were at the count's palace that evening as well, Lady Diana?" Lord Mandelton asked. He looked relieved.

"But of course," she said, eyebrows raised. "There were a number of English persons present, were there not, Count Zarcone?"

"Indeed," said Lord Arnside, putting his hands on his wife's shoulders and glaring at Antonio. "I was there myself."

Antonio glared right back at him.

What had happened, in fact, was that Caroline and Lady Diana had gained entrance to his palace under false pretenses because they wanted to have a look at the place. Unfortunately, the count was entertaining a party of the most wicked rakes in Naples at the time, and the ladies had been mistaken for common serving wenches.

The outcome might have been most unfortunate if Lord Arnside had not come to the rescue.

Antonio and Lord Arnside both knew that Caroline and Lady Diana had gone to the palace out of simple curiosity and that each had preserved her virtue in the end, but that hardly mattered. If it became known that they had disguised themselves as common Italian working girls and crept into his palace at night, their standing in society would be ruined.

Or rather, Lady Diana's position in society as the daughter of an earl and the wife of a tall and extremely muscular viscount was unimpeachable.

It was only Caroline who would be ruined.

Antonio hesitated, sorely tempted to let this happen.

It would be the truth, after all.

But the look on Caroline's face stopped him.

She expected him to betray her.

The truth would unquestionably make Lord Mandelton abandon his intention of marrying her.

"It is as you say, Lord Arnside," Antonio said, looking the viscount straight in the eye as he confirmed the lie. "The ladies were under your escort the entire evening, of course."

Lord Arnside nodded, satisfied.

"Shall we go, Diana?" he said to his wife. "We promised Stephen that we would come home before he is put to bed."

"Perhaps we should stay a while longer, Nicholas," she said, giving Antonio a straight look.

"I am certain there is no need, my dear," said her husband

with a questioning lift of his eyebrows at Antonio, who gave a brief nod of acknowledgment.

"As you wish," Lady Diana said as she accepted her husband's proffered arm. She paused to say her farewells to her hostess and friends.

She kissed Caroline on the cheek in order to demonstrate to everyone present where her sympathies lay.

"I will call on you tomorrow, Caroline, if you will be home," she said. "We have not been shopping together this age. Lord Mandelton cannot expect to monopolize all your time merely because you are to be married."

Then she sailed away on her husband's arm.

"Caroline," Antonio said involuntarily when she would have turned her back on him.

He could hear the note of pleading in his own voice and despised himself for it.

"I do not believe Mrs. Benningham has anything to say to you, Count Zarcone," Lord Mandelton said. He put his arm around Caroline's shoulders as if he would lead her away.

"I had not known until now that we must be enemies," Caroline said to Antonio. Her voice was trembling, but her chin was raised. "I must be very stupid, I think."

Most of the other guests had moved on, but Antonio could tell that some, despite the fact that their eyes were elsewhere, were straining to overhear further revelations.

"No. Never that, Caroline. I—"

"I believe you are engaged to me for the next dance, Count Zarcone," said Penelope Chalmers purposefully as she attached her small, dainty hand to Antonio's sleeve with a surprisingly hard grip. "Do come along, or we shall be too late to join a circle."

Caroline had already turned away with Lord Mandelton, who was talking to her in low, earnest tones, blast his eyes!

"There is nothing you can do," Penelope said in a kinder tone. "Anything you say now will make it even worse."

"I love her," he said simply.

Penelope's pretty green eyes were warm with understanding. "I know," she said. "Otherwise you could not have possibly handled the matter so clumsily. But she loves Lord Mandelton."

She does not, his heart cried. *She loves me! And I will prove it!*

He knew better than to say so now, however. He had made quite enough of a fool of himself for one evening.

Instead, he forced himself to smile and offer his arm to the girl.

"It would be my very great pleasure to dance with you, my dear Miss Chalmers," he said suavely.

His shoulder blades prickled, and he turned to see Miss Serena Mandelton looking daggers at him.

"You have failed," Serena said coldly when she cornered Count Zarcone in the refreshment room. "You said you knew something about her past that would disgrace her before all of society, and instead you point out an incident that appears to be perfectly innocuous."

Innocuous.

Hardly.

The gathering of artists and hedonists that Caroline and her friend had intruded upon that night could only be described as an orgy. Lord Arnside implied that the ladies were there under his escort, but, in fact, he had not exchanged more than two words with either of them until that evening.

Antonio had only to regale the gossips' ears with the truth to contradict his story, but he had not. The look on Caroline's face had stopped him dead.

Truly, he would have killed any other man who had so distressed her.

And now he was being upbraided by this vindictive child for showing mercy.

"Your father loves her," Antonio said heavily. Indeed, how could he not? Caroline was infinitely lovable. "He will not believe her unworthy of him unless he sees the evidence with his own eyes."

"What are you proposing?" the girl asked eagerly. "Something perfectly dreadful, I trust."

"Perfectly," he said. "I will lure her into a clandestine meeting, and you will arrange for him to discover us together."

"It will not work. She will simply invent some innocuous lie to account for it," Serena said with a sigh. "He is so besotted with her that he will believe her."

"I will seduce her," he said coldly. "And your father will discover us *in flagrante delicto.* There will be nothing she can say to redeem herself."

Antonio would disgrace Caroline in her fiancé's eyes. There was no other way to put an end to this ill-conceived wedding. But he would not disgrace her publicly.

"Oh, delicious!" Serena breathed. "This will be *so* much better!"

Certainly, Antonio thought disapprovingly. It was never enough for one so vindictive as Serena merely to win. She would not be satisfied until her opponent was lying at her feet in a pool of blood.

For all her youth and supposed innocence, Serena had the soul of a viper.

He was glad that when this was over, he need never see her again.

Antonio regretted the necessity of distressing Caroline, but this way was much better.

No one need know the circumstances of the breach between her and her fiancé. *He* certainly would not speak of it. He was too noble of heart, blast him, to gossip about a lady he once loved. In addition to this, the incident would show him in an unfavorable light. No man wished to be known as a cuckold.

Serena would keep her tongue between her teeth or Antonio would tell her father of her part in the conspiracy. It would hardly suit the girl's purpose for her father to learn that Caroline was innocent, after all.

Best of all, Caroline would realize she belonged with Antonio. Once he had her alone, he would convince her of it.

What need had she of London society's approval?

By the time the news of her broken engagement became common knowledge, Antonio would have swept Caroline away to the sunny Mediterranean to have his wicked way with her.

Chapter Eight

Caroline smiled when the pretty nosegay of pink roses arrived the next day. Lord Mandelton would escort her to a ball that night, and he never failed to send some floral tribute for her to wear with her gown. He was so old-fashioned and courtly.

There were definitely some advantages to marrying an older man, she told herself, even if he didn't send her pulses racing in the way that a certain Italian count did. Lord Mandelton would make her a perfect husband.

He was kind. He was considerate. He was just wealthy enough that no one could say he married her for her fortune. And she was still young enough to have children by him.

How shocked her acquaintances would be if they knew that she wanted the same things as every other woman did—a husband, a home, children. As Lord Mandelton's bride, she could have all of these things.

Count Antonio Zarcone, for all that he was capable of making her bones melt simply by smiling at her, was incapable of being loyal to any woman. Indeed, why should he be? He could have any woman in the world with the merest crook of his finger.

The hardest thing she had ever done in her life was to leave India with anger between them. She still felt her face flush with excitement whenever she beheld him unexpectedly at a party or in a crowd of people at the park.

Falling out of love with Antonio would get easier with time, Caroline told herself firmly. Indeed, just after she returned to

London she was prone to burst into tears at the sudden thought of him, and now she hardly ever did so.

Meanwhile, there was safe, solid, dependable Lord Mandelton.

Caroline had been evasive when he sought to set a firm date for their wedding, but now she was ready to reward his patience.

Tonight, she told herself.

Tonight she would tell Lord Mandelton that she would marry him as soon as he wished.

And thus the wicked temptation that was Count Antonio Zarcone would be removed.

Later that night at the ball, when most of the guests had filed into the supper room, Caroline detained her fiancé with a gentle tap on the shoulder. He turned with her at once and raised an eyebrow as she took two glasses of wine from a servant's tray and led him to a private parlor off the ballroom. Fortunately his daughter had gone on ahead to the supper room on the arm of a young man. This would be their only opportunity for private conversation, and she was determined to make the best of it.

"What is it, my dear?" Lord Mandelton asked, smiling, as Caroline seated herself on the sofa and indicated that he was to sit next to her instead of in the chair across from it. He was too proud to tell her that because his back had been paining him lately, the hard chair would be much more comfortable than the soft sofa.

When she smiled at him like that, he could refuse her nothing.

She was so lovely. Tonight she wore a gown of bright sapphire blue trimmed in lace. Diamonds glistened in her hair.

The high sticklers might say the gown was cut too daringly low, and that the skirt showed more of her shapely ankles than was strictly proper, but after their marriage, he was sure she would adopt more conservative dress.

"I have come to a decision about our wedding, my lord, and I hope you will agree with my wishes," she said.

"You may have anything you want, my dear," he said at once. "A large wedding or a small one. It makes no difference to me as long as you are happy."

"I wish it to be soon," she said. "Tomorrow, if possible."

He was delighted. Absolutely delighted.

"Certainly, Caroline, if that is what you wish," he said. "I shall see about procuring a special license in the morning. I regret to say that tomorrow might not be possible. Shall we say next week? Do you wish to make the arrangements, or shall I?"

"I shall, of course," she said. "It will be quite a small ceremony. Just your family and a few friends."

"How charming," he said. The deed would be done with no fuss, which suited him to the ground. He took her hand and raised it to his lips. "My dear, you have made me the happiest of men."

"I am glad," she said. Her beautiful dark eyes were moist with emotion. He raised his glass of wine as if in a toast and touched it to her lips. She sipped from it, and he turned it to put his own lips at the place she had touched.

"I wish to have children right away," she said, blushing a little at his romantic gesture.

Lord Mandelton nearly sputtered wine all over his shirt front.

"I beg your pardon, my dear?" he gasped.

"Children, my lord," she said, looking dismayed. "That is . . . I assumed that you would want . . . You do, do you not? Want children?"

"Actually, my dear Caroline," he said gently. "I already *have* children. Quite a lot of them, in fact."

Rather too many, if one wanted the branch with no bark on it. And all of them were driving him demented in their determination to discourage him from marrying Caroline.

Most of his contemporaries were courting young girls just

out of the schoolroom, for most men could think of nothing but filling their nurseries to bulging. His darling wife, rest her soul, had been fond of children and he had been powerless to resist her blandishments for more. He loved his children, and he had reared them the best he could without a wife, but it had been hard. Very hard, indeed.

When Lord Mandelton met Caroline, he knew she was the perfect bride for him. She was still young, although she had passed her thirtieth birthday, and there was no nonsense about her. She was worldly, she was intelligent, she was a brilliant conversationalist, and she was kind. He had naturally assumed that she did not particularly wish to complicate the pleasant life he anticipated in their marriage with children.

In this, he had assumed they were of one mind.

The thought of starting a second family made his blood run cold. And he remembered well his normally even-tempered wife's emotional outbursts that made everyone in the household walk on eggshells while she was increasing.

"Of course," he said, forcing himself to smile. "But it is early days to be talking of that. Will you think me terribly selfish if I tell you that I should like you all to myself for a year or two first?"

By then, he profoundly hoped, her desire for children might have passed.

She looked crestfallen.

"I thought you would be glad," she said.

"I am," he insisted, perhaps a bit too vehemently. "Nothing would make me happier, of course, than to accede to your wishes in the proper time."

"My lord, I do not have much time," she said baldly. "I am seven-and-thirty."

"I lost my first wife in childbirth," he reminded her. "Am I selfish for not wanting to risk you as well?"

"How thoughtless of me," she said at once as she patted his hand. "But I am a healthy woman. I am willing to take the risk. You need not fear for me."

"We shall talk of it later," he said evasively.

Egad, this was a pretty pass! He had proposed to her out of a desire for an entertaining woman's companionship into his old age. A few years hence, he might have deteriorated to the point where such a lovely creature would not look twice at him. He had seen their future as a serene one. A few parties, most of the year spent in the country where he could potter about the house and stables, raising his horses. Travel to one seashore or another during the summer. A month in London during the Season.

A handful of children definitely would ruin this pretty dream.

Indeed, he had not the strength to go through *that* again.

"Of course," she said, head bowed.

"My dear," he said, anxious to make amends, "let us not quarrel on this small point."

"It is not a small point to me," she said softly. Her eyes were moist with disappointment.

He took her in his arms and she raised her face for his kiss. He was a hairsbreadth from promising her that she could populate his house with several dozens of children, if she wished, when a cool voice interrupted him.

"Do I intrude?" asked Count Zarcone from the doorway.

"Yes," Lord Mandelton snapped. "Have you no decency, man?"

"We were, in fact, setting the date for our wedding," Caroline said with a brittle smile. "You may be the first to wish us happy. We are to be married next week."

"My felicitations," the count said coldly.

"Thank you," Lord Mandelton said, rising. To his embarrassment, his knees gave a loud creak when he did so.

Count Zarcone smiled.

Lord Mandelton took Caroline's hand and escorted her at once to the supper room.

When they were gone, Antonio sat down heavily on the sofa. He had to put his perfidious plan in motion at once, or his Caroline would be lost to him forever.

Chapter Nine

Count Zarcone was hosting a masquerade ball! It was a mark of his wealth and influence that the staff of the Clarendon Hotel was willing to accommodate what promised to be such a large affair at a moment's notice.

Everyone who was *anyone* would be there, and Caroline, it appeared, would be no exception.

She had intended to pen a note of polite regret to Antonio's invitation. The man had the gall to suggest a costume for her, in fact! A Spanish dancer, indeed! Never mind that she had appeared in just such a guise before him at a masquerade she attended several years ago, shortly after their first acquaintance.

Her gown had been red, and she had worn it with a black mantilla. She had carried castanets in her lace-gloved hands.

She still had the costume, as Penelope was quick to point out.

"You cannot mean it! It will be so much fun, Caroline," Penelope said in dismay when Caroline told her she intended to decline. "I would enjoy it of all things. And I cannot go if you do not."

Caroline looked—really looked—at her young friend.

Penelope had been in the first bloom of health and beauty when they left for India. Now she was pale and had lost weight. Her eyes practically burned in her face.

She did not look well, and Caroline knew why.

She was pining for the man she had been forced to leave behind in India.

The fact that Mr. Rivers was far beneath her socially and her guardian would never give his approval to her marriage to him was irrelevant.

Penelope was miserable without him, for all that she put a brave face on it.

If she wanted to attend a masquerade, Caroline would not refuse her.

"We will go, then, if Lord Mandelton approves," Caroline said. "After all, I am going to marry the man next week. I daresay Count Zarcone's path and mine will not cross all evening save for the receiving line."

"Thank you, Caroline," Penelope exclaimed, hugging her.

"Only if he approves, mind," Caroline said, smiling at Penelope's exuberance.

"He will," Penelope said, grinning. "He can refuse you nothing."

Indeed, persuading Lord Mandelton to attend a ball given by a man he thoroughly disliked was not difficult.

His daughter had already done the persuading for her.

"Serena's heart is set on it," Lord Mandelton said with a wry smile, "isn't it, my dear?"

Serena smiled sweetly at him.

"Yes, Father," she said. "It will be my first masquerade. All my friends will be there with their mothers."

"Quite the nursery party, in fact," Lord Mandelton said dryly. "After all, Caroline, there will be a great number of persons there, and all of the first respectability, if rumor is to be believed."

"The count is not so bad," Serena said, blushing a little. Caroline narrowed her eyes at the latest victim of Antonio's charm.

"He is, but we need not speak to the man overmuch," Lord Mandelton said. "Not with so many other guests there."

"And it will give a very odd appearance if we do not attend," Penelope said eagerly.

Penelope and Serena had no great liking for one another, it seemed, but they were united in their determination to attend the masquerade. They were already talking about their costumes, in fact.

"I suppose these giddy girls will give us no peace until we agree," Lord Mandelton said with an indulgent look at his daughter.

Indeed, Serena had taken the news that her father's marriage to Caroline would be so soon with surprising equanimity. Caroline began to hope that she might become resigned to the union eventually, and if she had no hope that the girl would ever regard her as anything but an interloper, she thought that perhaps in the future they might be able to live in the same house with some degree of civility.

"It is to be quite a memorable affair," Serena said enthusiastically.

"I am sure it will be," her father said with a resigned sigh.

He rose.

"I am afraid, my dear, that I must cut this visit short. I am engaged to pay a visit to my son and daughter-in-law to make the acquaintance of my new grandson."

"How delightful," Caroline said wistfully.

Lord Mandelton made his decision. His sons and daughters *would* accept Caroline with all the respect due to his wife.

They might as well start now.

"I would be pleased to have you accompany me, my dear," he said. "After all, you are soon to be a member of the family."

"I should be delighted," she said, rising at once.

If Mr. Mandelton was dismayed to see Caroline in his parlor when he and his wife entered the room with their infant son in his nurse's arms, he had the wisdom to hide it. He and his father had endured a long, heated discussion on the subject of Lord Mandelton's marriage. His son, of course, could not be expected to approve. He held the memory of his late mother with all the reverence that Serena did.

"Here is the young man," Lord Mandelton said with an enthusiasm he did not feel. Caroline's eyes were shining. He could tell she longed to hold the child in her arms.

That honor went first to Serena, however, as doting aunt, but she soon tired of clucking and cooing at the small, puckered face.

Lord Mandelton was next and then, it was Caroline's turn.

The baby, who had been as calm as a lamb until then, promptly cast up its milky accounts on her.

"It does not signify in the least," she said politely when the nurse rushed forward with a cloth to wipe the excess from the breast of her pelisse. Anyone could see that it would take nothing less than witchcraft to remove the stain from the expensive ivory fabric. "Oh, how fortunate you are," she said as she touched the baby's face.

He began to cry. Loudly. Caroline looked hurt.

The nurse removed the child from Caroline's arms. He stopped crying at once.

Lord Mandelton glared at Serena, which quite wiped the smug smile from her face.

"We must be going," he said, rising. "We do not want to tire the young man."

The truth was, the near proximity of an infant tired *him.*

He regarded with dismay Caroline's lingering caress on the baby's downy head.

It appeared that a close acquaintance with the true nature of infants would not be enough to discourage her from wanting one.

He looked with dread into the future of a household ruled by the tantrums of small children and the emotional volatility of a wife who was perpetually *enciente.*

I cannot go through that *again*, he thought.

But he could.

He must.

He had offered marriage to Caroline, and even though their engagement had not been formally announced in the newspapers—they had agreed that a small, tasteful announcement would appear after the deed was done—he would not draw back from his promise.

Such was the action of a cad.

All the *ton* knew of their intentions. He had made it clear to all his acquaintance that Caroline was his chosen lady, and anyone who slighted her need not expect to be recognized by him in the future. This included his own children.

He could only hope that she would come to her senses before it was too late. They could have such a wonderful life if only she would abandon this nonsense about having children.

"You are to go to Count Zarcone's masquerade ball?" his son asked with lifted eyebrows.

"A ball," his wife said with a sigh. "It will be months before I am able to attend such a thing."

"I shall tell you all about it the next day," Serena said with a marked lack of sensitivity. "I am to go as a shepherdess."

"How charming, my dear," her sister-in-law said. Lord Mandelton could see the envy plainly on her face.

Too bad he could not depend upon her to acquaint Caroline with the bald truth of what it was like to be a new mother. Unfortunately, his son's wife considered Caroline far beneath her notice and did not address her directly throughout the visit unless she could not avoid doing so.

"He is such a good baby," the new mother cooed. "Quite his mother's precious little man."

Lord Mandelton recognized this for what it was—putting a brave face on it. His son and daughter-in-law were both hollow-eyed from lack of sleep. The new mother's once-pretty face was bloated and blotched. Her gown rather resembled a green muslin tent—it was fashioned to accommodate the alarming amount of weight she had gained during her pregnancy.

The thought of Caroline appearing in such a state quite turned his blood cold.

By this time, the child had calmed, and Caroline had asked to hold him again. Exhausted from his tears, the child laid his little head on her breast and dozed off. His dark eyelashes formed feathery half-circles against his ruddy cheeks.

"So precious," Caroline sighed. The ruination of her pretty clothes was quite forgotten.

I cannot go through this again, Lord Mandelton thought again in despair as he regarded the pretty tableau of woman and child.

Chapter Ten

The day of the masquerade dawned clear and beautiful—or rather, it passed for beautiful in the eyes of the English because the sun, at least, was visible.

The air was cold and damp, however, as is usual for England in February. There were a few brave daffodils and primroses thrusting up from the soil, and here and there a thin, green shoot had fought its way through the brown grasses killed by the interminable winter, but Antonio was hardly impressed by these harbingers of spring.

In his country, the sunshine was bright in February, and his workers would already be engaged with the vines that would produce some of the finest wines in Italy. As Antonio rode through the fields, they would tip their hats to him.

People who knew his wicked reputation imagined he spent all his days in Italy sleeping off the debilitating effects of his night rakings, but he habitually greeted the day early. One of his blessings—or curses, depending upon how one looked at it—was the ability to function perfectly well with little sleep.

In England, with no estates to manage and no new wonders to enjoy, this only gave him more time to think of Caroline and how much he missed her smiles and laughter.

He could have distracted himself with other women, but once he had held Caroline in his arms, he knew that no other woman belonged in them. She was a creature set apart from these pallid English beauties.

Caroline was her own mistress, and this made her a stimulating and entertaining companion. But it also made her all the more stubborn in her determination to marry Lord Mandelton.

Lord Mandelton!

Antonio doubted the older gentleman had the strength of will to handle her.

Indeed, Antonio wondered if *he* did!

Antonio pulled his greatcoat collar about his ears and made his way to his rendezvous with a young lady who was beginning to vex him mightily. She had insisted upon such an early meeting in the belief that none of the members of the *ton* would be abroad.

The count was abundantly aware that in the eyes of the high sticklers he was no saint, but Serena Mandelton's insistence upon meeting him at inconvenient hours in secluded places was becoming tiresome.

He recognized her instantly on the path ahead, even though she was wearing a black walking dress and a veiled hat to conceal her features. When she saw him, she beckoned him to follow her to a bench in the public gardens. She seated herself on the stone, but he declined. The girl no doubt had wool petticoats on under her garments, but he did not.

Serena put her veil back and looked up at him.

"Mrs. Benningham will come to the masquerade," the girl said.

"Of course," he said with raised eyebrows. "Everyone will come. What is your news?"

As a rule, they did not waste polite greetings on one another. Serena had made it clear that they were not social equals in her eyes.

"That is all," she said, sounding a bit deflated. "I just wanted you to know that this stage of our plan had succeeded."

"My good girl," he said with a sigh, "I knew as much already, for she penned an acceptance to me and I received it last evening. If you were in doubt, you could have written as much in the note you sent to summon me to this meeting."

Then Antonio looked into her eyes and barely stopped himself from recoiling.

Serena's eyes were alive with excitement and anticipation.

She caught his hand.

He shrugged it off.

"If you have nothing more useful to impart," he said, "I will be on my way."

"I am here, all alone, and at your mercy," she said, leaning forward as her eyes fluttered closed. "Do you not want to kiss me?"

"No," he said baldly.

He should have known this would happen. The girl who insisted that he was too notorious for a respectable person to acknowledge in public wanted a taste of his wickedness.

It had happened often enough for him to feel more annoyed than flattered. Too many ladies who turned their noses up at him on the street were more than willing to meet him in private.

Hypocrites all!

Caroline, for all that some of these same ladies did not consider her their equal, would never snub a gentleman in public who she received in private.

Antonio regarded the flower of English womanhood before him with a lip curled in distaste.

Her jaw hardened, but he only laughed at her. With a huff of annoyance and cheeks aflame, she flounced off into the thin shrubbery.

Antonio turned in the opposite direction and walked back to the hotel.

Despite the cold, despite the wasting of his time by Lord Mandelton's spoiled daughter, his spirits lifted.

Tonight, Caroline would be his.

Caroline had butterflies in her stomach, and she had to get out of the house or scream.

Such foolishness.

She had encountered Antonio on many a social occasion in the past, and, for her sins, she no doubt would do so in the future, at least until he tired of persecuting her with his unwanted attentions and left England.

In one of their last amicable conversations he talked of going to Egypt once he left India and spending the early spring in Holland. He had playfully suggested he would enjoy making love to her in a field of tulips.

She had almost lost her determination to hold onto her virtue with that thought. She blushed now to think of it.

Caroline was no stranger to the seducer's art. She really had gone quite wild after Giles's death, but making love under the bright orb of the sun in nature was an experience she had not yet dared.

Antonio told her that The Almighty had bestowed her lovely form upon her as a gift to *him* for just such a purpose.

Such sweet blasphemy.

She tried, without success, to feel grateful that Lord Mandelton would never insult her by making such improper suggestions.

Thank heaven she was a widow. Otherwise, she would be compelled to have a female companion or maid with her today. Caroline did not wish to make conversation. She did not wish to pay social calls.

No, her fevered brain and restless limbs wanted exercise, and not the kind that came with a sedate stroll in the park or a gallop on horseback.

One could say that hunting was her sport, but not the kind that involved chasing some small, terrified animal on horseback or discharging a firearm.

Caroline's chosen sport was the hunting of bargains, and she excelled at it. With unflagging energy, she pursued her quarries in all of London's most exclusive shops with a single-minded determination that aroused Penelope's most devout admiration.

Darling Penelope had the attention span of a butterfly and

would dawdle through the shops and insist upon stopping at frequent intervals for tea and ices at Gunter's. Caroline could shop for hours without tiring or requiring sustenance of any kind, an ability that she demonstrated frequently in India in Count Zarcone's company as he pursued antiquities in the dusty shops of the merchants' quarter.

Antonio's eyes had sparkled with amusement as she haggled with the merchants with quite as much enthusiasm as he.

Caroline gave a sigh of vexation.

Did all roads lead to memories of Antonio?

She did not love him. She *would* not love him.

She would put him out of her mind at once.

Caroline was concentrating so hard upon putting Antonio out of her mind that she gave a faint scream when she suddenly came face-to-face with him in a dusty little shop known only to a few connoisseurs of antiquities off the main shopping avenues of the city.

She put a trembling hand to her throat and faced him, wide-eyed with dismay.

He was even taller and more handsome than she remembered. His full, sensual lips curved in a smile that quickly faded when she did not return his greeting.

She found she could not speak. Instead, she backed away from him, toward the door.

Antonio's happiness at seeing her so unexpectedly died. She looked at him as if her worst nightmare had come to life.

He, who had vowed to bring her only happiness.

"Caroline, my love, you do not need to be afraid of me," he said, stepping forward quickly to grasp her hand.

Her bosom heaved as if she had been running for a very long time, but his words loosened her tongue.

"I am not *your love*," she said huskily. "Unhand me at once, if you please."

"I do not please," he said, frowning, "but I will do so, if you wish it. *Do* you wish it, my Caroline? Truly?"

"I do, you insufferably conceited man!" she huffed. She

lost some dignity when she gave a mighty tug at the precise moment he released her. She staggered back, and he had to catch her arm to steady her.

"Caroline," he said reproachfully, "we can deal together much better than this."

"No, we cannot!" she cried. "I have told you over and over, we cannot, but you do not listen!"

"Calm yourself, my dear. You are distraught."

"I am not distraught. I am angry. Very, very angry. I am not one of those coy ladies who say no when they mean yes!"

His lips twitched.

"I, of all men, know that is true, to my everlasting gratitude. I will never forget that afternoon in India, with the hot sun beating down and your eyes melting with love for me. It was only the presence of some everlastingly tedious tourists that stopped me from—"

"Stop it! Stop it right there!" she cried. "I will not listen to such things! Let me refresh your memory, Count Zarcone! What stopped you was the indentation made by my parasol in your thick head!"

"True," he admitted. He could not stop a foolish grin from spreading over his face. Ah, but his Caroline in a flaming passion was a sight to behold. Never had he known a woman of such fire.

And such stubbornness, alas.

"At the risk of being insufferably conceited again, what has brought you to this shop, if not the prospect of seeing me?"

Caroline bit her lip and looked about her at the mounds of Oriental carpets, brass bowls, temple bells, shaggy animals that seemed to live again through the art of taxidermy, and intricately carved furnishings in a style that was not usually found in a lady's parlor.

Seemingly at random, she picked up an umbrella stand fashioned of an elephant's foot.

"This!" she declared. "I came for this."

"You did not," he said, grinning in disbelief.

"Yes, miss," the eager shopkeeper said, coming forward at once. "It is very fine. I will make you a very good price. Twenty pounds."

"I will take it," Caroline said, looking determined. Then her common sense exerted itself. "That is, will you take ten?"

"Miss, you rob me," the shopkeeper said, crestfallen. "Fifteen, and at that my children will have to beg—"

"Your children are comfortably situated at Harrow and at various expensive schools for young ladies at Bath, Khalid, my old friend," Antonio said. "Five, and not a penny more."

The shopkeeper gave him a reproachful look.

"From such a beautiful lady, I will accept it," he said with great dignity.

"Excellent. I will make a present of it to you, my dear," Antonio said as he put the amount on the counter and gestured for the shopkeeper to take the umbrella stand and wrap it.

"That is another thing you do not seem to be able to get into your thick head. I want no presents from you," Caroline said as she opened her reticule and withdrew the amount. She slid Antonio's money toward him with the edge of her gloved hand. She put her own money in its place.

"Caroline, you wound me," Antonio said, but he could not wipe the grin off his face. He had missed her so much.

"It is unnecessary to wrap it," she said to the shopkeeper as she plucked it from the nest of wrapping paper he had begun to construct around it. Antonio knew well that it was one of the man's tricks to take so long in wrapping a parcel that the customer would find something else to buy while he waited. "I will take it as it is. Good day, and thank you."

"Many thanks to you, gracious lady," said the shopkeeper, bowing.

She smiled at him.

"I shall enjoy my umbrella stand," she said kindly. "I am delighted to have found it."

One of the things Antonio loved about Caroline was that

even when she was in a temper, she never failed to acknowledge those who had done her a service.

Caroline favored Antonio with an inclination of her head and sailed out the door with her nose in the air.

What a woman!

Out on the street, Caroline regarded the umbrella stand with dismay.

Oh, she did not regret buying it. Partially due to Antonio's influence, she had developed a taste for exotic curios and antiquities. What a droll conversation piece it would make if she put it in her hall to greet visitors. But for a moment Caroline had forgotten that next week she would marry a very dignified and conservative gentleman and go to live with him in his stately mansion. He probably would not want an elephant's foot umbrella stand in his hall, which was furnished in Palladian elegance.

It was that dreadful man! Count Antonio Zarcone made her lose all reason.

And tonight she was engaged to attend his masquerade ball on the arm of her betrothed husband.

Chapter Eleven

Antonio put down his glass of champagne and walked forward to greet the red-gowned Spanish dancer. The dark-eyed beauty spread her black lace fan and fluttered her eyelashes at him.

Too short, he observed with a sigh of disappointment.

It was the fifth Spanish dancer to enter the ballroom in the past quarter of an hour, and none of them was his Caroline.

Then his heart started to beat faster. A sixth Spanish dancer in red entered the room alone, followed by an elder gentleman in a black domino and a young girl in a shepherdess's costume. The lady was certainly tall enough.

It had to be she!

He stepped forward at once.

"Good evening, madam," he said, bowing and extending his elbow. "Will you honor me with the first quadrille?"

She gave a regal inclination of her head and accepted his escort. When they were on the dance floor they stepped forward in the opening movement of the dance.

"Mrs. Benningham's costume becomes you, Lady Diana," he said genially.

"Wretch! How clever of you to guess," she said. "We are of a similar height and figure, and I was quite pleased with the effect of the dark wig."

"It is most admirable."

"So, how did you know? I made a point of entering the ballroom just ahead of Lord Mandelton and his daughter."

"I would know her anywhere, my lady," he said softly. "In any guise. In any place."

Lady Diana gave a sigh.

"My skin is too pale, I expect."

"That, too," Antonio agreed.

"I knew I should have darkened it," the lady said ruefully, "but Nicholas put his foot down at the suggestion. He was afraid that my skin would be stained permanently."

"Certainly, that would have been a great pity," he said, releasing her hand to complete the next figure. "As always, Lady Diana, I find you in great beauty."

"Even though you can see only half my face? Much as I adore hearing such sentiments, Count Zarcone, you waste your time in trying to turn me up sweet. I have no intention of telling you what costume Caroline has chosen."

"A crushing disappointment, of course, but I would know her anywhere. In any guise—"

"In any place," she finished for him. "You have said as much already. Count Zarcone, Caroline is quite determined to marry Lord Mandelton."

"She has made this plain to me," he said, smiling. "Surely you do not think I would do anything to jeopardize her happiness."

"I think you would do anything to get your own way," Lady Diana said.

Antonio laughed aloud.

"And you are right, my lady," he said, "but I have already lost this battle, and so I have only to wish Mrs. Benningham every happiness."

"I must say that is very civilized of you," Lady Diana said with narrowed eyes.

"We of Italy were civilized, my dear lady, while you English were still wearing clothes made of animal hides and threading bones through your noses."

"Why do I not believe you?" she asked pensively. "Oh, I believe you about the animal hides and the bones through our noses. We English were quite savage, and still are, I think you will find if you cross us. But I do not believe you have given up on Caroline. I have seen the way you look at her."

"If you knew how much I love her, you would pity me."

"I do pity you," she said at once. "But I will not help you because you are very, very bad."

"All of that is in the past. I have been reformed."

"Nicholas says a leopard does not change its spots."

"Your husband, my dear Lady Diana, is an inflexible man. Perhaps it is I who should pity you."

"My husband is *perfect*," Lady Diana said with some heat. "He is worth a thousand of you!"

"He is most fortunate to have such a lovely champion," Count Zarcone said with a bow as the dance came to a close.

"Have we danced long enough, my lady?" he asked. "We could join another set if Mrs. Benningham has not had enough time to enter the room and conceal herself from me.

"Do you listen at keyholes, Count Zarcone?"

He grinned at her.

She rapped him on the shoulder with her fan and sailed off to join her husband, if Antonio was correct in recognizing him in the tall, dark-haired man in the red domino standing near the doorway. His military bearing was unmistakable.

Antonio sighed as Lady Diana smiled up at her husband through the slits in her mask.

The fortunate dog.

Yet, Antonio did not pine for what might have been if Lady Diana had returned his interest in her before her marriage.

He would be much better off with his Caroline.

"Good evening, Lord Mandelton," the count said when he had approached that gentleman. He looked pointedly at Serena. "Miss Mandelton."

"You were not supposed to recognize me," she said, flustered. "In my costume, I mean," she added quickly, lest her father consider her words suspicious.

Lord Mandelton's eyebrows rose.

"I had not known you were formally acquainted with one another," he said.

"My error," Antonio said at once. "We are not, of course."

"In that case," Lord Mandelton said reluctantly. "May I present my daughter, Miss Mandelton?"

"*Enchanté, mademoiselle*," Antonio said with sweeping bow. "May I have this dance?"

"Count Zarcone," she acknowledged. "Yes, thank you. I would like to dance, if Papa has no objection."

"None at all," Lord Mandelton said, but he didn't look happy.

"You are ready?" Antonio asked the girl as he guided her toward a set with three couples in it. "When you see me leave the room with her, you will wait a quarter of an hour and then come to the small parlor six doors away from the ballroom. The door will be closed, but unlocked. All I need to do is find her."

"But is *she* not—" she said, indicating Lady Diana.

"A decoy. I recognized her at once as such," Antonio said. "Mrs. Benningham is not yet in the room."

"She insisted upon driving here in a separate carriage," the girl complained. "She said she wanted to surprise my father with her costume. But if that is not she, how will we know her?"

"You may leave that to me. Be ready. I will signal you when—ah," he gave a significant nod toward the doorway and Serena turned in the direction he indicated just in time to see a dark-haired gentleman and two ladies, one a blonde and one a brunette, enter the room. He went ahead with the blonde, who was dressed in a pretty blue brocade gown in a Medieval design with a towering henning and trailing veils.

The brunette stopped and hesitated in the doorway for a moment. She was dressed as a Turkish dancer in silk veils, draped strategically to protect her modesty, and a headdress of nodding plumes.

"I believe we have discovered her," Antonio said.

"The shameless hussy," Serena said in disgust.

The brunette circled the room, exchanging pleasantries with several gentlemen. Serena watched her progress covertly.

When the dance came to a close, Antonio escorted Serena to her father and bowed.

Then he sauntered off toward the brunette, who turned and batted her eyelashes at him.

He walked by her to touch the blonde in the blue Medieval costume on the shoulder.

She turned to him with a gasp of dismay.

"Two decoys," Antonio said. "Very clever. My congratulations, madam, on your costume."

"It is all right, Christopher," she said to her escort, who looked as if he might like to take exception to Antonio's presence. "He is our host, after all."

"I do not believe I have had the pleasure—" Antonio said to the gentleman as the brunette Turkish dancer came to join them.

"Count Zarcone, may I present my dear friends, Mr. Christopher Warrender and Mrs. Warrender?"

"Delighted," Antonio said, smiling graciously at them. Now that he was closer to Mrs. Warrender, he could tell that she was wearing a wig.

"If you will excuse us," he added as he took Caroline's elbow and whisked her out of the room. He surreptitiously looked toward Serena Mandelton, who gave a nod of her head to indicate she was watching.

He had a quarter of an hour to manipulate the woman he loved into a compromising situation, one that would demean her in the eyes of the man she was to marry.

"Caroline," he said when she would have extricated herself from his grasp. He stopped, took her shoulders, and looked into her eyes. "My dear, I must speak with you. If you still want your Lord Mandelton after you have heard me out, I will importune you no longer."

Her eyes narrowed.

"You will keep your promise? If I listen to you now, you will bother me no more?"

"I promise. I am, in many ways, not a good man, Caroline. But I do not break my word. All I ask is a quarter of an hour. You will not be missed for a quarter of an hour."

"All right, Antonio," she conceded. "You have a quarter of an hour."

Chapter Twelve

As soon as they stepped into the room, Antonio pulled Caroline into his arms and feasted on her sweet, red lips. Her fisted hand struck his shoulder, but he kept right on kissing her until she became pliant in his arms.

"You are a beast, Antonio," she said huskily when he stopped to draw breath. "You promised you would not do this."

"No, I did not," he said, breathing hard. "I promised I would let you go after a quarter of an hour. The thought of having you in my arms again is all that has sustained me in this wretched climate. This is the first time I have been warm since I left India."

He tipped her face up to his and stroked her cheek with his hand.

"I gather from the heat in your beautiful skin, *ma belle*, that I am not the only one. Does your English lord kiss you as I do?"

"That is none of your business," she said, pushing against him. He held her tighter. She stomped on his foot.

With a cry of surprise, he released her. A gentleman's dancing slippers were no protection from a lady's hard heel jammed into his instep.

"Caroline, my Caroline," he said, bursting into laughter. "Oh, how I have missed you."

She pulled the bodice of her square-necked gown into a more decorous position.

"Antonio, you are making this so difficult. I will *not* be your mistress."

"Not my mistress, but my love. My queen."

She threw her hands up in exasperation.

"It is the same thing, you ridiculous man! And when you tire of me, you will turn to others."

"Never. How could I want another after I have had you?"

"Because I will grow old and ugly!" she cried. "It has already started."

"It has not. You will be beautiful when you are ninety," Antonio said as he framed her face with his hands. "Beauty has nothing to do with age. It is bred in the elegant bones of your face and in the purity of your heart."

"Purity? I?" she scoffed. "Have you not heard that I am the wickedest woman in London?"

"Nonsense. Those who say these things are merely jealous of your independence. You have a kind and generous heart. I cannot say better than that of any woman. What has happened to the intrepid lady who vowed she would shoot a tiger and ride elephants in India instead of conforming to society's expectations?"

"I do not wish to die alone," she said softly. A tear coursed down her cheek. Antonio produced his handkerchief and gave it into her trembling hand.

"Caroline, my love, you are not ill?" he asked. The thought of a world without his Caroline horrified him. "We will consult the best physicians. At once."

"I am perfectly well," she said, "but I am growing older."

"So am I. Let us not waste any more of our precious time in this dismal climate."

"No! I am going to marry Lord Mandelton. Next week."

"Is that why you are marrying him? So you will not be alone?" he asked.

"He is an honorable gentleman. He would never cast me off for another once he has married me."

"But will he love you as I do?"

"Love? Giles claimed to love me, but he pursued other women behind my back. He could not help himself. Women threw themselves at him, and he was powerless to resist them. He could not be faithful to me long enough to give me a child."

"And you think I am such a man?" Antonio asked indignantly. "Your husband was a pig! I spit on his memory!"

"You are cut from the same cloth."

"Do not marry your Englishman, Caroline. If you do, my heart will break."

"More pretty words," she said with a sigh.

The woman was so stubborn. And Antonio knew exactly how to deal with a stubborn woman. He seized her in his arms again and began kissing her. He was exploring her throat with his lips when she dragged his face back to hers by his hair and began kissing him back with a passion that left him breathless.

He practically dragged her to the sofa, where he began untying the laces of her gown.

"You have won. I will not marry Lord Mandelton," she said.

"Then you will go to Rome with me!" Antonio said, seizing her hand and covering it with kisses. "You have made me the happiest of men."

"No, Antonio, I will not go to Rome with you," she said, straightening up and putting her clothes in order.

"But why not? If you are not to marry Lord Mandelton—"

"My conscience will not permit me to marry Lord Mandelton while I am in love with another man. It is not fair to him."

"Then marry *me*, my love!" Antonio cried.

Caroline gave a gasp of surprise.

"You are not serious," she said.

"I am perfectly serious," he insisted. "I have neglected to marry in all this time because I never found the perfect woman. Not until now."

"No. I refuse to ruin Lord Mandelton's life by marrying *him*, but I refuse to ruin my own by marrying *you*."

"You do not want to marry me?" he asked in disbelief. "You lie."

"I want a home. And children. And a faithful husband. Can you give these things to me?"

"Yes. And more!"

"I do not believe you," she said, standing. "You would say anything to get me into your bed."

"This is true," he said. "There is nothing I want more than to make love to you right now," he said. "If this must be farewell—"

"Antonio, we must not," she said halfheartedly.

He kissed her, and she gave a little moan of surrender. His fingers were busy at her laces again. Soon she was gasping, half reclining on the sofa, completely responsive to his will.

"No. I cannot do this," Antonio said abruptly.

With an effort, he drew back and pulled her to her feet. Deftly, he retied her laces.

"Forgive me, Caroline. I lured you here deliberately so your Lord Mandelton would find the two of us in a compromising position. His daughter is to bring him here to discover us in a moment or two. I thought I would do anything to prevent this marriage, but I was wrong."

"Antonio—" she breathed. Her eyes were still clouded with passion.

"No," he said. "I will leave for Italy tomorrow. I will not bother you again."

A moment after he was gone, Lord Mandelton barged into the room with Serena right behind him.

"My lord?" Caroline said as she self-consciously straightened her wig, which she suspected was all askew.

He looked embarrassed.

"I thought—" He looked around the room. "I had expected—"

Serena, who had entered the room with a smug look on her face, drooped with disappointment.

"Forgive me, my dear," Lord Mandelton said with a hard

look at his daughter. "I was told . . . something spiteful and untrue by someone I once trusted."

Serena could not have looked more hurt if he had slapped her across the face.

"You were told, in fact, that I was not alone in this room," Caroline said deliberately. "And your information would have been correct. Count Zarcone was alone with me here until a moment ago."

"I see," Lord Mandelton said. His jaw hardened.

"I cannot marry you, my lord, for my heart belongs to him," Caroline said. "I am sorry."

Lord Mandelton's shoulders slumped.

"I honor you for telling me the truth," he said.

He kissed her hand.

"I must go," she said. "I do regret—"

"As do I, my dear," he said wistfully. He squeezed her hands before he let her go.

When she was gone, he faced his daughter.

"Are you very hurt, Papa?" Serena asked in a small voice. "I did not mean for you to be hurt. I only wanted you to know the truth about her."

"No, my child," he said with a sigh. "In fact, now that it is at an end, I will admit to you that I have been regretting my engagement to her."

"Truly, Father?" she said, brightening. "I knew it! You finally came to your senses and realized that she is unfit to fill my mother's shoes!"

"Wrong. I have discovered that Mrs. Benningham wants children, my girl, and I have quite enough of *those,*" he said grimly. With that, he took his daughter's arm and ushered her out of the room.

"We are going home, Serena," he said. "I hope you enjoyed the ball, because it is the last one you will attend in some time. Tomorrow morning I am going to write to your grandmother to give her the delightful news that you will spend a month with her in Tunbridge Wells instead of spending the Season in London this spring."

"But *why*, Papa?" she cried. "You said you had been regretting your engagement!"

"True. But I have become quite accustomed to the idea of marrying. I must now ask some other lady to be my wife, and I want you far away from London when I do!"

Chapter Thirteen

Nature should have been raging to match the turmoil in Antonio's soul.

The wind should have been howling in despair.

Lashing rain should have been beating against the earth and tearing the first hopeful spring grasses to shreds.

He would have welcomed it. Embraced it. A storm so violent that it tore the flesh from his very bones, for what was his life without Caroline?

At the very least, lightning should be arcing against the sky.

He would dare it to strike him and burn his body to a cinder. Then, perhaps, she would feel remorse for rejecting his devotion and his centuries-old name.

But, no.

On this day that Antonio stood before his rented house in traveling dress, waiting for his servants to place the last of his baggage on the roof of the coach, Nature provided a mere spattering of mixed rain and snow.

How pathetic.

It was early. Just past dawn.

He had promised Caroline he would leave today. All the world knew he was not a good man, but he did keep his word.

Perhaps Caroline could have reformed him. He certainly would have tried to be a good man. For her.

He entered the coach and rapped his silver-headed walking stick against the roof for the coachman to begin.

Caroline, no doubt, would marry her Englishman now that Antonio was gone from her life. He could have crushed that possibility last night by permitting her fiancé to discover her in Antonio's arms.

But, no. Chivalrous to the core, he had to do the honorable thing and save her from disgrace.

He could have persuaded her to fly away with him. In the teeth of her humiliation, she would have had little choice. Once he had her in Rome, he could have swept away all her silly protestations and made her his slave.

Antonio had been weak. And now she was lost to him.

Fool! Imbecile! Idiot!

The coach veered sharply, then pulled over to the side of the road.

Antonio was about to demand to know why the coachman had stopped when the door was wrenched open by a breathless lady in damp riding dress. Her nose was red with cold, her hat was all askew, and her hair was blowing in messy tendrils all about her face. He could see her horse standing by the side of the road.

Antonio had never seen so beautiful a vision in all his life.

"Come out of there, you coward!" his beloved cried.

Bemused, he obeyed. He took her in his arms and would have kissed her, but she thumped him hard on the chest.

"You were going to sneak out of London, were you not, Antonio? You made me a proposal of marriage last night. Were you going to leave without hearing my answer?"

"I heard your answer. You said no," he said curtly.

She gave a great sigh of exasperation.

"Honestly, Antonio. For all of your much vaunted experience with women, you know *nothing*! I have reconsidered. I will marry you after all."

"My darling! You have made me the happiest of men!"

He took her in his arms and began kissing her in the rain. He felt a great weight lift from his heart and his mind.

She would be his, after all!

"My Caroline! What do you wish to see first? Rome? Egypt? Corfu? I will lay the world at your feet!"

Antonio could feel Caroline's body tremble. At first he thought it was from passion. But, no. She was laughing.

"Antonio, enough! I am much obliged to you for the world, but all I want to see now is the inside of your coach. I am freezing!"

Antonio grinned.

"It will be my very great pleasure to warm you," he said as he handed her into the coach and took her in his arms.

Epilogue

"I am *so* jealous," said Penelope as she made foolish faces to entertain Caroline's six-month-old daughter as the adorable infant cooed and smiled at her.

The Neapolitan sun was on the descent, and lush, green shadows dappled the magnificent blue-and-green mosaic on the floor of the outer court of Antonio and Caroline's palace.

Before them on a low, intricately carved table was a bowl of ripe peaches and green grapes. Red wine glistened in crystal glasses.

"I have been so blessed," Caroline replied as she took the infant, who was beginning to grow restive, from her friend's arms and placed a kiss on the baby's soft cheek. "I do not know what good I have ever done in my life to deserve such happiness."

"You truly are happy, are you not?" Penelope asked, looking anxious.

"Abundantly. Deliriously," Caroline said, laughing. "I am touched beyond measure that you came all this way to make sure I was not miserable with longing for England."

"Do not be," Penelope said. "I must say that the prospect of staying with you in this lovely sunshine was quite enough incentive to make the journey. It was absolutely miserable in England."

"Of course it was," said Antonio as he walked in from the main house and kissed Penelope's hand. "My Caroline was not there."

Caroline smiled fondly at him.

The wicked rake she had expected to reform turned out to be not so wicked, after all. He was an attentive husband and a devoted father to their darling little Diana Penelope.

He was dressed in the first stare of elegance today in honor of their guest—dark coat, spotless linen, his dark hair tamed with Russian oil.

Who would have thought that when they had no guests, he spent most of his leisure time dressed in a comfortable but threadbare old coat, cataloguing his vast collection of antiquities and poring over dusty old tomes.

He even wore spectacles now, although he was too vain to do so in front of guests.

"I am to be married, too," Penelope announced.

"Are you, my dear? How delightful," Caroline said at once. "You know Antonio and I wish you much happiness."

"This calls for a celebration," Antonio said genially as he poured wine all around. "Who is the fortunate man?"

Penelope looked down at her hands.

"As to that," she said slowly, "I am not precisely certain."

She looked up, and Caroline's heart sank at the sorrow in Penelope's beautiful green eyes. Her chin was hardened, as if she expected an argument.

"I have been extremely foolish to pine away for Bernard Rivers all this time," she said. "Seeing Diana's happiness and now yours has brought me to my senses."

"My dear girl—" Caroline began.

Penelope gave a sigh and favored Caroline with a brave smile.

"I must forget all about him and go forward. Indeed, I should have done so long ago," Penelope said.

"If you want him, little one, I will get him for you," Antonio offered. His tone was fierce. He could not bear to see any innocent suffer. "I will send a letter by courier today and have him cast before you on his knees."

"You are reverting, my darling," Caroline said softly, and

he looked sheepish. She turned to Penelope. "Of course you must be married, if that is what you wish. But I implore you to choose carefully. From my experience I can tell you that being married to the wrong man is worse than having no one at all."

She bent a radiant smile on her husband, who had taken the baby from Caroline's arms and was cuddling her in his lap. His face, formerly so closed and haughty, beamed with open pleasure.

"And being married to the right man is heaven."